Songs of Home
A River Falls Novel

Valerie M. Bodden

Valerie M. Bodden

Visit me at www.valeriembodden.com

River Falls Series

Pieces of Forever
Songs of Home
Memories of the Heart
Whispers of Truth
Promises of Mercy

River Falls Christmas Romances

Christmas of Joy

Hope Springs Series

Not Until Forever
Not Until This Moment
Not Until You
Not Until Us
Not Until Christmas Morning
Not Until This Day
Not Until Someday
Not Until Now
Not Until Then
Not Until The End

A Gift for You

Members of my Reader's Club get a FREE book, available exclusively to my subscribers. When you sign up, you'll also be the first to know about new releases, book deals, and giveaways.

Visit www.valeriembodden.com/freebook to join!

Do not fear, for I have redeemed you; I have summoned you by name; you are mine.

Isaiah 43:1

Chapter 1

"I'll make you proud," Lydia whispered to the empty outdoor amphitheater. She'd said the same words from every stage before every performance for the past year, though Mama and Daddy would never hear them. The old fear that this would be the time she didn't live up to their legacy gripped her around the gut, and she tried to ignore it. But it was harder today than usual. Maybe because it was her birthday? And for the first time in forty years, her parents wouldn't be here to say they loved her.

Lydia peeled a sticky lock of hair off her neck—the Nashville humidity was brutal today, just as she'd warned Dallas it would be when he'd scheduled this tour stop. She supposed she should be grateful—at least she'd get to sleep in her own bed tonight. With a muttered, "happy birthday" to herself, she made her way backstage, trying to shake off the unsuitable melancholy. It was her birthday, she was on the last leg of what so far had been a massively successful national tour—one poised to launch her and Dallas to the levels of fame Mama and Daddy had achieved—and she was in love.

With a man she hadn't seen since their sound check a few hours ago.

Maybe he was preparing a surprise for her. A tingle went up her spine. Maybe the surprise would be a ring.

She pushed the thought away. Just because they'd been dating for a few years didn't mean Dallas had to propose. He would do it when he was ready—and she wouldn't pressure him. Though he *had* been acting

1

different lately—kind of nervous. And he'd said something about things changing the other day that had made her think that . . . maybe.

She shook off the hope.

At any rate, there wouldn't be time for him to do it before the concert—she had her hair and makeup to do yet, not to mention squeezing herself into the silver dress Cheyenne had insisted would be perfect for tonight's concert. Lydia cringed just imagining trying to pull it on. She loved that her best friend was also her backup vocalist and guitarist, but maybe she should replace her as fashion adviser. Eight years younger than Lydia, Cheyenne might still be able to get away with wearing tight sequined dresses. But Lydia was starting to feel ridiculous in them.

What if he did it on stage? The question filtered through her thoughts. She pressed her hands to her cheeks, which suddenly felt too warm.

Stop it. You don't even know he's going to do it at all.

But she knew who probably did know: Cheyenne. Somehow, the woman was the first to know every piece of gossip that floated through the band, the crew, even the audience sometimes.

She rushed for the dressing room, determined to find out what her best friend knew. It might ruin the surprise, but her nerves were already frayed to the point of breaking after the exhaustion of three months on the road.

The door stuck, but she shoved hard and it opened. "Hey Chey, do you think—"

Her words got caught in her chest as she grabbed for the door frame. A wave of dizziness nearly knocked her to the ground.

She couldn't make sense of what she was seeing.

A woman with a blonde braid hanging to her waist. A man with a shaggy mop of dark hair.

She couldn't see much else since their lips were pressed together, their arms locked around each other.

Kissing. The word swam at her through the fog, smacking her in the face with a cold splash.

"Dallas. What are you— I don't— Cheyenne." She had to stop to gasp for air. Who had sucked all the oxygen out of the room?

Cheyenne jumped back from Dallas with a quiet shriek. His reaction was less pronounced, a calm turn and a grimace.

"I don't— What are—" Lydia tried again, blinking a few times as if that would change the frame frozen in front of her.

"Lydia—" Cheyenne's hands were on her lips, as if she could hide the evidence of what she'd been doing. "This isn't what it looks like." But the guilt in her best friend's eyes didn't lie.

"Actually—" Dallas stepped forward. "It is. I'm sorry, Lydia. I wanted to wait until after the tour. But maybe it's best if you know now. Cheyenne and I are . . ." He looked at Cheyenne, and Lydia could already tell.

"In love," she filled in dully. How, oh how, had she not seen it before? All those nights she'd gone to bed early and they'd stayed up to "work on songs." All those tour stops where she went for a walk alone, only to get back to the bus and find the two of them gone. All the time Cheyenne spent gushing to her about how great Dallas was.

"This doesn't change anything, Lydia." Cheyenne reached for her, but Lydia took a step backward.

Didn't change anything?

It blew up her whole life.

Again.

The only two people she had left in the world were saying they had chosen each other over her.

"I know this isn't ideal." Dallas took a step toward her, and she snorted. Not ideal was having a show on her birthday. Not ideal was squeezing into a dress she could barely breathe in. Not ideal was the humidity that would slick her in sweat the moment she stepped onto the stage.

But this?

This was way beyond not ideal.

"But," Dallas continued. "We have appearances to keep up here. This isn't the time to fall apart."

Lydia blinked at him. "Who's falling apart?" She steeled her spine, same way she had for every show since Mama and Daddy's deaths. She shoved down the urge to run out of the amphitheater and never look back. That wasn't an option.

Instead, she kept her shoulders stiff, lifted her head higher, and skirted around Dallas and Cheyenne to grab her dress and makeup bag. Then, without a word, she made her way back into the hall and down to the ladies' room. For tonight, this would be her dressing room.

By the time she'd gotten ready, an appealing numbness had settled over her. As long as she didn't have to see Dallas and Cheyenne, didn't have to talk to them, she could put herself in a little bubble and pretend none of what had just happened was real. At least until the concert was over.

But the moment she emerged from the bathroom, Cheyenne pounced at her. "Lydia, I really think—"

Lydia spun on her heel and burst back through the bathroom door. She dove into the first stall, ducking over the toilet just in time to avoid vomiting on her glittery cowboy boots.

When she was done, she wiped her face, flushed, and stepped out of the stall to wash her hands and rinse her mouth.

She'd half-expected Cheyenne to be there, holding out a paper towel as she had at every show, making the same stupid joke she made every time about how much Lydia's vomit would be worth on the internet. But the bathroom was empty, and when she emerged, so was the hallway.

She let out a long, slow breath. She'd seen her parents perform through the flu, a massive tabloid uproar, and even appendicitis. She was going to get through this concert and make them proud of her tonight if it killed her. There'd be time to deal with her emotions later.

Dallas and Cheyenne were in the wings, Cheyenne holding Dallas's arm and whispering earnestly. She cut off abruptly as Lydia approached.

"Thirty seconds," a panicked looking stage manager said, pressing Lydia's mic into her hand.

"Give us a minute." Dallas's low rumble held a command Lydia had never seen anyone ignore.

She smoothed a hand down her dress. "We don't need a minute."

"Lydia, I think we should—" Cheyenne started. But the stage manager was waving them onto the stage.

Dallas's hand grabbed Lydia's, and the shock of his touch almost drew tears. She needed to avoid contact if she wanted to keep this bubble around her.

But he squeezed tighter and leaned toward her, his hot breath brushing over her ear. "As far as these people know, we're supposed to be in love. That's what they came to see."

"Yeah," Lydia murmured. "We're supposed to be."

And then they were on the stage, the lights dazzling, the crowd cheering, the music beating. Lydia tugged her hand out of Dallas's and ignored the choreography they'd rehearsed, instead letting herself get caught up in the rhythm of the song. She stepped to the front of the stage to touch fans' hands, something she usually avoided. Lights flashed brilliantly over her, and she let herself get sucked into the magic that was the show.

She could get through this.

And she almost did.

But as the lights lowered and the music slowed for the final set of the evening, Dallas moved to her side, sliding an arm behind her back, as the choreography called for him to do.

Lydia attempted to slip away, but his grip tightened and he leaned over to whisper in her ear, "Personal problems aside, you know that."

When he pulled away, he offered her an intimate smile that she knew was entirely for the benefit of the crowd.

She tensed as his deep baritone with its light twang carried the first notes of the song:

Once upon a time, I promised you forever,
But darling, I didn't mean what I said.
Because forever would never be enough
To show you every ounce of my love.
So tonight, let me make a new promise, hon:
Tonight I promise you forever plus one.

She slipped out of his grip. But she could feel his eyes on her, feel the sigh of the crowd, feel the light wisp of wind on her sweaty back.

She forced herself to turn her head toward him like she was supposed to and drew in a shaky breath. But when she opened her mouth to begin her verse, her usually rich alto broke on the first note, and a painfully loud sob reverberated through the mic.

Slapping a hand to her mouth to hold the rest of her cries back, she chucked her microphone, noting with a detached sort of satisfaction that Dallas had to step aside to avoid getting hit. She spun on the heels of her cowboy boots and sprinted for the wings, humiliation hot on her heels.

As she fled down the hallway, she heard Cheyenne's voice take up her part, and it hit her—the song had probably been meant for Cheyenne all along.

A fresh wave of desperation and adrenaline drove her straight toward the exit.

Chapter 2

Liam leaned against the front of his van, head tilted toward the dark sky, watching the play of lights from the other side of the amphitheater reflecting off the clouds. He'd finished the job, finished packing his gear into the van, and yet he couldn't make himself get in and drive away. This was his last night in Nashville, and he felt an overpowering need to soak it all in.

The city held some of the best memories of his life—the years with his wife, the birth of their daughter Mia, and the fast-paced adrenaline of setting up the lighting for shows like this one.

Life in his hometown of River Falls would be nothing like this, he knew that. But what choice did he have? After her fall, Mama needed him to help care for the house, and he needed to get Mia away from the bad crowd she'd fallen in with—especially that delinquent of a boyfriend. If that meant a three-hour move away from everything he'd come to love over the past twenty years, then so be it. He'd promised Molly he'd do whatever it took to make sure Mia never drifted from the faith—and right now he was failing miserably at that. Actually, it felt like he'd been failing miserably at everything when it came to parenting for the past year or more.

"I sure wish you were here to help me figure this out," he murmured into the dark, unable to keep himself from talking to his wife even six years after her death.

The sound of pounding footsteps yanked his gaze to the path that ran from the amphitheater to the parking lot. A woman in a silver dress barreled toward him at full speed, jerking to a stop at the last second as her eyes landed on him. She let out a small, low-pitched squawk, staring at him with wild eyes, black makeup lines streaking her wet cheeks.

Something about the brokenness in her gaze tugged at his heart, and he pushed off the van to step toward her.

She squawked again but seemed unable to move.

"Are you okay?" He kept his voice gentle. "Can I get you some help?"

She shook her head but didn't move, and he took a step closer. "Are you sure? Maybe I could call someone for you? The police or . . . someone."

She lifted her hands to her cheeks, spreading the streaks of makeup all the way to her hairline, her eyes roving the parking lot as if searching for her car.

"Actually—" Her voice was deeper than he'd expected, resonant and warm. Almost like the cello his wife used to play. "I could use a ride."

He pulled out his phone. "I'll call a taxi for you."

But she gave him a desperate look. "I can't wait for a taxi. I need to get out of here right now."

"Why? Are you sure I can't call the police?" He peered behind her. He didn't see any signs of anyone chasing her. Maybe she was running *from* the police.

"Not unless they can arrest a cheating jerk and my best friend." She sniffed but managed the smallest grimace of a smile.

"Ah." A protective instinct flared in his chest, and he took a step closer to the building, then stopped himself. What was he going to do, deck a guy he'd never met?

"Look. I know this is a lot to ask. But could you give me a ride? I rode here with said jerk and friend." The woman turned her eyes on him. Where

VALERIE M. BODDEN

Molly's had been a light, sparkling blue and full of laughter, this woman's were as deep and full and soulful as her voice. And yet they seemed to have an equivalent effect on him—a desire to shield her.

"You're not really asking a complete stranger for a ride, are you? Because that isn't exactly a safe thing to do. For all you know, I could be a serial killer or a kidnapper or a . . . a litterer."

The woman managed a small laugh. "I'll take my chances. Besides, I can tell you're a good guy. You've probably never littered in your life. Come on." The woman moved toward the passenger door of the van bearing the logo of his electrical company. "I'll pay you. A thousand dollars. Please."

"I don't want your money."

But the woman was already opening the door and climbing into the van.

Liam blew out a hard breath. He knew he wouldn't hurt her. But *she* didn't know that. He really shouldn't let her . . . But if he didn't give her a ride, someone else might. Someone with less innocent intentions.

"Fine." He opened the driver's door to find the woman huddled in the passenger seat, wiping at her eyes again. "You're sure you're all right?"

She nodded with a loud sniffle. "Sorry. I'm fine." She gave him her address, then leaned her head against her seat.

Liam backed out of his parking spot and navigated into the street, trying to keep from looking at her too often—and failing miserably. Her silver dress was glittery, her boots even more so—but that wasn't what kept drawing his eyes to her. It wasn't even the natural beauty he could discern under her streaked makeup. It was the sense of familiarity he got looking at her. But for the life of him, he couldn't place it.

"You don't like music?" The woman's voice broke into the silence.

"I— What makes you say that?"

"You don't have the radio on," she pointed out.

"Oh." Aside from hymns in church, Liam avoided music as much as he could these days. It held too many memories of Molly. "You can turn it on if you want."

"I'm not the biggest fan of music at the moment either." The woman's laugh was sharp, before she fell into silence. After a few minutes, her eyes closed, and Liam took it as a sign that she wasn't interested in talking.

They drove the rest of the way like that, until Liam pulled into the driveway at the address she'd given him. He couldn't help letting out a low whistle as he drove past the sprawling, perfectly manicured lawn toward a brick home fronted by tall white columns. A place this big could only be called a mansion.

He cut off his whistle as he realized it probably wasn't the most sophisticated thing to do. His gaze slipped to the woman, but she hadn't opened her eyes.

In that case . . . He gaped openly, noting the full wraparound porch and the bubbling fountain and the tropical-looking flower beds.

Who *was* this woman?

He slowed the van to a stop alongside the house, then turned to her to say . . . Well, he wasn't sure what to say. "Goodnight" or "good luck" or "your boyfriend was clearly an idiot." But her eyes were still closed, and her lips were parted the smallest crack, moving slightly as tiny puffs of air slipped out of them. A faint pulse went through his heart as he watched her, the tiniest sign of life where there had been only a dead circuit for the past six years.

He ignored it.

He had no desire for his heart to come back to life—not without Molly.

He cleared his throat, hoping that would be enough to wake the woman in the passenger seat. When it wasn't, he touched a hand to her shoulder, ignoring its soft warmth as he shook her gently.

But she still didn't stir.

He eyed the walkway from the driveway to her front door. He supposed he could carry her, but what would he do once he got her to the door? Break in so he could set her down?

Fortunately, the moment he took his hand off her shoulder, her eyes popped open. She gasped, looking around wildly and reaching for the door.

"It's okay." He kept his voice low so as not to startle her further. "You fell asleep. But we're here."

Clarity came back to the woman's eyes as they fell on him. "See, I told you that you're a good guy."

He frowned. "It's a good thing too."

She nodded, her eyes meeting his. Something in the air between them sparked to life, something Liam felt right down to that new pulse in his heart.

He looked away.

"Oh, let me get you your money." The woman pushed her door open.

"I don't want your money. Really. Just—"

The woman blinked at him. "Just what?"

"Are you going to be okay?" It probably shouldn't matter to him, but it did.

"You must think I'm crazy." Though she delivered the words with a laugh, there was a certain vulnerability behind them.

He let his eyes flick to her, offering a small smile. "A little, maybe. But crazy isn't always such a bad thing."

Her laugh was edged with regret. She got out of the van but didn't close the door. "At least let me offer you some sweet tea as a thank you. And some cake. It's my birthday." Her lips twisted with irony.

Oh man. Her boyfriend had cheated on her on her birthday?

Go home. He had a lot to do yet tonight to make sure everything was ready for the movers tomorrow.

But how could he make her eat birthday cake alone? "All right." He reached for his door handle. "But only a slice."

He followed her to the backyard, which felt cozy and secluded despite the imposing house.

"Have a seat." The woman gestured to the cushy patio set under a wooden pergola. "I'm going to run in and make some tea." She disappeared into the house, and Liam lowered himself onto the patio couch, trying to pretend her smile wasn't still zapping through his veins. He was leaving tomorrow and would never see this woman again. Which, given the way his heart seemed to be attempting to jump-start itself, was probably a good thing.

He tilted his head back to peer through the slats of the pergola above him. Was this the same sky he'd been looking at half an hour ago when this woman—he realized he hadn't asked her name—had crashed into his life?

The clouds from earlier had cleared, and millions of lights twinkled down at him. He picked out Virgo, which had always been Molly's favorite constellation because she said it looked like someone playing a cello. He'd never been able to see the resemblance, but he'd loved her passion in describing it to him.

With a start, he brought his gaze back down to earth.

What was he doing here?

After six years of barely so much as speaking to a woman outside of work contexts, he was sitting in the backyard of some strange—beautiful, granted, but strange—woman's house.

He pushed to his feet. If he left now, he wouldn't have to explain why it was a bad idea for him to be here.

But then he pictured the tears that had streaked her face as she'd run toward his van earlier. She'd already been hurt once tonight. He couldn't do that to her again.

He'd wait for her to come outside, apologize, and then go home.

Go home and not think about her again.

Just like he wasn't thinking about her right now.

The moment he heard the door open, he sprang to his feet. "Look, I should—"

"I wasn't sure if you liked frosting or not. So I brought one piece with lots and one with a little. You choose." She'd changed into jeans and a loose-fitting t-shirt, and her hair fell around her shoulders in thick, dark waves. She'd washed the streaks of makeup off her face, and her eyes were warm and bright.

And Liam completely forgot what he'd been about to say.

"I'll take the one with less frosting," he finally stammered, waiting until she'd set the tray of tea and cake down and taken a seat to sit as well.

She poured the tea into glasses, then handed him one. He took it, careful not to let his fingers brush hers. He'd eat a slice of cake and *then* go.

"This is an amazing place." Liam eyed the giant house as he took a bite of the cake, the perfect blend of fluffy and sweet mingling on his tongue.

"Thanks." She scooped a bite of cake—complete with a giant frosting flower—into her mouth, a streak of purple dotting her lips as she brought her fork down.

Liam was seized by the oddest urge to wipe it away, but fortunately she picked up a napkin and rubbed her lips before he could do something stupid. He directed his eyes to his plate, studying his cake so he could get his thoughts under control.

"It's ridiculously big for me. I think I use like three rooms." She set her cake down to sip her tea.

"You live in this big place by yourself?" He cringed as he heard how the question must have sounded. "I mean—"

But she laughed gently. "It was my parents'. They left it to me when they died."

Nice one, Liam.

"I'm so sorry." He couldn't stop himself from touching her hand. But the jolt to his middle made him pull back immediately.

The woman didn't seem to notice. "I should probably sell it. But I'm not quite ready yet."

Liam nodded, resisting the urge to wrap his hand protectively around hers. He knew too well how hard it was to let go of a place that held so many memories.

"Anyway." She seemed to chase away the thoughts. "What about you? You live in Nashville?"

"Until tomorrow. We're moving back to my hometown." He sighed as a thousand images of his life hit him at once. "I'm going to miss it here. Lots of good memories."

She gave him a bemused look. "I think about leaving sometimes. But I don't know where I would go."

He had a crazy urge to invite her to come to River Falls. Fortunately, his mouth was full of cake, and by the time he'd swallowed it, his common sense had returned. "I love Nashville. My wife and I came here for college and never left. But—"

"Your wife." The woman looked horrified. "I'm so sorry. I didn't mean to keep you from being with your family on your last night in town. You should go." She reached for his plate, but he switched it to his other hand.

"My wife died. Six years ago."

The horror in the woman's eyes transformed to compassion. "I'm sorry. That must have been so devastating."

His eyes went to hers, and he could tell it wasn't a platitude. She hadn't said it because it was expected. She'd experienced it too.

"Yeah." He cleared his throat. "My daughter Mia has been struggling, and I think I need to get her out of the city. Plus my mama fell and needs some help, so . . ."

"I'm sure your hometown isn't such a bad place." She settled back into the couch, as if she planned for him to stay and chat a while.

"It's not. It's where Molly and I met, actually. I only hope I'm doing the right thing for Mia."

The woman frowned. "I'm sure you are. How old is she?"

"Sixteen. I don't know what happened." He set his empty plate down, and the next thing he knew, he was telling her about Mia and about Mama and even about Molly.

Whenever he tried to direct the conversation toward her, she deflected.

Finally, they fell silent and the woman covered a giant yawn with her hand. Though it had to be well past midnight, Liam wasn't tired in the least. But he should let the poor woman get some sleep.

Regretfully, he got to his feet. It felt like an invisible tether had woven between them over the past couple hours, and he was reluctant to break it.

"Thanks for the tea and cake." He gestured toward the table with the empty dishes, then tucked his hands in his pockets. "This was . . ."

"Surreal?" The woman's smile was sweet and a little wistful as she stood too.

He chuckled. "Surreal but nice."

"Yes it was. Thank you for being a good guy." She stepped forward and, before he could react, dropped a quick kiss on his cheek.

His hand lifted involuntarily to the spot, the pulse in his heart strengthening into a full-out throb.

"I don't even know your name." Not that it mattered at this point. He would never see her again.

"Maybe it's better that way." Her throaty whisper curled around him, making him want to sit back down, but he nodded and took a step backward.

"Maybe it is." He made his feet turn and carry him toward his van. When he reached it, he peered into the backyard, but there was no sign of the woman.

With a sigh, he ran his hand over his cheek.

He might never see this woman again—but he wasn't likely to forget her anytime soon.

Chapter 3

What was today's painkiller of choice going to be?

Lydia gnawed her bottom lip as she contemplated the vast selection in her freezer. Good thing she'd stocked up yesterday.

Store brand vanilla wasn't going to cut it today. Maybe triple chocolate mocha?

She grabbed the pint of ice cream and a spoon. No point in bothering with a bowl.

But she'd no sooner settled at the giant, empty dining room table than her phone let out a loud peal. With a mixed groan and sigh, Lydia fished it out of the pocket of her sweats. She didn't have to look to know who it was. There was only one person who ever called her anymore.

"Hi, Becca." She struggled to put some pep behind her words because she knew that was what her manager would be looking for.

"I hope that ice cream is worth it."

"What?" Lydia craned her neck around the dining room. She wouldn't put it past Becca to install spy cameras in her home.

"Have you been on social media yet today?" Impatience snapped through Becca's words. "Of course you haven't. Otherwise you would have already posted the smiling, happy, optimistic picture I told you to post."

"It's on my list of things to do today." First, she had to figure out how to put on a smiling, happy, optimistic expression—hence the ice cream for breakfast.

"You'd better get on it. Unless you want people to permanently think of you as the ice cream queen."

"What are you . . ." Lydia pulled the phone away from her ear and put it on speaker, then opened her social media accounts.

"Your little trip to the grocery store yesterday was immortalized," Becca said, even as Lydia's eyes fell on the picture.

It was her, wearing sweats, sunglasses, and a baseball cap—which had clearly not done enough to mask her identity—her cart loaded with a dozen pints of ice cream. Only so she wouldn't have to go back out anytime soon. It wasn't like she was going to eat them all in one day.

Former country star Lydia St. Peter appears to have traded in her microphone for a spoon, the caption read.

Needles stung Lydia's eyelids. Why did anyone care how much ice cream she bought? What business was it of theirs?

She blinked the moisture away as she closed the app. "So what do you want me to do?"

"You know what I want you to do." Impatience crackled in Becca's voice. "It's been, what, ten months? Dallas and Cheyenne's album is all over the place."

Like Lydia needed the reminder.

"It's time to snap out of it." Becca's tone gentled. "Write some new songs. Get back on the stage."

Lydia shook her head. Did Becca think she hadn't tried? But she was like a rubber band that had been stretched too far. She had no snap left.

"Look—" Becca's voice held that same gentleness, and Lydia wanted to tell her to stop acting so nice. It unnerved her. "You have to decide if this is what you want or not. If it's not, that's fine. You're entitled to make your own decisions about your future. But if you *do* want this—"

"I do." Her parents had worked hard to make this possible for her. They'd used their own fame to launch her career. She had their legacy as country music legends to live up to. She couldn't throw that away.

"Then upload a video today. It's been months since your last one. Do a cover of one of Dallas's songs. That will show him."

Lydia pressed her fingers to her eyes. The reason she hadn't done a video in so long was that the two she'd uploaded months ago had fallen flat. She'd felt it—her heart wasn't in the music. And her fans had felt it too—as they'd been vocal about in the comments.

"You know I'm not going to do any more videos." Just the thought of failing in front of the whole world again was enough to make her break out in hives.

"Whatever." Becca clicked her tongue against the roof of her mouth. "But at least take a shower, put on some makeup, get yourself all cute, and put up a post that says you're doing great."

"Who says I haven't already showered?" Lydia ran a hand through her knotted hair, searching again for hidden cameras.

"And then get to work on some new songs. I want to see something by . . ." Becca's voice grew muffled, and Lydia could hear the shuffling of the giant calendar that took up most of Becca's desk. "The end of summer. Let's say September 1 at the latest."

"But that's only . . ." Lydia ran through the months in her head. "Two and a half months from now."

"Any longer than that, and you might as well forget it." The impatience was back in Becca's voice. "People aren't going to wait around for you forever. *I* can't wait forever."

Lydia heard what she was insinuating. "So you'll drop me if—"

"I want to keep managing you, Lydia. So give me something to manage. Now go take a shower. I expect to see your post within the hour." The phone went silent, and Lydia pulled it slowly away from her ear.

She glanced down to find her now melting pint of ice cream creating a pool of condensation on the table.

"Fine." She pushed her chair back, snatched the ice cream, and carried it to the sink.

Then she went to take her shower.

By the time she'd emerged from the shower, she'd come to one conclusion: She needed to get out of Nashville. Sure, it was a beautiful city, but over the past year, it had started to feel like a gilded cage. She couldn't go out without fear of being recognized. Couldn't stay in without feeling like she was going to go crazy with loneliness.

But where would she go?

She'd seen some pretty places on tour over the years. But she didn't know anyone anywhere else.

She was rootless—a piece of dandelion fuzz drifting aimlessly on the wind, without a soul to care where she landed.

She dried her hair, applied a light layer of makeup, then marched into the much-too-formal living room to keep her promise to Becca. But as she positioned herself on the stiff sofa, her eyes fell on the bank of windows overlooking the backyard. An involuntary smile lifted her lips, just as it did every time she saw the comfy patio furniture and remembered that amazing night she'd spent talking to a complete stranger.

She'd wished more than once that she'd gotten his name. Because as it was, she sometimes wondered if she'd dreamed the whole thing. Her only proof that it had actually happened was the crumpled receipt from Curly Q's that she'd found on the couch the next day.

She got up and headed for the door. If Becca wanted a picture of her looking happy, maybe she should take it in the spot she last remembered *being* happy.

And safe. Even though he was a complete stranger, she didn't remember ever feeling so safe with anyone. And a good thing too, since she must have been out of her mind to accept—no, demand—a ride from a stranger. Every time she thought about what a less noble man might have done in that position, a shiver coursed through her.

She'd toyed with the idea that maybe the guy had been an angel sent by God to rescue her. Until she'd remembered that God had abandoned her just as thoroughly as everyone else in her life. The guy had simply been exactly what he seemed—a good guy.

A good guy she would never see again.

The thought made her frown, ruining her first attempt at a selfie. She tried again, this time thinking of the dazed look he'd worn when she'd kissed his cheek. The memory worked, resulting in a picture with a semi-nostalgic but hopeful smile.

That should satisfy Becca.

Lydia quickly posted it, along with a caption: *A beautiful day, a beautiful life. A beautiful song in my heart.*

A lie, maybe, but she'd learned it was what everyone wanted to hear. If she didn't post often enough about how amazing she was doing, the rumors about her "breakdown" started circulating again.

The sound of a car door slamming startled her out of the thought. The houses in this neighborhood were spaced far enough apart that she rarely heard noise from any of her neighbors. And that door had sounded close—like in her driveway.

Her heart skipped.

Had her mysterious stranger returned?

She snorted at herself and pushed to her feet. Whoever it was, she wasn't in the mood to chat. She ducked into the house just as the doorbell chimed. She froze in the kitchen, out of sight of the front windows, and waited for them to go away.

The doorbell chimed again.

And then a third time.

In her experience, there was only one type of person who was that persistent—paparazzi. Probably here to ask about her ice cream binge.

She marched toward the front door. She'd tell them what they could do with their ice cream story.

Poised, polite, proud. Becca's mantra went through her head, and she gritted her teeth. Why should she bother being polite? They were going to write whatever they wanted anyway.

The doorbell rang a fourth and fifth time before she reached the foyer.

"What?" she snarled as she yanked the door open. That was as polite as she was going to manage today.

A dark-haired woman stood on the porch, fidgeting with something in her hands. But the moment her eyes fell on Lydia, she gasped and covered her mouth. Next thing Lydia knew, the woman was crying.

Lydia took a step backward, grabbing for the door. But for some reason, she couldn't close it on the woman's face. She obviously wasn't paparazzi, but why was she standing on Lydia's doorstep, crying?

"Are you okay? Can I get you some help?" It felt strange to hear her rescuer's words coming out of her own mouth.

The woman shook her head, laughing as she wiped at her eyes. "Sorry. Lydia St. Peter?"

Lydia glanced around nervously. Was the woman a stalker? She tightened her grip on the door and felt in her pocket for her phone.

The woman took a breath. "My name is Grace Donovan. Well, my maiden name is Calvano. I saw your post on the Adoption Reunion page. I've been trying to message you, but when I didn't get any answer . . . I recognized who you were from your picture so I thought I'd come in person instead. I don't want to intrude or anything. . . . It's just, I really wanted to meet you."

Lydia blinked, trying to catch up with the woman's words. "Grace? The Adoption Reunion page?" she repeated dumbly.

"You were adopted forty years ago? From Nashville?"

Lydia nodded numbly.

"And Lydia is your given name? Your adopted parents didn't change it?"

Again Lydia nodded. Aside from sitting her down when she was eight or so to tell her she was adopted, her parents had rarely spoken of it, but that much she knew. They'd kept her name as a thank you to the woman who had given her up so that they could have a child. More than once over the years, Lydia had wondered about her birth mother. But it had always felt disloyal to Mama and Daddy to ask for more information. She loved them dearly, and she was so grateful they had chosen her. She wouldn't be who or where she was without them.

But sometimes, especially since their deaths, she'd found herself longing to know where she'd come from. Where she belonged. That was why she had finally worked up the courage to post on the Adoption Reunion site.

She hadn't anticipated the small knot of guilt she'd feel every time she thought about the post. Which was probably why she'd stopped checking her messages months ago.

"I think—" Grace touched a hand lightly to Lydia's arm. "You might be my half-sister."

"Sister?" The word came out as a strangled whisper.

Grace nodded, swiping a hand under her eyes. "I think it's possible, yes. My mother gave up a baby girl named Lydia in Nashville forty years ago. And now that I see you in person . . ." She passed Lydia the object she'd been fidgeting with, and Lydia realized it was a photograph.

It was obviously old, but the woman in it had the same dark hair as Lydia, the same hooded eyes and thin nose, even the same tiny indentation under her lip that showed when she smiled.

"That's my mama," Grace said. "Your mama."

Lydia licked her lips, her heart throbbing a sudden sharp staccato beat.

Maybe the woman in the photo was her mother. But that made her one more person who had abandoned Lydia.

"I know this is a lot to take in," Grace said kindly. "But I was hoping you'd be willing to talk. Well, honestly, I was hoping you'd be willing to meet the rest of the family."

"The— Um. The rest of the family?" The word felt foreign on Lydia's lips.

Grace laughed, the sound nearly an exact duplicate of Lydia's laugh. "I—we—have six brothers. They'd all love to meet you."

Six? Was that even possible, outside of the Brady Bunch or the Partridge Family?

"My mother?" The words croaked out of her.

Grace's face fell. "I'm so sorry. She passed away a few years ago. She told me about you shortly before she died and gave me her blessing to look for you. I've been searching so long. I just can't believe I finally found you. How many times have I seen your picture on TV and the internet, but I never put two and two together. I mean, why would I think . . ." She stopped. "Sorry. I'm babbling."

Lydia shook her head. This had to be a joke. A trick. Some kind of scam. Grace had said herself that she'd seen Lydia on TV and the internet. She probably wanted to get her hands on the fortune Mama and Daddy had left.

Just because Lydia looked like some woman in an old photo didn't mean they were family.

"I think you should go." The words didn't come out as forcefully as she'd hoped, but Grace seemed to get the message.

Her smile faded, and her shoulders fell. "Please. I know this is a lot, but . . ."

"It's too much." Lydia grabbed the door.

"Wait." Grace stepped forward, holding out a hand.

Lydia didn't know why she obeyed.

Grace pulled a small notebook and a pen out of her purse and scribbled something on a page. Then she ripped it out and held it toward Lydia. Reluctantly, Lydia took it, glancing at the neat handwriting that was eerily similar to her own. It was a phone number and an address.

"Our—my—family is all in River Falls. It's a small town in the Smokies, about three hours from here. I'll be there for another week or so, before I go back to my home in Wisconsin. Please, will you consider coming?"

Lydia pressed her lips together and held the photograph out to Grace. But Grace waved it off. "You keep it."

With a nod, Lydia closed the door. Then she let out a shaky breath. She couldn't keep her eyes from locking on the picture in her hand.

Was this really her mother?

Lydia fiddled with the charm bracelet Mama and Daddy had given her the first time she'd ever performed with them. They were her family.

But they were gone now.

Her phone dinged with a text from Becca. Good. She could use a pat on the back from her manager right about now.

But instead, Becca had sent a screenshot of Dallas and Cheyenne's names at the top of the Billboard chart. *We need a song*, her text read. In case her message hadn't sunk in this morning, apparently.

Before she'd consciously decided to do it, Lydia's fingers were tapping out a search for River Falls.

The pictures that came up looked quaint—idyllic, even—with the Smokies as their backdrop. It might just be the perfect place to write a song.

She clicked her phone off.

Now was not the time to be indulging in wild fantasies.

Chapter 4

"I'm going and you can't stop me." Mia crossed her arms in front of her, treating Liam to her most defiant stare.

"Want to bet?" Liam's voice rose, even as he pondered collapsing on the couch behind him and dropping his head into his hands. After a long day of upgrading the lighting at a nearby park, he just wanted a warm shower and a cold glass of water. He supposed he should be thankful he'd gotten home before Mia had made it to the car and taken off. Honestly, sometimes he wondered if moving to River Falls had helped at all. After ten months here, his daughter seemed to resent him more than ever. And now that she had her driver's license, it felt like a full-time job keeping tabs on her.

"Those car keys are not a right, you know. They're a privilege. And right now, they're a privilege you've lost." He held out his hand, waiting for her to drop the keys into it.

Mia's mouth opened, but she silently gave him the keys, then spun on her heel and stalked out of the living room. She waited until she was in the hallway to drop the bombshell. "Why couldn't you have died instead of Mom?"

Liam forced himself to keep his back straight and his mouth shut until Mia's bedroom door had slammed.

Then he dropped onto the couch, pressing his fingers into his face and running them down his cheeks. Sometimes he asked himself the very same question.

"Keep praying for her." Mama made her way into the room, navigating her walker carefully around the furniture in spite of the fact that her eyesight had deteriorated to the point that she could no longer pick out the large oak tree through the back window. But he supposed fifty years of living in the same house had imprinted its layout permanently in her mind.

Liam blew out a breath. "I haven't stopped praying for her since the day she was born." For all the good it had done. It'd gotten to the point where he had to force her to go to church on Sundays. And still he wasn't sure it was enough. If giving up his own faith would have helped bring Mia back, he would do it—but that wasn't how it worked.

"God is faithful." It was Mama's favorite line, and Liam had heard it probably a million or more times in his life. And yet, right now, he had to admit he appreciated the reminder.

"You're proof of that," Mama added.

Liam made a face. He'd had his moments of rebellion as a teen, yes—far too many of them. But fortunately, he'd met Molly and started attending Bible study just to spend more time with her. Who could have known he'd start listening to what Pastor Calvano said?

God knew.

"I know, Mama." He took her arm to help her into the rocking chair, trying not to notice how frail she seemed compared to the Mama he'd grown up with. The fall last year had taken a toll on her.

"All I'm saying is, don't give up. God is strongest when we are weak."

"And thank the Lord for that." Liam moved back toward the couch. He'd let himself sit down for five minutes, then go shower and make some dinner.

But before he'd lowered himself to the cushion, the doorbell chimed. With a sigh, he straightened mid-sit. "I'll get it."

That was one thing he'd forgotten about living in a small town—people tended to drop by whenever they felt like it. Not that he minded. It was kind that folks stopped by to chat with Mama. But sometimes a person wanted their space.

As he reached for the door, he prepared a smile—Mama's friends were always asking after Mia, and he needed to be ready to tell them how well she was doing here in River Falls. Because if he said anything else, they'd be only too ready with their well-intentioned but utterly outrageous advice. Mrs. Stanton had actually suggested that he send Mia to military school. Liam had smiled politely, thanked her, and said he didn't think they were quite at that point. To which she'd raised an eyebrow and given him a knowing look.

Please don't let it be Mrs. Stanton, Lord, Liam prayed before he opened the door.

But as his eyes fell on the woman standing there, his breath caught on the edges of his lungs, and his lips moved into a pointless circle.

Because this wasn't Mrs. Stanton at all. Or any of Mama's silver-haired friends.

This woman had dark hair and darker eyes.

Just like he remembered.

This time he knew her name.

Who didn't?

One of the biggest stars in country music. At least until that day they'd met. When he'd seen the headlines the next day, he'd felt like an idiot. He'd been pouring out his problems to a celebrity—a celebrity with her own problems. And yet, she had listened and sympathized and seemed to really *care*. It was hard to believe that had been ten months ago.

Probably because he couldn't get that night out of his head, no matter how much time went by.

"What are you doing here?" He winced. He could have at least found a politer way to ask. And he could have found time for that shower.

The woman's expression changed—she looked startled, and for half a second, he thought she might recognize him, but then the look passed. Of course she didn't recognize him. She was *Lydia St. Peter*, and he was some forgettable electrician she happened to talk to one night almost a year ago.

"I'm here about the carriage house."

If Liam had any doubts about the woman's identity, her full, resonant voice answered them.

"The carriage house?" he asked blankly. What did she care about the apartment above the old carriage house—now the garage?

"I called and spoke to someone about renting it for the week."

Renting it? Liam had only just started fixing it up. The idea was to rent it out to vacationers someday—but it was a long way from being ready for that. "I'm sorry, we're not—"

"That was me, dear. Welcome. I'm Helen." Mama greeted the woman as she marched her walker toward the door. "Don't mind me, I'm a little slow getting around these days."

Lydia looked relieved. Because she didn't have to talk to Liam anymore?

"You must be Grace Calvano's sister." Mama stopped at Liam's side, smiling at their visitor.

Liam eyed his mother. She'd known the Calvanos forever. "Mama, you know Grace doesn't have—"

"Yes, ma'am. I guess so," Lydia said tentatively.

Liam bit back his reply. She guessed so? What kind of answer was that?

"Oh, none of that ma'am business here," Mama scolded. "You can call me Helen. Or Mama, if you want. I answer to either. And this is my son, Liam."

Lydia's eyes lifted to his, and she offered a small smile. The circuits of his heart jumped to life. Did she recognize him after all?

"Liam." Mama lifted her hand off her walker to nudge him. "Where are your manners?"

"Sorry." He cleared his throat. What was he supposed to say? *Remember me? From that incredible night last August?* "Nice to meet you."

Mama gave him a look that said she wasn't impressed. "Liam will grab the keys to the carriage house and help you with your bags," she said to Lydia.

"Mama, the carriage house isn't ready for renters yet," he said firmly, then turned to Lydia. "I'm sorry." And was he ever. He might not understand what Lydia St. Peter was doing on his doorstep asking to stay in his carriage house. But he did understand the way his heart had jolted to life again the moment he'd opened the door and found her there.

"Oh." Lydia's face fell. "Is there somewhere else . . ." She looked over her shoulder, as if a hotel might spring up in the field next door.

"Nonsense." Mama tapped his arm. "It's got plumbing and electrical, right? I'm sure Lydia doesn't need much else."

Liam worked not to cringe. If only Mama had seen the house this woman owned. He could only imagine what the carriage house would look like to her.

"As long as there's a bed and a coffee maker, I'm good." Lydia smiled the same smile that had run through his memories for the past ten months.

Liam considered putting up more of an argument. But it would be pointless. Mama always won in the end.

And besides, he couldn't help wondering if it was more than a coincidence that had brought Lydia to his door.

Right, Liam. Because God thinks you really stand a chance with Lydia St. Peter.

"I'll grab the keys and walk you over there," he muttered, escaping to the kitchen and taking more time than necessary to grab the keychain out of the drawer. Buck, his golden retriever, looked up from his spot on the rug by the back door.

"Sorry, boy, not suppertime yet. Want to come outside?" At least that way he'd have something to focus on other than the fact that the woman he was never supposed to see again had just showed up at his front door.

He shook his head in disbelief, then steeled himself and made his way back to the entry, where Mama and Lydia were chatting like old friends.

He held up the keys. "Ready?"

Lydia nodded, and Mama squeezed her arm. "Don't be a stranger. You come over here anytime you want a cup of tea or just a chat."

"Thank you, ma'am. I mean, Miss Helen. I will." Lydia offered Mama a warm smile, then stepped out the door.

Liam followed, wondering suddenly what on earth he was going to say to Lydia St. Peter as they walked the fifty yards to the carriage house. Buck sprinted toward the field, so he'd be no help with the conversation.

"Are your bags in your car?"

"Yeah."

"Okay."

Well, this was a brilliant conversation. Only forty more yards to keep it up.

"Sorry." He couldn't hold the question back. "*How* are you related to the Calvanos?"

Her laugh was wispy. "I'm not sure I understand it myself. But their mama, Heather Calvano, was my mama too. I don't know all the details, but she gave me up for adoption." There was a brokenness in her voice that made Liam want to reach out to her.

He pressed his hands to his sides. "How did you find them?"

"Grace found me. Through the Adoption Reunion app, which I had given up on. Until she showed up at my door yesterday."

He laughed. "That sounds like Grace."

"You know the Calvanos?" Lydia's eyes brightened.

"It's a small town. Everyone knows everyone. And—" He pointed across the cornfield on the other side of the carriage house. "They grew up right across the field. Their daddy still lives there. The oldest, Simeon, was best man at my wedding."

"Are they . . ." Lydia trailed off as if afraid to finish the sentence.

"Nice?" Liam supplied.

Lydia nodded.

"No." He chuckled at her alarmed expression. "Nice doesn't do them justice. They're the best."

Lydia blew out a breath. "I closed the door in Grace's face. Probably not the best first impression."

Liam's hand accidentally brushed the back of hers, the contact feather-light but electric. He shoved his hand in his pocket. "Trust me. She won't hold it against you. I promise there's nothing to worry about."

They reached her car, and she opened the trunk. Liam pulled out the single suitcase. "This is it? I always figured celebrities traveled with more than this."

Her sharp inhale was audible. "You recognize me?"

He laughed. "I don't think there's a person alive who wouldn't recognize you." The real question was, did *she* recognize *him*? He watched her, but her face had gone blank at his last statement, as if he'd offended her.

He closed the trunk and hefted her suitcase across the gravel driveway to the stairway that led up to the second floor of the barn-shaped carriage house. Buck romped out of the field and charged up ahead of him. At the top of the stairs, Liam unlocked the door, then pushed it open, passing

34

Lydia the keys. He stepped inside and flipped on a light, throwing the dingy space into high relief. He cringed at the dated countertop in the kitchen, the drab maroon on the living room walls.

He set the suitcase down and swiped a layer of dust off the table that held a pile of his tools. "When are you planning to meet the Calvanos?"

"Grace asked me to come over to her father's for lunch tomorrow, so . . ." She bit her lip and tucked a strand of hair behind her ear, looking adorably nervous.

"I'll plan to come by while you're gone and get some things done. I probably won't get to the painting, but I can at least clean up some of this mess." He gestured to the table.

"It's really fine. Please don't put yourself out for me. I'm just grateful for a quiet place to stay."

"You're welcome to stay as long as you like." Wait. Where had that come from? He took a step toward the door. "I'll, uh, let you get settled. But I'm over at the house if you need anything."

"Thank you, Liam." Her smile seemed to loosen from the inside out, and it was almost like he could see the tension in her face melting away.

He strode out the door before his heart could melt too.

Chapter 5

Lydia's eyes sprang open at the sound of a dog barking, and it took her a second to place the unfamiliar surroundings. But then her gaze fell on the window, and she spotted a man tossing a ball for a golden retriever.

"Liam," she whispered into her empty room. It was nice to finally put a name to the face that had lingered in her thoughts for the past ten months. She still couldn't quite understand how he lived next door to the family she hadn't even known she had.

All she knew was that the moment she'd seen him, the constant cloak of tension that had engulfed her in Nashville had eased. And a good night's sleep in this beautiful four-poster bed—old but obviously well cared for—hadn't hurt either.

And to think, she almost hadn't come.

But after Grace had left her house yesterday, the giant mansion that surrounded Lydia had grown more and more oppressive, until she'd found herself dialing Grace's number and throwing clothes in a suitcase.

And now here she was, about to meet her family.

She stretched and got out of bed, letting herself watch Liam pet his dog for a moment before closing the curtains to dress. By the time she'd pulled on her favorite pair of jeans and a white blouse and reopened the curtains, Liam and Buck were gone. She ignored the twinge of disappointment. As nice as it was to see a familiar face here, she was in town to meet her family, not fall in love with some guy she barely knew.

Not fall in love at all, she reminded herself.

She'd learned her lesson in that department. It didn't matter that as far as she could tell, Liam was everything Dallas hadn't been—she wasn't going to invite yet another person to abandon her. Which was why she'd already decided to stay only a week. That would give her enough time to get to know her half-siblings without getting too attached. And if a week wasn't long enough to get attached to her family, it certainly wasn't long enough to get attached to Liam.

She got a pot of coffee going, then wandered onto the balcony that wrapped around the entire second floor, drifting to the portion that looked out over the large backyard. Scattered trees dotted a slope that led down to a quietly flowing river, and in the distance, lush hills created a perfect cocoon around the valley. She felt tucked away here. Anonymous. She pulled in a deep breath. The air smelled like summer and flowers and hope. Contentment settled over her as she envisioned herself sitting out here writing a new song.

The sound of the coffee percolating reached her ears through the open door, and she stepped back inside to fill a mug and bring it out to the balcony. As she sipped it and listened to the birds call, a tiny, broken shard of her heart seemed to put itself back into place. There were thousands more like it that remained shattered, but at least it was a piece.

When she'd finished her coffee, she strolled the yard for a bit, glancing toward the house every now and then to check if Liam had come back outside. In between glances, she fought off the nerves brought on by the thought of meeting her family. What were they expecting? Would they like her? Would they ask why she didn't sing anymore? Had they read all the stories online? Did they already think she was crazy?

Finally, it was time to go over there. A fresh dose of panic hit as she moved toward her car.

She wouldn't have to go. She could get in her car and drive back to Nashville right now. It wasn't like she owed them anything. They were the ones who had abandoned her.

The bang of a door at the other side of the yard drew her attention, and her lips lifted. The tension in her shoulders released as she waved to Liam.

He waved back, his pace quickening as he got closer. Buck had been lying under a tree, but apparently the sight of Liam excited him, and he jumped to his feet, loping first toward Liam, then changing directions and charging at her.

"Buck, come," Liam called.

But the dog didn't so much as turn its head. It had zeroed in on Lydia and was coming at her full tilt. She scampered halfway up the carriage house steps.

"Buck, sit." Liam's voice was commanding, and Lydia took her eyes off the dog to find Liam sprinting, his long legs swallowing up the ground.

Her eyes went back to the dog, who had stopped right at the bottom of the steps and was sitting with his head cocked to the side, tail wagging, tongue lolling.

She couldn't help cocking her head to the side too. Fine, he was a little bit cute. But that didn't mean she trusted him. Dogs acted like they loved you—but in the end, they always left you. Just like people.

"Sorry," Liam puffed as he drew to a stop behind the dog. "He's harmless. But he can look scary when he barrels at you like that."

"I wasn't scared." Lydia trounced back down the steps to prove her point.

Liam raised an eyebrow at her. "But you're not a dog person?"

She shrugged. "I had a dog as a kid, but he ran away."

"Ah. Well, Buck likes to explore, but he knows where he's got it good. Don't you, boy?" He scratched behind the dog's ears, and Buck groaned.

Lydia laughed. "I see that."

"I thought I'd work on the carriage house now. If you're headed to the Calvanos."

Lydia let out a quick breath. "Yeah. I'm kind of nervous." She looked away. She hadn't meant to confess that. She was supposed to say everything was fine.

"Hey." His hand touched her elbow for only a second, but it was long enough to make her stomach leap the same way it had the first night they'd met. "It's going to be great."

Lydia bit her lip, twisting the bracelet on her wrist. "It's just strange. One day, you think you're completely alone in the world. And the next day, you find out you have seven siblings." She looked at him. "I don't even know how to be a sister."

"I imagine it's a lot like being yourself, just with a bunch of other people around." Liam's warm smile soothed some of the nerves.

But not all of them.

"I've been dreaming about my birth family since I learned I was adopted. Not that I didn't love my adoptive parents," she rushed to add.

But Liam nodded as if he understood. "And you're afraid they won't live up to your expectations."

"More like, I won't live up to theirs."

"Trust me, they'll love you."

"You think so?"

"Absolutely." As they'd been talking, they'd somehow moved closer together, but Liam took a step back and cleared his throat. "I should let you get going." He gestured for Lydia to move past him, and she was gripped with a desperate urge to grab his arm and ask him not to make her do this alone.

"You said you know the Calvanos well?"

"Yeah." He gave her a strange look.

"Well enough that it wouldn't be odd for you to join a family lunch?"

Surprise registered on Liam's face. "It wouldn't be odd, no."

Lydia bit her lip. Did she have the guts to go ahead and make the ask?

"Do you want me to come along?" Liam asked before she could work up the courage.

Relief coursed through her, but she tried to remain casual. "I mean, it might be nice to have a familiar face over there. And I already know you're a good guy." She toed the ground with her sandal. If he didn't remember her, he was going to think she was crazy. And if he did remember her—well, then he already knew she was crazy.

She let her eyes meet his, which slowly crinkled into a smile. "I wasn't sure you remembered."

"Our surreal night?" She let the laugh that tickled the back of her throat escape. "I remember. But I didn't expect to see you again. Here, of all places."

"Likewise." He tucked his hands into his pockets, his eyes still on hers. "That night— I had no idea you were . . ."

"In the middle of a breakdown?" she said wryly.

He shook his head. "I was going to say famous."

She clutched the music note charm on her bracelet. "It was nice not to be famous for a night. I've always wanted to thank you for that."

His smile seemed to reach for her. "You're welcome."

Chapter 6

The walk from the carriage house across the field to the Calvanos had not been nearly long enough to prepare Lydia for this. As she and Liam reached the edge of the narrow tree line that separated the field from a large yard, Lydia drew to a stop, her eyes taking everything in.

Half a dozen grown men played a loud game of football on the front lawn. A slightly smaller group of women gathered on the porch with an older-looking man. Lydia swallowed. There were so many people. Were they all her . . . family? A lump the size of a guitar formed in her throat, and she blinked a few times. Liam had already seen her cry enough the first night they'd met.

"So Simeon is the shortest one. Kind of a sore spot with him, since he's the oldest." Liam had stopped next to her, and she caught a whiff of the clean, outdoorsy scent she'd noticed on him that first night. She followed his finger, which was pointing toward the man about to snap the football.

"And that's Levi Donovan." Liam's finger shifted to the guy who had received the snap and was going back to throw. "Grace's husband. Used to play in the NFL." Liam's eyes came to her. "So I guess they're used to having famous people in the family."

In spite of her nerves—or maybe because of them—a laugh spilled out of Lydia. "I don't know if that should make me feel better or not."

"It should." His eyes crinkled into that smile again, before he moved to point out the rest of the brothers. "Zeb is the big guy. Joseph is the lanky one. Asher is the one with the beard. And Benjamin is the baby face. He's the youngest. Currently studying to be a chef."

Lydia counted in her head. "That's only five brothers and one brother-in-law."

Liam frowned. "Judah hasn't been home in years. I would guess that you won't see him at all."

"Why?" From everything Liam had said so far, Lydia had gotten the impression that the Calvanos were the perfect family.

"I'm not sure anyone really knows. He went off to college, fell away, and stopped coming home."

"Fell away?"

"From the faith. Their dad is a pastor, so I don't know if something happened there or . . ." His expression was grave. "Broke their mama's—your mama's—heart."

Lydia swallowed. What if they found out she hadn't been to church since Mama and Daddy's funeral? Would they kick her out of the family?

She straightened her shoulders. She'd grown up going to church. She knew all the right things to say. And it wasn't like it would kill her to go to a service, if it came down to it.

"And that's their daddy, on the porch by Grace?" She squinted toward the older gentleman, who looked kind, at least from here.

"Yep. Best preacher you ever heard. You're going to love his sermons."

Lydia made herself nod. "And what about the other women?"

"Let's see." Liam pointed. "That's Zeb's wife Carly. Simeon's wife Abigail. Joseph's wife Ava. And Asher's wife Ireland." He waited a few beats, then asked, "You ready?"

Lydia licked her suddenly dry lips and turned to him, panic shooting through her chest and nerves popping in her belly. "What if they don't like

me? According to Grace, she didn't even know I existed until her mama—"
She fumbled over the words. "My mama, I guess, was dying."

Liam eyed her. "She came looking for you, right? I don't think she would
have done that if she didn't want to meet you."

"But the others. I don't know if . . ."

Liam squeezed her arm, his fingers warm and somehow grounding her.
"They're going to love you. Come on."

Before she could reply, he was stepping into the yard and calling out
greetings to the Calvanos.

A surge of adrenaline went through Lydia as she followed him, making
her want to giggle. But she clamped her lips together. The last thing she
needed was for her new family to think she'd lost it.

Everyone stopped talking, and the familiar pre-show nausea rolled over
her. But then she made eye contact with Liam, who gestured her forward.
She took a step toward him, letting herself draw strength from the smile in
his eyes.

"I'm so glad you came." Grace practically leaped off the porch. For half
a second, Lydia was afraid she would expect a hug, but Grace stopped in
front of her, smiling. Apparently Liam had been right. Grace didn't seem
to hold Lydia's rudeness yesterday against her.

"Everyone, this is Lydia," Grace announced as the family converged on
them, so many smiles and warm greetings flying her way that Lydia could
barely catch her breath.

"We figured out who she is, Grace," one of the brothers said. "Why don't
you tell her who we are?"

"Oh yeah." Grace gave her an apologetic smile, but before she could
start the introductions, Lydia pointed to the brother who had spoken.
"Benjamin."

A surprised laugh burst out of him, and he nodded.

She pointed to the other men in turn: "Simeon, Joseph, Asher, Zeb. And Levi. Grace's husband."

Benjamin let out a low whistle as the others grinned at her. "You've done your homework."

Lydia let herself relax enough to smile. "It helps that Liam just pointed y'all out. And I have an uncanny memory for names."

"Really? Me too." This time it was Joseph who spoke.

"Yeah, but you remember animal names, not people names," the woman who had moved to wrap her arms around Joseph's waist teased. Now that she was up close, Lydia could see that one side of the woman's face bore what looked like burn scars. As Joseph dropped a kiss onto the woman's head, Lydia's chest tightened. Liam had been right. This did seem to be the best kind of family.

"You must be Ava, right? And—" She pointed to the other women one at a time. "Carly and Abigail. And Ireland."

"You got us all." Grace beamed at her. "And this is our daddy. Abe Calvano." She gestured to the older gentleman with the slightly rounded middle who had stepped forward.

"Pastor Calvano." Lydia moved toward him tentatively. She had so wanted to meet at least one of her birth parents. But when she'd called Grace back yesterday, she'd learned that her birth father had left her mother when he found out she was pregnant as a teen. That was how Lydia had ended up at the adoption agency. And why Pastor Calvano had every reason to hate her.

"Please, call me Abe." The man's eyes watered through his smile. "You have your mother's eyes."

Lydia had to look away, blinking hard, before she could return his smile. Growing up, people who didn't know she was adopted used to say that to her, and she would always smile and say thank you, though she'd known it couldn't be true. But after seeing the picture of her birth mother, she knew Abe's comment was sincere.

"Come on," Grace broke in. "Lunch is ready." She took Lydia's arm and led her toward the front door. "We'll make sure you get some first. Having these animals for brothers means you have to fight to get fed."

"I'm just glad Grace isn't the only girl anymore," Benjamin called from behind them. "Now she can't keep using that as an excuse to be treated like a princess."

Grace stuck her tongue out at her brother. "Like you've ever treated me like a princess."

An unfamiliar sense of belonging went through Lydia. So many times in her life, she'd wished for siblings to laugh with and tease with and even fight with. Would the Calvanos treat her like that eventually?

She looked over her shoulder at the brothers—*her* brothers—who were involved in some sort of scuffle that seemed to involve Asher's baseball cap.

"Boys," Grace muttered.

Lydia laughed, but her heart filled. She'd met celebrities, sung before sold-out stadiums, even walked the red carpet. But this felt bigger.

Her eye caught Liam's, and his smile sent a warning flutter through her.

This might seem big right now. But her career was bigger. She'd stay here for the week, then get back to her real life.

Chapter 7

Liam had gotten sucked into a game of football with the Calvano boys after lunch, but his eyes kept drifting to the porch, where Lydia was poring over old photo albums with Pastor Calvano and the women. She looked so . . . happy—so much less tormented than the first night he'd met her—that it made something in Liam's heart lighten just to look at her.

"Liam, heads up," Benjamin called, and Liam spun just in time to catch the pass sailing his way. He ran with it toward the edge of the yard, which served as their end zone, but he was half a dozen yards short when Zeb brought him down with a thud.

"I'm getting too old for this," he groaned as Zeb jumped to his feet, then held out a hand to help him up.

"Or too distracted," Simeon joked as he jogged up to them.

Involuntarily, Liam's eyes darted to Lydia, but he forced them back to the guys gathering around for the next play.

"Yeah seriously," Benjamin gave him a mock shove. "Stop staring at our sister. Or Zeb will have to have a talk with you."

"You should have seen Levi when Zeb told him he better not hurt Grace," Asher filled in. "Not such a tough football player then." He elbowed his brother-in-law, and the Calvano men all laughed.

"Scariest day of my life," Levi deadpanned.

Liam shook his head. He highly doubted that the former quarterback had been intimidated by Grace's brothers. Though he knew they were fiercely protective of their family—and he sure wouldn't want to be the one to cross them, close as he was to them.

And anyway, this conversation was preposterous. He had no reason to worry about the Calvano brothers because he had no interest in their sister.

"Are we going to play or what?" He took his position, and the rest of the guys followed suit. He ran long, and this time he was ready for the pass Benjamin spiraled his way. He made it across the goal line before Zeb could stop him.

Benjamin and Asher tackled him in a celebratory heap, and Liam couldn't help grinning. He may miss Nashville sometimes, but moments like this made him glad he'd come back.

Of their own accord, his eyes went to Lydia yet again. She was facing their way and smiling, looking perplexed by their antics but also pleased.

Next to her, Grace said something and Lydia nodded, then got up and followed her sister into the house.

As their game broke up, Simeon fell into step next to Liam.

Liam had known his friend long enough to realize he had something to say. He drew to a stop and turned to Simeon. "What?"

Simeon raised his hands at his sides but laughed. "It's pretty clear you have a thing for Lydia."

Instead of the denial he had planned in his head, Liam blurted, "She's the one."

"The one?" Simeon gawked at him. "Until now, you haven't so much as looked at another woman, and now she's the one?"

Liam shook his head impatiently. "Not *the one*, like that. The one from that night in Nashville."

He'd told Simeon about his bizarre but enchanting encounter with Lydia months ago, though he hadn't mentioned who she was because he'd figured Simeon would think he was crazy—or had hallucinated the whole thing.

Simeon's eyes widened into a skeptical look. "You're telling me the mystery girl who wouldn't tell you her name was Lydia St. Peter? Why wouldn't you have said something sooner?"

"Because I figured you'd react like this."

Simeon frowned in thought. "Good point. So you're being serious?"

"One hundred percent."

"What are the chances?"

Liam shrugged. "I don't know. What are the chances Lydia St. Peter would be your sister?"

"Another good point. And now she's here and you're wondering what it means and what you should do."

"No, I'm not. I already know what I should do. Nothing."

Simeon shook his head. "So the woman you've been dreaming about for the past year walks back into your life, and you're not going to do anything."

"I have not been dreaming about her for the past year." It had only been ten months. And it wasn't like he thought about her *every* day.

"You forget how well I know you, man. Like right now, you're thinking you want to deck me."

"Sure, but that was an obvious one."

"I'm just saying—" Simeon glanced toward the house, where Lydia and Grace had stepped back onto the porch.

Liam ignored the way his heart surged.

"You'd be an idiot if you let her get away again," Simeon finished.

"No, I'd be an idiot to pursue anything with her. She's Lydia St. Peter, for crying out loud. A little bit out of my league. And anyway, I have enough on my plate, between Mama and Mia and work."

"Excuses." Simeon gave him a hard look. "It's okay to think about your own happiness once in a while too, you know."

"I'm happy enough." At least most of the time. Aside from the occasional night when the ache of missing Molly sharpened into a hard point in his chest. But that happened less frequently as the years went by, and he had learned to deal with the loneliness.

"Look." Simeon clapped a hand to his shoulder. "All I'm saying is, if you want to ask her out, you have my blessing. I'll leave the talk about not hurting her to Zeb. But I know you wouldn't."

Of course he wouldn't.

Liam thought again of the tears that had streaked her face the first time he'd met her. The way he'd wanted to pound whoever had done that to her.

But just because he wouldn't hurt her—just because he wanted to shield her from anything that could ever make her sad again—didn't mean he wanted to date her.

He glanced her way again, his heart filling at the joy on her face.

She looked up, catching his eye with a smile, and he couldn't help the thought: *There could be something there.*

And then he snorted at himself. She was Lydia St. Peter. Not just a little out of his league. Way out.

Chapter 8

Lydia surveyed herself in the full-length mirror, frowning, then slipped her sunglasses over her eyes.

That was better.

She'd gotten so used to going out in public in incognito mode that the thought of letting people see her sent a shiver of dread up her spine. But if she kept her head down, maybe people wouldn't recognize her.

She wondered briefly if it would be rude to keep the sunglasses on during the church service.

She shook her head at herself.

Church.

What had she been thinking, accepting Grace's invitation to the service?

That a family like the Calvanos wouldn't have any interest in a lapsed believer, that was what. Judah's name had only come up a couple of times during the past week, but every time it did, she felt the tension that rippled through the family.

So she'd smiled and thanked Grace for the invitation, then gone so far as to agree to attend the church picnic afterward. Which she was very much regretting right now, though she didn't see any way out of it.

But it was her last full day in River Falls, and if that was where her family was going to be, it was where she should be too.

She sighed—the heaviness in her heart grew every time she thought about leaving this quiet little town and returning to her non-life in

Nashville. But what was she going to do—stay here and impose on the Calvanos, and Liam, indefinitely?

With one more glance in the mirror, she grabbed her keys and stepped out the door. She'd told Grace she'd meet her at the church, since Grace was going early to help set things up for the picnic. She typed the address her sister—they had taken a DNA test earlier in the week that confirmed their relationship—had given her into the phone, then plodded down the steps. Already, humidity hung heavy in the air, and Lydia glanced up, half hoping it would rain and force them to cancel the picnic. But the few clouds that hung in the sky were soft and wispy, not stormy.

As she reached the bottom step, she caught sight of movement at the other side of the yard. One tall, broad form, one much smaller, slightly stooped one.

Involuntarily, Lydia's feet slowed as she watched Liam help his mama navigate down the porch steps, then turn and call something over his shoulder. A second later, a teenage girl slammed out the door and clomped across the porch, gesturing as she said something Lydia couldn't hear, then stomping across the yard toward the driveway.

Liam shook his head, then took his mother's arm in one of his and led her much more slowly behind the girl.

Something in Lydia's heart stirred at the care he showed his mama, and the thought went through her again that he was different from other men she'd known. Different from Dallas, who, she saw in retrospect, had rarely shown care for anyone but himself.

As if Liam felt her eyes on him, he looked up. Although he was in the shadow of a large tree, she could make out the smile on his face, and that stirring in her heart grew stronger. She'd only seen him in passing most of the week, as he came and went from work and she came and went from spending time with the Calvanos. But Friday night she'd come home from playing video games with Benjamin—she still wasn't sure how he'd talked her into that—to find Liam installing a new light fixture in the carriage house kitchen. Though she'd been planning to curl up in bed with a book, she stayed and watched him work instead. They'd ended up sitting at the table long after he was done, talking about the Calvanos and his electrical business and Mia. It hadn't been quite as surreal as that night in Nashville. But in some ways it had been better. Because she knew who he was now. Knew he was exactly the good man she'd taken him to be.

Careful.

But Lydia didn't need to give herself the warning. She already knew that she wasn't going to go getting feelings for this man. It was just nice to have a friend, that was all.

"Good morning," she said to the teenage girl who was now scudding her feet across the gravel driveway. She'd met Mia earlier in the week but had yet to get a word out of her. If Mia's glare could talk though . . .

The girl ducked into the back seat of the sedan parked in the driveway and slammed her door shut behind her.

"Sorry about Mia," Liam called, guiding his mama onto the gravel of the driveway and steering her toward the passenger side of the car. "She wasn't exactly thrilled to get up for church." He gave her a wry smile, but she could hear the concern in his voice.

"That's okay. I'm not a morning person either." Lydia scurried to open the car door for Helen, and Liam gave her a grateful smile as he helped his mama navigate the space.

"You hide it well. You look . . ." He cleared his throat and ducked his head, as if he hadn't meant to say that out loud.

Lydia pressed her lips together to keep her grin from escaping. It was kind of cute, seeing him flustered. Her cheeks warmed, wondering how he'd been planning to end that sentence, but he recovered and said, "Until you growl at me first thing in the morning, I'll consider you more of a morning person than Mia. I mean—" Liam looked flustered again. "I didn't mean for that to sound like I'd see you first thing in . . ."

Helen squinted up at Liam with a laugh and an eye roll, then turned to Lydia. "Headed to church?"

Lydia nodded, though something made her want to confess to them what a fraud she was.

"Climb on in," Helen said. "No sense taking two vehicles when we're all going to the same place."

"Oh, that's okay, I—"

"Nonsense, dear. The parking lot is going to be packed today, what with the picnic and all." Helen gestured for Liam to open the back door, as if the matter had already been settled.

Liam gave her an apologetic look. "I'm afraid there's no use arguing with Mama. You'll just waste your time and your breath. She always wins in the end."

"Trust him," Helen said. "He's been losing arguments to me for forty-two years."

"Mama, I highly doubt I was arguing with you the moment I came out of the womb." Liam grinned at Lydia and muttered, "Watch this."

"There you go again," his mama said. "Starting another argument you can't win. You were the most cantankerous baby anyone ever saw. We had plenty of arguments even then. You just don't remember it."

"See, what'd I tell you?" Liam chuckled, his eyes lighting on hers. "You might as well get in." He closed his mother's car door, then pulled the back door open for Lydia. "If you're brave enough to sit next to Mia," he muttered under his breath.

Lydia gave him one more hesitant look. Was it weird to go to church with him? But she wasn't going *with* him. Just getting a ride from him.

And his mama and daughter.

She ducked into the car. Mia spared her half a glance before looking out the window again.

The ride to church was pleasant enough, with Helen pointing out the local sights along the river, including Daisy's Pie Shop, Joseph's veterinary practice, and Henderson's art gallery. Lydia interjected politely, unwilling to ruin Helen's fun as tour guide by telling her that she'd spent the day in town with Grace and her sisters-in-law yesterday. They'd walked along the river that ran behind the shops, bought t-shirts at the Sweet Boutique, and had pie at Daisy's. It had been possibly the most perfect day she'd ever spent.

By the time Liam pulled the car into the parking lot of the church, Lydia had nearly forgotten her nerves, but they rushed at her afresh.

She pressed her lips together as she examined the large brick building. It looked a lot like the church Mama and Daddy had taken her to whenever they weren't on the road.

Liam parked the car and hopped out, then rounded the vehicle to open her door and then his mama's. With a sigh clearly meant to convey her irritation, Mia opened her door as well. Taking a deep breath, Lydia stepped outside, checking that her sunglasses were secure on her nose, grateful that even if she wouldn't be able to hide her eyes during the service, no one would be able to see the truth in her heart—that she didn't belong here.

With Mia, she trailed behind Liam and his mother as they led the way to the church, ducking her head and letting her hair fall over her face, looking up only occasionally to make sure she wasn't going to trip.

As they stepped into the building, she forced herself to push her sunglasses onto the top of her head but kept her gaze directed down.

"I'm glad you could make it." Abe appeared at her side and squeezed her elbow, then shook Liam's hand and Helen's. "I think Grace is finishing up a couple of things, but she should be in shortly. The rest of the family is sitting up there." He pointed toward the front of the church, and Lydia swallowed. Of course the pastor's family would be in an exposed spot.

"But feel free to sit wherever you want." Abe seemed to sense her hesitation.

"Okay." Lydia forced the word out as she spotted a middle-aged woman eyeing her, as if trying to figure out where she knew her from. Lydia ducked her head and turned away to find Liam watching her.

She gave him a weak smile. "I guess I should go sit down."

"We'll come with you. Mama likes to be close to the front so she can see better."

Gratitude swelled in Lydia's chest. She didn't know why she felt more secure when he was around—and it was probably best not to examine that feeling too closely.

She followed him to the pew behind the Calvanos, who all turned around to greet her as if she was part of the family.

She noticed Simeon raise his eyebrows toward Liam in an unasked question and Liam shake his head. But before she could figure out what that was all about, a breathless Grace appeared at the end of the pew.

"I'm so sorry," Grace whispered as Lydia slid over, her shoulder accidentally bumping into Liam's arm before he slid over too. She ignored the tingle of the contact.

Grace settled into the pew next to Lydia as Abe greeted the worshipers and announced the first song.

"Did you make it here okay?" Grace whispered as she flipped her hymnal open.

Lydia nodded. "I rode with Liam and Helen and Mia."

"Oh good." Grace turned her focus to the music in front of her, her voice rising above those around her in a pure alto that made Lydia lift her head in surprise. Apparently, dark hair wasn't all she had in common with her sister. Grace had an incredible voice—and more than that, Lydia could hear the passion in it. She really believed what she was singing—really loved it.

Lydia hadn't felt that way about a song since before her parents had died. She let her eyes go to the words of the hymn, even though she knew it by heart. She'd sung Amazing Grace with Mama and Daddy a thousand times—many of them on stage. But today, as hard as she tried, she couldn't make herself open her mouth. Fortunately, no one around her seemed to notice.

After the hymn, Abe moved into prayers and readings from the Bible. Lydia watched her half-siblings in the pew in front of her. Watched the way Asher wrapped an arm around Ireland's shoulder. And the way Ava looked up to whisper something to Joseph that made him smile. And even the way Benjamin nudged Zeb to pass him a Bible. A familiar sense of loneliness went through her. Because even if the Calvanos had welcomed her and accepted her, she didn't really *belong* with them. She would never have the same backstory and memories as they did.

Liam shifted, his shoulder bumping hers as he leaned closer to whisper, "Everything okay?"

She gave him a questioning look, and he gestured to the worship folder that she'd crumpled in her fist.

"Yeah," she whispered back, smoothing the paper on her leg and sliding over so their shoulders no longer touched. "I'm fine."

Of course she was. She had made an art of being fine.

She folded her hands in her lap so she wouldn't crumple the paper again as Abe stepped into the pulpit. He looked around the church with a smile that made Lydia relax into the pew in spite of herself. Abe seemed to be just as welcoming from the pulpit as he was in person.

"This morning I have to tell y'all a story I've managed to keep secret for over forty years." Abe's voice rang out, and Lydia's head snapped up. She glanced down the row of Calvanos in a panic. He wasn't about to tell this whole congregation about how his wife had given her up for adoption, was he? She only just resisted the temptation to pull her sunglasses back over her eyes, but the paper in her hand crackled loudly. She ignored Liam's glance and made herself set the paper down.

"It's quite possibly the dumbest thing I've ever done," Abe continued. "And if you've paid attention to many of my sermons, you know I've done a lot of dumb things."

The congregation chuckled—no one harder than the Calvano siblings, and she relaxed. This couldn't be about her.

"See, I was helping my daddy make a new dining room table for my mama. And he kept telling me, 'Watch your thumb, watch your thumb' when I was using the table saw. But I was twenty years old, and I knew everything." He held up his hand, drawing a line in a circle above the knuckle on his thumb. "If you look up close, you can see the scar from where they reattached the part I cut off."

Lydia winced and felt Liam do the same next to her. She looked his direction and accidentally met his eyes. He smiled, and she pulled her gaze away but not before her tummy tickled.

"Funny part is, my daddy knew the moment it happened," Abe said from the pulpit. "He asked if I was okay. And you know what I said?" He paused, shaking his head. "I said, 'Yes, sir, I'm fine.'" He let out a hearty laugh at his own expense. "There I was, clutching my severed thumb in my other hand, bleeding all over the place, and I'm like, 'I'm fine. Never better.'" Many in the congregation were laughing outright now, and Lydia felt herself smiling. If nothing else, Abe was an engaging preacher.

"I don't know who I thought I was fooling. He was my daddy. He knew exactly what had happened. I probably deserved a knock upside the head for that one. But instead of hollering at me, my daddy wrapped an arm around me and took me to the hospital to get stitched up." Abe leaned against the pulpit, his eyes sweeping the congregation. "I've thanked God many times that my daddy was smart enough to know when I needed him."

Abe's voice grew serious. "You ever do that? Someone asks you how it's going, and you're like, 'Fine. Never better.' Even though it's not fine. Maybe you didn't cut your thumb off. But there's a bill on the table at home that you don't know how you're going to pay. Or the doctor just gave you the news no one wants to hear. Or you're worried about your kid."

Next to her, Lydia felt Liam tense, and she glanced in his direction. His jaw was clenched and he stared at the pulpit as if his life depended on hearing this sermon. On the other side of him, Mia sat with her arms crossed, her expression a mix of rebellion and boredom.

"Why is it we do that, do you think?" Abe asked. "Is it because we know the world is waiting to see us fail, and we don't want to give them the satisfaction? Is it because we think if we admit we have problems, it's like saying God has removed his favor from us, maybe proof that we're not good enough? Or is it pride? We're too stubborn to admit that we don't have it all under control? That we can't do it alone?"

All of those. Though she hadn't intended to take the sermon to heart, all of those things rang so true that Lydia couldn't help the bob of her head.

But what could she do about it? It wasn't like she could go around letting people see she didn't have it all together. It would destroy her image. An ironic smirk twisted her lips at the thought of how Becca would react if Lydia posted a confession of what a mess she really was.

"And you want to know what the really dumb part is?" Abe continued. "It's when we try to hide those things from God. Instead of going to him in prayer, we try to muscle through on our own. We try to come up with our own solutions, find our own way." He shook his head. "He's our Father. Don't you think he already knows all of our problems and struggles? What good is it doing us to pretend everything is fine when really what we need is for God to take us into his arms?"

Lydia stiffened. This was where he lost her. Because, in her experience, God didn't take her into his arms when she needed help.

"I know what you're thinking," Abe said, and Lydia's heart jumped—she could swear he was looking right at her.

"You did go to God with your problems, and he didn't take care of them. He left you out there on your own. Left you to fall flat on your face." He picked up his Bible. "You think you're the only one who ever felt like God was nowhere to be found? Well, I have news for y'all. No less a Biblical hero than David felt that way. Do you know how many times he called out to God, asking where he was, when he was going to come and rescue him?" He flipped the Bible open and read, "'How long, Lord? Will you forget me forever? How long will you hide your face from me?'" Abe flipped a few more pages. "'I am worn out calling for help; my throat is parched. My eyes fail, looking for my God.'" Flipping again, he read, "'So my spirit grows faint within me; my heart within me is dismayed.'"

Abe looked up. "There are plenty more, but you get the idea. Those don't exactly sound like the words of a guy called a man after God's own heart, do they?" He paused, looking thoughtful. "But, you know, that's exactly what they are. Because when David faced trouble, he didn't say, 'I'm fine, God. I've got this.' He said, 'I'm not fine, God. But *you've* got this.' Because see, his Psalms didn't stop with his despair. He poured out his worries and fears and problems to God. And then he said—" Abe directed his eyes back to the Bible. "'But I trust in your unfailing love; my heart rejoices in your salvation.' And, 'I have put my trust in you. Show me the way I should go, for to you I entrust my life.' And, 'Your righteousness, God, reaches to the heavens, you who have done great things. Who is like you, God? . . . My lips will shout for joy when I sing praise to you—I whom you have delivered.'"

Again Abe set the Bible aside, leaning forward with a gentle smile. "Who is like our God? That same God who delivered David, who redeemed his people—he has redeemed us. He has sent his Son to save us from our sins. And he promises to be with you in everything—even when you're not fine. *Especially* when you're not fine. So the next time you're tempted to hold it all together yourself, to put on a brave face and say everything is fine, to think you have to be the one to fix it, remember that. Turn to the Lord instead. Trust him with your life. And be okay with saying, 'I'm not fine, God. But you've got this.'"

As the sermon concluded, the words rang in Lydia's head. She could easily admit that she wasn't fine. But she wasn't quite sure she was ready to trust that God had it.

Chapter 9

Liam should be worried right now.

Benjamin Calvano—one of the best young quarterbacks to ever play for River Falls High—was currently poised to take a shot at the dunk tank in which Liam sat. But the feeling of relief from this morning's sermon was still with him. He had so desperately needed the reminder that it was okay to admit he didn't have it all together—and to trust that God did. Based on the way Lydia had reacted next to him as Pastor Calvano delivered the sermon, he had a feeling that she'd needed it too. He only hoped it had brought her as much peace as it'd brought him.

His eyes scanned the crowd gathered in the large green space behind the church, which had been transformed with tents, tables, and games for the picnic. Finally, he found the person he was looking for—Lydia had stopped outside one of the tents and appeared to be attempting to make conversation with Mia.

Good luck to her.

Liam couldn't remember the last time his daughter had uttered a word that wasn't snarky. And getting her to get ready for church this morning had been a nightmare—one that had culminated in him threatening to confiscate the car keys for a month if she didn't go. He wished he knew when she'd started to look at church as a punishment, rather than a gift. Probably around the time she'd started seeing that no-good boyfriend Zack in Nashville. Liam should have been more alert, insisted on getting to know the kid better.

He'd hoped that after almost a year apart, Zack's influence would have worn off. But if anything, Mia had only gotten more resistant since the move. Mama had reminded him this morning that someday Mia would thank him for taking her to church even when she didn't want to go. He only hoped that someday came soon. Because he wasn't sure how much longer he could do this. If Molly had been here . . .

Liam's eyes went again to Lydia and Mia, and he nearly fell off the dunk tank seat as Mia cracked a smile.

Lydia's lips moved as she said something, but before Liam could catch Mia's reaction, the seat dropped out from under him, and icy water closed over his head. He hadn't been ready for the hit, and it took a moment before he managed to get his feet under him and push to the surface. By the time he'd stopped coughing and cleared the water from his eyes, Lydia and Mia were no longer standing in the same spot.

"Get back up there," Benjamin called. "I have two more throws."

Liam shook his head but took his place on the narrow seat once again. He'd volunteered for this, after all, so he didn't have much of a choice.

Over the next hour or so, he was dunked more times than he could count—mostly by the Calvano brothers, who seemed to have made it their mission to keep him in the water. Not that Liam could complain—it was a hot day, and the ticket sales were going to a good cause. His only regret was that he'd been so busy climbing up and down from the seat that he'd lost track of Lydia.

Which was probably for the best.

"So how do I do this?" The throaty, feminine voice caught at his ears, and before he could turn his head, he felt his lips responding with a smile.

But when his eyes landed on her, he gaped. If he hadn't heard her voice, he wouldn't have recognized her. A giant glittery butterfly covered her entire face, from her forehead, across her cheeks and nose, and down onto her chin. The design was intricate, outlined in bold strokes of black, with dark pinks and purples filling in the open spaces. She looked like a princess out of a fairytale.

"Hit the bullseye." Benjamin stood next to her, pointing. "And he goes under. Trust me, it's a lot of fun."

Liam made a face at the youngest Calvano but clapped for Lydia. "Come on. Let's see what you've got."

The butterfly paint gave a quality of mystery to her smile, but her throw didn't make it anywhere near the target.

"Try again." Benjamin passed her another ball.

"I'm getting warm up here," Liam called. "I could use a refreshing dunk."

Again Lydia's throw went wide.

"Shake it off. You have one—" But before Liam had finished the sentence, he was underwater. His mouth had been open as he went down, and he came up spluttering and coughing.

"I'm so sorry. Are you all right?" Lydia rushed forward, holding a hand out toward the glass tank that enclosed him.

Liam shoved the hair out of his eyes. "I'm great," he managed. Despite the coughing, he really meant it. That electrical feeling in his heart was back, and he was finding less of a desire to fight it.

"You want me to take over?" Benjamin came up behind Lydia. "It's almost my shift anyway."

Liam's stomach rumbled. "If you wouldn't mind. I want to check on Mama. And I'm starving."

He climbed out of the tank and grabbed his beach towel off the chair, rubbing it over his face and hair. His wet t-shirt and shorts would have to dry in the sun.

"Nice towel." Lydia's voice was thick with a suppressed laugh, and Liam groaned as he pulled the towel away from his face.

He hadn't been able to find his own beach towel this morning, so he'd grabbed Mia's old one—which sported a shimmering mermaid tail.

"Thanks. I thought it went well with my hair."

Lydia's laugh burst out at that. He'd only heard the sound a few times before, and every time, it surprised him. He always expected it to be low and quiet, but it was bright and melodic.

"You eat yet?" He hadn't been planning to ask the question, yet he didn't want to take it back.

She shook her head. "I was waiting for Grace, but she's had a steady stream of customers at her face painting tent."

"I bet. I barely recognized you."

"That was kind of the point."

"You don't like to be recognized?"

She shrugged. "By people who think they know me because they've heard a few of my songs? Who think that gives them the right to every detail of my private life?" She cut off, her smile rueful under the makeup. "Sorry. That sounded really bitter."

"Nah. Only a little bitter. And understandable." He'd seen the way she'd been skewered online for what everyone called her breakdown. He often wondered why she'd never revealed the truth about that cheating scumbag.

"You wanted to check on your Mama?" The bitterness had left her voice—now she only sounded sweet and thoughtful. A dangerous combination if he didn't want his heart to take over.

"Yeah." He pointed to the food tent. "I'm going to go grab a plate and sit with her. You want to join us? I'm sure Mama would like that. She said you had tea with her the other day."

"Oh. Yeah." Lydia looked embarrassed. "I needed to borrow some tape, and she invited me in. I hope I wasn't overstepping or anything."

Liam let himself touch her arm. "No. She enjoyed it. She doesn't get out much anymore. I try to be around as much as I can, but . . . Anyway, thank you." Mama had been full of Lydia's praises when he'd gotten home that night. None of which he could refute. Except her suggestion that he ask Lydia to dinner.

"I should be the one thanking you. Your mama's a fascinating woman. And some of the stories she told me about you—"

Liam stopped in his tracks and swiveled toward her. But she was chuckling.

"Mama told you to say that, didn't she?"

Lydia laughed harder, and the melody of it made him want to go ahead and tell her one of those embarrassing stories, just to keep her laughing.

They reached the food tent, and Liam touched a hand to the small of her back to let her enter in front of him. The contact sent tingles through his fingers, making him pull his hand back and shove it in his pocket.

By the time they'd gotten their food and taken a seat by Mama, the feeling still hadn't completely passed, and he had to concentrate on not fumbling his meal. Fortunately, Mama monopolized Lydia's attention, asking her what she thought about River Falls and relaying some of the town's history, so Liam could focus on his food—and maybe the occasional glance at Lydia. But every glimpse only confirmed it: she was way out of his league.

"Oh, there's Betty. I'm going to go say hi." Mama slid her chair back, and Liam reached for her walker.

"I'll help you over there."

But Mama waved him off. "I'm not helpless yet, Liam."

As she shuffled away, Lydia chuckled. "She's quite a lady."

"That she is." Liam opened his mouth to say more, but suddenly everything he'd been thinking about saying sounded foolish in his head.

"I'm going to go grab some dessert," he burst out. "You want anything?"

She shook her head, but he'd only made it two steps from the table when her voice stopped him. "Actually, you know what, I do. Think they have any apple pie?"

Liam laughed. Did they have any apple pie? That was like asking if the North Pole had any elves. "Yeah. I think they do."

At the dessert table, he loaded a plate for himself with a slice of apple pie and a brownie, then put together another plate with the same for her. If he couldn't convince her to eat the brownie, he'd make the sacrifice and take it off her hands.

As he turned away from the table, he nearly crashed into his daughter, who was glaring at him with arms folded across her chest. "What are you doing?"

"Getting dessert. Did you have any?"

"I mean with *her*." Mia nodded toward their table, where Lydia was taking a drink of water.

"Oh. Eating. I saw you two talking together before. That was nice."

Mia rolled her eyes. "You're so dense sometimes." Then she stalked away.

Liam shook his head. *Lord, help me to understand my daughter*, he prayed for the umpteenth time. It was so much easier when she was younger. She'd been ten when Molly died, and she'd been his little pal then, accompanying him to jobs and cheerfully holding his hand at the zoo. But the last couple of years . . .

He wondered if all teenage girls were this hard to deal with or if he'd just been particularly blessed.

As he approached the table, he spotted Grace making a beeline for Lydia, and his heart fell a little—which made no sense, since he liked Grace just fine and was sure she wanted to spend as much time with her sister as possible.

Grace reached the table before he did, but he came up behind Lydia in time to hear Grace's apology for getting caught up in the face painting tent.

"No problem," Lydia said, her back to him. "Liam's been good company."

Liam's chest lit up. He slowed his footsteps so she wouldn't know he'd overheard.

But as he passed her the plate, her warm smile forced him to admit it. She may be way out of his league. But Lydia St. Peter was firmly in his heart.

Fortunately, she was returning to Nashville tomorrow, so he wouldn't have to worry about making a fool of himself by asking her out.

Chapter 10

Lydia couldn't remember the last time she had been this exhausted. Or this content.

It had turned out to be a good day after all, and the church picnic had been more fun than she'd expected.

But now it was over, and she was standing face-to-face with Grace, wondering how to say goodbye to the sister she'd just met.

"I can't believe we have to go already." Grace swiped at her eyes as they stood in the driveway of the carriage house. Liam had taken his mama home a couple hours ago, but Lydia had stayed with the rest of the Calvanos to help clean up. Grace and Levi had given her a ride back to the carriage house on their way out of town.

"Do you think— Could I—" Grace opened her arms, and Lydia realized she was asking if she could hug her.

"Oh. Uh. Of course." Awkwardly, Lydia stepped forward, letting Grace wrap her arms around her. After a moment, Lydia's arms went around Grace's back, and she found herself squeezing her sister tight. She closed her eyes against the unexpected rush of emotion.

"We'll be back in a couple months," Grace said as she let go. "Maybe we can stop in Nashville to see you?"

"Of course." Lydia watched Grace and Levi get in their car and drive away. She couldn't figure out how she could already miss someone she'd just met.

A drawn-out breath slid out of her. She should go pack too. She was supposed to leave in the morning.

She trudged up the steps to the carriage house and opened her suitcase. But her eyes fell on the untouched notebook on the table next to the bed. The week had been so busy that she hadn't had a moment to even attempt to write. She grabbed the notebook and rummaged in her purse for a pen, then took both outside. She surveyed the balcony, the trees, and the house across the yard, finally settling on the cozy circle of Adirondack chairs under a tree halfway between the carriage house and the main house. She curled into one, watching the river beyond the property slip toward the setting sun.

She hadn't attempted to write in months. But for the first time since everything had happened with Dallas and Cheyenne, she felt like maybe she could.

It only took a few minutes to realize how wrong she was.

She set her pen to the paper a dozen times, only to pick it back up again, the sole sign of her efforts a few blue dots on the page.

"Here, Buck." Liam's voice cut through the dusky air, and Lydia couldn't stop the smile it brought to her lips—because it gave her an excuse to put aside this fruitless endeavor. "No, boy. Come."

Even the jingle of Buck's collar closing in on her spot didn't make her tense tonight.

"Hey, boy." She leaned aside as he sniffed at her, then tentatively reached a hand to pet his head. His fur was softer than she'd expected, and he made a face that she interpreted as a smile.

"Sorry. Once he decides he likes someone, there's no holding him back." Liam's warm drawl, combined with his warmer smile, sent Lydia's tummy rushing toward her chest.

"We didn't mean to interrupt you," Liam added. "Looks like you're busy."

"Not really." Lydia sighed. "Just trying to write a song."

"Yeah?" Liam stepped closer, snapping a leash on Buck's collar. "How's it going?"

She made a face and turned the empty page toward him.

He chuckled, the sound a sweet harmony to the crickets that had begun their evening chorus. "That good, huh? Buck and I are going to take a walk, if you want to join us. I always find it clears my head."

Lydia jumped up from her seat so quickly that she would have crashed right into Liam if he hadn't made a swift sidestep.

He chuckled again. "Boy, you really don't want to work on that song anymore, do you?"

Lydia laughed along. Yes. That was why she was so eager to walk with him.

It had nothing to do with the new piece of her heart that had slipped back into place the moment she'd heard his voice tonight.

Chapter 11

"Can I ask you something?" Liam asked hesitantly. They'd made their way to the quiet riverbank on their walk. Although night had fallen around them at least half an hour ago, they'd kept going, Buck trotting cheerfully between them.

"Yep," Lydia answered immediately, and Liam let himself glance at her—though he'd been trying to limit how often he did that so he wouldn't creep her out. But she seemed so different tonight from the guarded woman who'd deflected all of his questions that night in Nashville.

"Why didn't you defend yourself? When all those stories came out about your so-called breakdown? Why didn't you tell them Dallas had been cheating on you?" His jaw tightened. More than once, he'd been tempted to call up some reporter and set the story straight. Except it wasn't his place if she wanted it to remain private—not to mention, no one would believe that he knew anything about it.

Lydia sighed. "You sound like my manager."

The exhaustion in her voice made him want to reach out a hand to her. Instead, he wrapped Buck's leash tighter around his fingers. "I'm not saying it's a bad thing. I think it showed a lot of integrity. I just hated all those horrible things they were saying—" He broke off. She probably didn't need a reminder.

"You're sweet." Her voice was soft. "But honestly, I don't think they were that far off. I'd been pushing through for so long that I think I finally just snapped. I wish it hadn't happened onstage in front of five thousand people, but . . ." Irony dripped from her laugh. "Becca, my manager, thinks if I get some new songs written by the end of summer, she'll be able to launch my solo career. But you saw how that's going. I was hoping the change of scenery would spark something this week, but . . ."

"You could always write a song about fireflies." Liam gestured toward the flickering lights along the riverbank. "Or Buck here. He's very song-worthy."

Lydia's laugh encouraged him to keep going. He was probably making a complete fool of himself with these wacky suggestions, but if it made her happy he'd do it all night. "Oh wait. I've got it. You could write a church picnic song."

"Trust me, if I could come up with a church picnic song right now, I'd write it. Watch—"

Liam's foot slid through something soft and slippery and skidded right out from under him. Next thing he knew, he was on his backside in wet mud. He'd been so busy watching Lydia that he hadn't been looking where he was going and must have stepped into one of the low-lying areas along the river that never completely dried out.

He tried to scramble to his feet, but Buck found it a great game to pounce on his chest with muddy paws.

"Are you all right?" Lydia did a terrible job hiding her laugh.

"You know, if I was hurt, you'd feel bad for laughing."

"You're right. I would." But she laughed harder as she stepped closer. "Here." She held out a hand to him.

He contemplated it. It looked soft and delicate and . . . way too clean.

Deftly, he scooped a handful of mud, then plopped his hand into hers.

She shrieked and stumbled backward, staring at him as if she couldn't believe what he'd just done. And suddenly, neither could he. He had never been the kind of person to pull pranks—let alone on a celebrity.

"Lydia, I'm sorry. I—" He gasped as a wet blob hit him right in the middle of the chest. He looked down to find a glob of mud splattered across the front of his t-shirt, then looked up to find Lydia bent in half with laughter.

"Oh. It's on." He grabbed another fistful of mud, then scrambled to his feet, taking off after her as she ran back in the direction they'd come from. The first handful of mud he threw went wide. But the second one hit her in the shoulder.

"Ouch." She grabbed at her arm, but she was still laughing. She stopped running as he caught up, Buck leaping at his side as if he wanted them to do it all over again.

"For the record, you started that," he said, puffing.

"You're the one who slapped mud into my hand when I was trying to help you up," Lydia protested.

"Yeah, but you're the one who dunked me at the picnic." He shook the remaining mud off his hands, then rubbed them on his shorts before wiping the thickest spots of mud off her shoulder. He had to force himself to pull his hand away as she smiled at him.

"So that's what this is about? Revenge?"

"Yep. Be sure to put that in your song."

"Only if I can put in the part about you falling in the mud too."

"Sure, why not." He shrugged. "Maybe something like, 'He was walking and talking, didn't see the puddle. Fell right into that there—uh—muddle."

Lydia's laugh rippled across the river. "Into the muddle?"

73

Liam let his laugh join hers, trying not to notice the way they harmonized, like a cello and a violin. "You think you can do better?"

"Let's see." Lydia chewed her lip, and he had to look away because suddenly he was way too interested in that lip. "Riversong singing, moon shining bright. He couldn't see, didn't notice the light. Walking along, he didn't know. Fell right into that mud hole."

"All right, fine. That's better than mine. What comes next?"

She closed her eyes, and he took her arm so she wouldn't trip as they kept walking. A small smile played over her lips. It transformed into a great grin as she opened her eyes again and turned to face him. "Riversong singing, dog at their side. She saw it coming, she saw the light. But that old mud hole it got her too. And the one she blames, well, it's you."

He laughed. "You started it," he said again.

"Shh." Lydia's grin didn't falter. "Do you want to hear the rest or not?"

"Yes. Definitely."

"Good." She made up a few more lines, as did he, and by the time they reached his backyard, they were both laughing so hard, they were huffing and puffing more than Buck.

"So how does the song end?" Liam asked quietly, his feet slowing to a stop. Much as he wanted to know the end of the song, he didn't want *this* to end.

"Hmm." Lydia stopped too and looked out over the river. She hummed a few bars, a lilting melody Liam had never heard before. Then, her voice fuller than the river, she sang, "Riversong singing, moon shining bright. They walked along after that mud fight. Laughing and talking and feeling fine, trying to figure out how they would write the next line."

Her voice trailed off, and she gave him a smile at once wistful and hopeful. "Or something like that."

"That was perfect." He cleared his throat, seeking to break the spell her voice had cast over him. Because if he didn't, he might do something outrageous—like kiss her or ask her to stay here forever. "What time are you planning to leave tomorrow?" He started across the yard toward the house.

Lydia speed walked a few steps to catch up with him. "Is there a time you want me out by?"

"No. Of course not." Way to play it cool. "I mean, whatever works for you is fine. It's not like we have a waiting list or anything. I'll probably finish fixing the place up before we rent it out again."

Lydia had been such a good sport about the condition of the carriage house, but he couldn't guarantee the next guest would be. And he was quite sure he wouldn't enjoy spending time with them nearly as much as he did with her.

"Do you think—" As abruptly as she'd begun the question, Lydia cut off. "Never mind."

They'd reached the driveway, and they both drew to a stop at the foot of the carriage house steps.

"Do I think what?" That he wanted to hear everything she had to say? Yes. That they should walk together like this every night? Yes. That—

"Do you think I could stay a little longer? In the carriage house?" Her look was ridiculously earnest.

And his heart was ridiculously bursting into song. "How long were you thinking?" Not that it mattered. The answer was a very emphatic yes.

"A week? Maybe two? If that wouldn't be too inconvenient for you?"

Liam nearly laughed out loud. Seeing her longer most definitely wouldn't be inconvenient. "Sure. That should be fine." There. Much better in the playing it cool department. "Is it because of the awesome song we wrote?"

She didn't laugh like he'd expected. Instead, she nodded. "I think you may have gotten me out of my slump. So thank you." She leaned forward to kiss his cheek, the same way she had that night in Nashville, her pomegranate scent cloaking him. And then she was gone, with a final, "Goodnight, Liam," at the top of the stairs before she stepped inside.

Behind him a car door slammed, and Liam jumped. He hadn't heard Mia pull up.

"What was that about?" Mia's footsteps scuffed the gravel as she marched toward him. "Did she just— What happened to you?" She pointed at his mud-covered clothes.

"Long story. Lydia will have to sing you her song about it."

Mia made a disgusted noise and traipsed toward the house. Liam jogged to catch up with her. "You don't like Lydia?"

"Does it matter?" Mia muttered.

"Matter to what?" Why did talking to his daughter always have to feel like speaking in riddles?

"Never mind. She's leaving tomorrow, right?"

"Nope." There was no disguising the lightness in his voice. "She decided to stay another week or two. She wants to try to write some songs."

"Can't she do that in Nashville?"

"I guess not. What's your problem with her?" Liam stopped at the bottom of the porch steps, hoping to have a longer conversation with his daughter.

But Mia stomped up them. "I don't have a problem with her. As long as she doesn't start acting like my mom."

"What? Mia—" But she had already let the front door slam behind her.

All the joy that had built up from his walk with Lydia seeped out of Liam.

As if the fact that Lydia was a celebrity wasn't enough to make a relationship with her impossible, now he had his daughter's disapproval to worry about.

Chapter 12

"Dare I ask how the songwriting is coming?" Benjamin faked a flinch as he passed a plate to Lydia.

"Funny." She took a piece of the leftover chicken he had cooked up for dinner last night. There were definite perks to having a brother in training to be a chef. And after two weeks in River Falls, she was getting used to her youngest brother's goofiness too. Despite their twenty-year age difference, she felt closer to him than to any of her other brothers, largely because he was off of school for the summer, so they'd been able to spend time together most days. Abe usually joined them for lunch too, but today he had a meeting. Joseph and Ava had finally embarked on the honeymoon they'd deferred to meet Lydia. And Zeb, Asher, and Simeon and their spouses were all at work.

"It's going okay." She'd managed to catch a snatch of melody here and a few random lines there, but she had yet to figure out how to pull it all together. Sometimes she wondered if all her previous songs had been flukes.

"It'll come." Benjamin shoved a gigantic bite into his mouth.

"What if it doesn't?" The thought had haunted her more and more frequently over the past few days. She'd stayed in River Falls because she thought she could write here, but maybe it was time to face it: It wasn't the place. It was her.

Benjamin spoke around another bite. "Then you'll stay here. Hang out with your family. Live happily ever after."

"I don't think it's that easy." Lydia took a long swallow of water to ease her dry throat. It wasn't like the idea didn't have a certain appeal—a strong appeal, if she was honest. But it wasn't only herself she had to think about. She'd promised Mama and Daddy she'd make them proud. She had a legacy to live up to.

Benjamin shrugged. "It's only as complicated as you make it."

Lydia stared at him. There was no way those were his own words. Not that he wasn't wise, but . . . "Another one of Mama's sayings?"

Benjamin laughed. "Yeah. I guess so. Some of them have become so engrained that I forget I didn't come up with them."

Lydia laughed too, even as she rubbed at her heart. What she wouldn't give to have heard those words from her mama's mouth, just once.

"Anyway." Benjamin finished off his chicken and carried his plate to the sink. "If you want to take a break, a buddy is home from college, and I said I'd go game with him. You're welcome to come. You're getting pretty good."

She snorted. She now managed to make it about thirty seconds without dying in a good match. "I think I'll pass. Thank you though. It was sweet of you to include me."

"What are brothers for, right?"

"Right." Lydia had to look at her plate to keep from getting emotional. The Calvanos had made her part of the family so readily, and she couldn't imagine how she'd ever go back to Nashville and not see them every day.

She brought her plate to the sink and helped Benjamin clean up, then headed back to the carriage house. Her heart dipped at the sight of the empty driveway. She'd hardly seen Liam all week—he had a big job in Brampton, which was an hour away, so he'd been leaving well before Lydia was awake most mornings. They'd spoken a few times in passing when she "happened" to be outside when he got home, but he'd seemed exhausted and preoccupied. At any rate, they hadn't had another night together like the night they'd taken Buck for a walk.

It was for the best, as far as her heart was concerned. But she wouldn't have minded if he kick-started another song for her, maybe one that actually made sense this time.

As she reached the carriage house, the grumble of tires on gravel caught her ears, and she turned eagerly toward it. But instead of Liam's work van, it was the car Mia generally drove. Lydia considered making a quick retreat into the carriage house—it was probably safest. But something about the girl made Lydia want to reach out to her. Maybe because she saw in her the same brokenness she'd gone through when Mama and Daddy died. Only Mia was so much younger to have to deal with that kind of pain.

Mia opened her car door, not even glancing in Lydia's direction.

"Hey, Mia." Lydia made herself step toward the girl.

Mia sent her a disdainful look but said, "Hi."

"What are you up to?"

"I'm not 'up to'"—she made air quotes—"anything. Not that it's any of your business."

Defensive much? But Lydia made herself keep smiling. "How was the play?"

During the few minutes Lydia had spoken to Liam the other night, Mia had been on her way to see a local production a friend was in.

Mia gave her a blank look. "The play?"

"The other night?"

"Right." Mia nodded, biting her lip. "It was good."

Lydia studied the girl. She'd never been a parent, but something didn't sit right about that answer. "Which of your friends was in it?"

"Um. Sierra." Mia didn't bother to say goodbye as she stalked toward the house.

Lydia watched her retreating form. She was almost sure she'd said the other night that it was Heidi who was in the play.

Should she mention something about it to Liam?

No. She was probably remembering wrong. Besides, Liam had plenty to worry about the way it was.

She saw how he carried everyone else's burdens. His mama's health. Mia's attitude. His clients' needs. Even Lydia's struggles. She only wished there was something she could do to help him.

She climbed the carriage house stairs and flopped onto the couch. Her eyes fell on the painting supplies Liam had left in the corner, with the promise to paint the room soon.

She jumped up.

That was it.

That was how she'd ease his burden.

She crossed the room to pick up a paint can—which was heavier than she anticipated—and spun to examine the space.

She'd technically never painted a room before. But how hard could it be?

Chapter 13

Liam knocked on the door of the carriage house, a tingle of anticipation going up his back. He'd finally managed to finish his job in Brampton, and he needed to see if Lydia minded leaving for a little bit so he could spend the evening painting over here.

Then again, she could always stay . . .

He glanced down at his jeans and work shirt. He probably should have changed first, but he hadn't exactly been thinking straight when he'd gotten out of his van. All he could think about was the few quick hellos he'd exchanged with Lydia during the week—and how those moments had left him wanting more.

He couldn't explain it, the way his heart seemed to come to life whenever he was around her. Like the tingling of a foot that had fallen asleep and was waking up again. It ached something fierce, and yet it was the kind of ache that told him he was starting to have feeling again—feeling he'd been sure would never return.

As the door opened, a shot of nerves went through him, but he ignored it. He was simply a landlord coming to ask his tenant if he could paint her place. It was natural enough. There was no way she would realize his feelings went beyond that.

"Hey, Liam." Her smile was wide and warm, but that wasn't what made him stare.

She was completely covered in paint. Flecks all over her shirt, along with one big blotch on the hem. Her dark blue jeans were now polka dotted with light green, and there was even a streak of paint across her cheek—not to mention an entire lock of hair that stood out white against her dark strands.

"What— How—" He shook his head. "What are you doing?" And why did she still look so beautiful, even when she was a mess?

"Painting."

"*Yourself?*"

She glanced down at her clothes as if she hadn't realized she'd turned herself into a living Picasso. "Painting's messier than I anticipated. But no, I'm painting the living room." She stood back and gestured toward the room. "What do you think?"

"You didn't have to do that. I was planning on doing it tonight." He stepped past her to examine her work. Actually, maybe she *shouldn't* have done it. Sporadic drip marks tracked down the wall. Fortunately, she'd only gotten a small section done.

"I know. I wanted to surprise you."

"Oh." Forget the drip marks. It was worth it to see her smile like that.

"But if you wanted to help, I wouldn't be opposed." Lydia scooted toward the spot where the paint can sat on the drop cloth. Liam gave a silent thanks that she'd used one, since it was covered with more paint from her one day of use than Liam had gotten on it in an entire year. "No one ever told me that painting takes *forever*."

He stared at her. "You've never painted before?"

"Do I look like someone who knows what she's doing?" She spun in a circle, indicating her clothes. But his eyes got caught on the way her hair waved around her shoulders and the way her laugh hung in the air around her.

She stooped to pick up a brush, then dipped it in the paint can all the way to the handle and pulled it out, still dripping.

"Whoa, whoa, whoa." He rushed at her and grabbed her hand, easing the paint brush out of it. "If you're trying to prove to me that you've never done this before, I believe you."

"What?" She looked at the spot where sparks zapped from her hand into his. "Isn't this how you do it?"

Liam let go of her hand, the electricity of the touch still playing at his heart. "Give me five minutes to change into some painting clothes, and I'll teach you." Gingerly, he set the overloaded brush on the edge of the paint can.

Lydia reached for it, but he caught her hand again.

"Maybe take a break until I get back."

"Am I that bad at it?" She gave him a half-hurt look but didn't pull her hand away.

"Uh." Liam had to concentrate on the question. He let go of her hand. "Yes."

"Hey." But her laugh was full and throaty.

"It's nothing you can't learn. Just give me five minutes."

He ducked out the door into the warm evening and jogged down the steps outside the carriage house, then across the yard. All the exhaustion from the work week disappeared into a pulsing, supercharged energy.

He reached the porch just as the front door banged open and Mia emerged.

"Hey, kid, haven't seen you around much lately. You're not leaving again, are you?"

Mia rolled her eyes. "No. I just felt like coming outside and carrying my keys around."

Liam sighed. He'd assumed when she'd entered the sarcasm phase a couple years ago that it wouldn't last long. He'd been wrong. "Where are you going?"

Mia blinked at him, then glanced over his shoulder. "What were you doing up there?"

"Up where?" He followed the direction of her gaze. "Oh. I was planning to paint the carriage house. But Lydia already started. Sort of. She has more paint on herself than on the wall." He couldn't help laughing. "I'd better get changed and go help before she—"

"You're not going to date her or something, are you?" Mia's interruption was sharp.

He studied his daughter. The answer was probably no. She was Lydia St. Peter, after all. But maybe . . . "Why do you ask? Would that be weird for you?"

She shrugged. "Do what you want. It's not like you've ever cared what I think. Otherwise we wouldn't be here." She jumped down the steps.

There was no winning at this parenting thing. "You didn't tell me where you're going."

"I have to work."

"About that. I thought you were going to post a copy of your schedule on the fridge."

"Yeah. Whatever."

"Hey." Liam waited for her to turn toward him. "One: I do care what you think. And two: I'm proud of you. I know it's hard to work so much when your friends are all going out, but it'll be worth it."

"Yeah." With another eye roll, Mia stalked away. But then she stopped and hit him with a hard stare. "And since you care so much about what I think, you might want to think about Mom once in a while."

Oof.

Liam took a step backward. Did she really think that he didn't think about Molly every day?

But the truth was, no matter how much he thought about his late wife, she was never coming back. Not dating wouldn't change that. Not that he'd ever had a desire to date before, but now . . .

He shook off the thought.

Even if he did decide to date again eventually, it was unlikely to be with Lydia St. Peter. Her last boyfriend had been a superstar—not a great guy, but still not exactly something Liam could live up to.

With a sigh, he opened the door and stepped inside. But he got caught in the entryway as he spied the wedding picture of him and Molly that had been hanging there for nearly twenty years. He looked slightly dazed in it, and she looked radiant, as always. He lifted a hand to wipe away a small spot of dust on the frame.

"She'd approve, you know." Mama's voice was quiet, but it made him jump.

He dropped his hand from the picture. "Approve of what?"

Mama made a face that said she knew that he knew exactly what she was talking about. "Of you moving on."

"I moved on a long time ago, Mama." He stepped around her, but her hand fell on his arm.

"She wanted you to be happy, Liam. Not to be a martyr."

"I'm not being a martyr." He rubbed at his temple. He didn't have time for this conversation right now.

"Is that why you spend all your time working or taking care of me and Mia?"

"I'm not sure you can call being ignored by Mia taking care of her."

"You're a good father, Liam. And a good son. But you're a man too. And you're allowed to want a new relationship."

"Mama, I don't—"

But Mama lifted a hand to his cheek. "I may be losing my *sight*, Liam, but I'm not losing my ability to *see*. You like Lydia. And that's a good thing."

"Mia doesn't think so." The slap of his daughter's words hit him again.

"I love Mia." Mama patted his arm. "But she needs to start thinking about other people instead of only herself."

"She's not—" Liam felt like he should defend his daughter.

But Mama shook her head. "It's part of growing up. You went through it too."

Liam snorted. He was certain Mama could list examples all day of how he'd been selfish at Mia's age, but he was pretty sure that wouldn't make him feel better right now.

"I have to go change. I told Lydia I'd help her paint the carriage house. I should be back by dinnertime."

"Don't rush on my account. I'm going to dinner with Betty, remember? She'll be here to pick me up in a bit. You and Lydia should get some pizza or something."

"Mama, I'm not going to get pizza with Lydia. I'm going to rescue my living room from her massacre of a paint job. That's all. Anyway, I'm sure she already has other plans."

He tried not to resent the Calvanos for taking up so much of her time. After all, they were her family—and the whole reason she was here.

If it weren't for them, he may never have seen her again after that night in Nashville.

Which, in retrospect, may have made things easier. Because when she had been only a memory, he had never had to think about the possibility of something more.

Chapter 14

Lydia's shoulder ached, and the paint fumes were starting to make her woozy—or maybe that was hunger. Or being so close to Liam for so long.

She dipped her roller into the paint tray and rolled it back and forth like Liam had taught her. He'd been right that it was much more efficient than using a paint brush—and less messy too. They had only one wall left, and then they'd be done.

She let herself glance over at him. His focus was on the wall, but his brow was wrinkled, as if he was thinking about something else. He'd been like that since he'd come back from changing. She'd debated asking him what was on his mind a thousand times, but each time, she dismissed the thought. As someone whose privacy had been invaded most of her life, she knew better than anyone the value of being allowed to keep your private thoughts to yourself.

Instead, she let her mind drift. A line worked its way into her head, and she froze with her roller halfway through a stroke, repeating it to herself. *Didn't know it could be like this.* She could hear the melody too. Ignoring the splotch of paint that landed on her foot as she dropped the roller into the tray, she dashed across the room for the notebook that sat on a table next to the couch.

"What was that about?"

But she ignored Liam's question. She had to get this down before she lost it. She scribbled the words onto the page, but more ideas kept coming. Her hand raced to keep up.

By the time her pen finally slowed, she'd written almost two verses. They were rough and had no meter—and she wasn't one hundred percent sure they made sense—but a feeling of relief swept over her as she closed the notebook.

At last she had managed to write something she might actually be able to shape into a song.

She got up and moved to grab her roller again—but it was missing. As was Liam.

"Liam?" She spun in a circle, hoping her mad dash to write hadn't scared him away.

"What's up?"

Oh, thank goodness.

She followed the direction of his voice to the kitchen, where he stood at the sink, washing out the paint brush she'd used earlier.

"What are you doing?"

"Cleaning up."

"But—" They were so close to done—and she wasn't ready for him to go yet. "Shouldn't we finish it?"

He nodded over her shoulder, and she walked back into the living room. Sure enough, he must have finished the last wall while she was writing. Which meant there was no longer a reason for him to stay.

"Did you get something down?" Liam asked.

She bit her lip and nodded. What if he wanted to read it? She never showed anyone her songs in progress.

But he smiled. "Good. I knew you would."

"That makes one of us." But the glow of finally getting words on paper hadn't left her.

Her stomach chose that moment to give a loud rumble. She ducked her head and pressed a hand to it, but it seemed to take that as encouragement to rumble louder.

Liam's laugh was warm and understanding, not mocking. "I'm starving too. Are you having dinner with the Calvanos tonight?"

Lydia shook her head. "They all have other things going on tonight. I'll probably just have some cereal or something."

"Oh no." Liam gave her a mock horrified look. "Mama would never forgive me if I made you have cereal for dinner."

"You're not *making* me. I'm choosing to."

"That's not the way Mama will see it. She went out to dinner with a friend. I was thinking about getting some pizza, if you want to . . ." He trailed off, moving to the paint can and applying the lid, rapping on it with a hammer. "Never mind."

"Wait a minute." Lydia stepped forward. "You can't say pizza to a starving woman and then say never mind."

Liam lifted his head, his smile stretching his lips. "So you want some?"

"That's a very definite yes. Do you want me to call and order it?"

"That's okay. I can do it. Unless you want to go . . ." He stood and tucked his hands in his pockets, not looking her way.

She waited for him to finish the sentence. "To go . . ."

"Never mind. There's just this great place up on the ridge overlooking the town. Great pizza and an even better view. But I don't want to take up your whole night."

Lydia chewed her lip. He wasn't talking about a date, right? Just two people eating dinner. And pizza did sound a lot better than cereal.

Plus, she'd been wanting to get a view of the town from above. Who knew—maybe that change of perspective might inspire a song.

"That sounds fun." She glanced down at her paint-spattered clothes. "I should maybe clean up a bit first."

"I don't know. I think you could start a new trend." His glance skimmed over her clothes but settled on her eyes with a warm smile. "How long do you need?"

"Fifteen minutes?"

Liam whistled. "I don't think Mia can even pick out her clothes in fifteen minutes."

"It helps that I only brought a limited selection with me." Her extended stay had necessitated a lot of re-wearing, some clever outfit combos, and a few purchases from the Sweet Boutique downtown.

"Meet you out front in fifteen minutes." Liam left the carriage house, and Lydia moved to the bedroom to study her options. She almost grabbed the sundress she'd purchased the other day, but that might seem too date-like. Instead, she grabbed a pair of green linen shorts and a soft white top.

It took longer than she'd anticipated to scrub the paint off her skin, and by the time she had pulled on the clothes, a good thirty minutes had gone by, and she hadn't even done anything with her hair and makeup. She glanced into the mirror, then gathered her hair into a large butterfly clip, making sure to tuck the painted strand under others to hide it. In lieu of makeup, she grabbed her sunglasses. So far, the few times she'd gone out in public here, no one had bothered her, but you could never be too careful.

She took one more look in the mirror. She certainly didn't look glamorous. But she did look happy.

"This is the best pizza I've ever eaten." Lydia savored a bite of tangy tomato and cheese as a soft evening breeze stirred her hair. The restaurant patio was more crowded than she liked, but fortunately, no one seemed to recognize her. Or if they did, they didn't care.

Even so, she double-checked that her sunglasses were firmly over her eyes.

"Told you." Liam grabbed another large slice of the deep dish pizza, lifting it straight to his mouth.

A drop of tomato sauce fell onto his chin, and she patted her own chin in the same spot to clue him in.

"Oh." He grabbed his napkin and wiped it with a sheepish look. "And the view?" He swept a hand toward the panorama below them.

Lydia pushed her sunglasses onto the top of her head so she could take in the full effect. The patio literally perched on the side of a mountain, which dropped away to offer startling views of the river winding past the buildings of the town below, its slow waters reflecting the wine and gold hues of the setting sun.

"Spectacular." She leaned back in her chair, a rare relaxation making her feel like she could float right up over the hills.

"How was everything?" A perky waitress in her twenties approached the table, and Lydia wondered for a second about setting her up with Benjamin.

"It was excellent." Liam's eyes remained on Lydia, and for some reason she felt her cheeks warm.

Careful, she reminded herself. This wasn't a date. And she didn't want it to be a date. She'd learned the hard way that dating only led to heartbreak.

Lydia turned toward the waitress just for somewhere else to look as Liam continued to watch her. "It was delicious."

"Oh my goodness, you're Lydia St. Peter." The waitress's eyes widened, and Lydia realized too late that her sunglasses were still on top of her head. She slammed them back onto her nose.

"Yeah." She kept her voice low. "It's nice to meet you."

"Oh wow. I can't believe it. I am such a fan," the waitress squealed. Apparently she hadn't picked up on Lydia's attempt to keep her identity quiet.

The other diners looked their way.

"Do you think I could get your autograph?" The waitress held out her pad of paper and pen, as if Lydia had already said yes.

Swallowing back her annoyance, Lydia took them and scribbled a signature.

But as she passed them back to the waitress, a teenage girl approached the table, a middle aged couple close behind her.

She grimaced, her glance going to Liam. Did he want to flee as badly as she did? But his expression was more bemused than panicked.

She took a breath, her manager's voice pounding against her head. *There's always time for your fans. They're the reason you have a job.*

"Sorry," she muttered to Liam. "I'll make it fast."

"I'm in no hurry." He sipped his water and sat back in his chair.

Lydia signed a handful of autographs and smiled for a few selfies with fans, then glanced around the patio. "I think we should go now, while we have a chance."

"Sure." Liam gestured for the check, and the same perky waitress who had started the whole thing came over.

"So." The woman spoke as loudly as she had before. "Did you really have a breakdown?"

"I—" Lydia blinked, caught completely unprepared.

"No." Liam pushed his chair back and stood. He shoved a pile of cash at the woman. "For our bill. Keep the change."

He stepped around the waitress, pulling Lydia's chair back and wrapping a hand around her elbow, not letting go as he led her around the building to the parking lot.

"That happen often?" He was breathing heavily, and his voice was hard, protective.

Lydia's heart sped up, keeping rhythm with her breaths. But she forced herself to shrug it off. "It's the first time it's happened here."

His jaw tightened. "I'm sorry. I shouldn't have suggested we come."

"It's not your fault. Anyway, it's fine."

He eyed her.

She sighed. "All right, it's not fine. But I'm used to it. Sorry you had to be dragged into it." Except he hadn't been dragged. He'd stepped willingly to her defense. Her heart accelerated as they reached the van, his hand still on her elbow. He watched her a moment, and though she knew she should get in the van before someone tracked them to the parking lot, she couldn't make herself move.

But then Liam let go of her arm and opened her door.

"Thanks," she whispered, climbing in.

He closed the door, and she sat back against the seat, feeling cocooned and safe in spite of what had just happened.

They drove silently, twilight falling against the canopy of trees that cloaked the road, and Lydia could almost pretend the rest of the world didn't exist. When they reached River Falls, the streets were mostly empty. But a few cars turned into the parking lot of a long, squat building Lydia had never noticed before.

"What's that place?"

Liam glanced in the direction she pointed. "Bowling alley."

"Oh. Have you ever been?"

"Bowling?" Liam shrugged. "Of course. Who hasn't— You've never been bowling, have you?"

She shook her head with a rueful laugh. "Nope. I saw it in a movie once though."

Liam snorted and made a hard right turn into the driveway they'd nearly passed.

"Oh but—" Lydia protested. She hadn't meant they should go bowling *now*. Or ever.

Liam slid the van into a parking spot and shut off the engine. "Everyone has to go bowling at least once in their life. It's a rite of passage."

Lydia chewed her lip. She did want to go bowling. It was such a normal thing to do. But after what had happened at the restaurant . . .

"Here." Liam reached past her into the back seat, his outdoorsy scent making her want to lean closer. When he sat back, he held a baseball cap in his hand. He passed it to her.

"O'Neill Electric." She read the insignia on the hat.

"Since it's kind of dark for sunglasses. I have a big, oversized work shirt in the back if you want that too. I might even have a jumpsuit if you want to go all out."

Lydia settled the hat onto her head. She tucked her hair into it. "Do I look like a normal person?"

"You look . . ." Liam cleared his throat. "That will work." If it weren't for the look in his eyes, she might have been offended. Instead, heat rushed to her face, and she had to get out of the van before she could give in to the temptation to ask what he meant.

Chapter 15

"Best three out of five?"

Liam laughed at the way Lydia's eyes gleamed. They'd bowled two games already. "You're sure you can handle another loss?" he teased.

"Maybe I've been hustling you. Did you ever think of that?" With her hair tucked haphazardly into his baseball cap and her playful smile, she looked relaxed and happy. And . . . gorgeous. There was no point in denying that—anyone could see it. But fortunately, no one else seemed to be paying any attention to them. At the restaurant, he'd initially been flattered on Lydia's behalf when people lined up to get her autograph. But when that woman had presumed she had the right to pry into Lydia's personal life—even the memory of the hurt and fear on Lydia's face was enough to form a bowling-ball-sized rock in his stomach.

He reset the computer and watched her bowl her first frame. Three pins, followed by two more.

"Hustling me, huh?" He stood to pick up his bowling ball, passing closer to her than necessary, mostly so he could catch a quick whiff of her tantalizing pomegranate scent.

She rubbed her hands on her arms, and he caught sight of the raised flesh.

"Are you cold? Maybe we should go."

Lydia smirked. "Are you saying you forfeit?"

He pointed to her arms. "You've got goosebumps the size of blueberries."

She rubbed her arms faster. "That's because the temperature in here is subarctic. But I can handle it if you can."

"Oh, I can handle it." He picked up his bowling ball, made a perfect approach to the line, and released, concentrating on his follow-through. The ball rocketed down the lane . . . and hit four pins.

"You've got to be kidding me," he muttered, wiping his hands on his shorts.

"Don't let me win," Lydia warned from behind him. "I want my victory to be totally honest."

He laughed, his eyes getting caught on the strand of hair that had fallen out of the cap.

"Your ball is ready." Lydia pointed to the ball return.

Right. Liam forced himself to focus on the pins in front of him instead of the beautiful woman behind him.

This time, his release was off, but he still managed to pick up three pins.

"Nice one." Lydia stepped forward and held up a hand for a high-five.

Liam swallowed. He knew what was coming.

Sure enough, the instant his hand made contact with hers, a series of jolts went through his fingertips, electric as the zaps he'd gotten in his early years on the job. But much more pleasant.

Lydia stood in front of the ball return, rubbing her hands on her arms again. If anything, her goosebumps had grown to the size of eggs.

"Oh, for heaven's sake. I'll be right back." He kicked his bowling shoes off and pulled on his street shoes.

"Wait. Where are you going?" A flash of panic washed across Lydia's face.

"Don't worry. I'll be right back. Go ahead and take your turn." He waited until she returned to the lane and picked up her ball, then jogged toward the door.

Outside, it was a perfect early July night, warm but not humid, quiet aside from the crickets, the sky filled with stars. Liam paused for a second, pulling in a deep breath and asking himself what he thought he was doing.

He should be home in bed. Not out on the town with Lydia St. Peter.

It's bowling, Liam. He did a mental eye roll at himself. *It's not like you're asking her to marry you.*

Whoa. Where had that thought come from? It wasn't a date, much less a proposal. It was just . . . fun.

He tried to recall the last time he'd had so much fun, but he'd probably have to go back to before Molly died to find that.

He yanked the back door of the van open and rummaged around until he found the shirt. Then he strode back to the bowling alley, his eyes drawn instantly to Lydia.

But her eyes were on someone else, and she was smiling. A shot he recognized as uncomfortably close to jealousy went through him as he tracked the direction of her gaze. But the only people he noticed were a young couple in the next lane. The man bowled a strike, then swept his date into a kiss.

Liam pressed his lips together, trying to remember what it felt like to kiss a woman. It had been so long. . . .

His gaze returned to Lydia, who faced his way now, and suddenly he couldn't stop noticing her lips. When they rose in a smile directed at him, he had to avert his eyes. He may be bowling with Lydia St. Peter, but there was no way he was going to kiss her.

He directed his eyes toward the scoreboard as he reached their lane.

He stopped and gaped at her. "A strike?"

"What can I say? I improved while you were gone." Her grin widened, but she shrugged as if it were no big deal.

He glanced toward the door. "How long was I gone?"

"Hey." She swatted his forearm with icy fingers. "Where did you go? I thought you were going to abandon me here." The slightest hint of uncertainty ran below her words.

"Of course not. Though I guess you would have been fine. A strike." He shook his head and held out the denim work shirt he'd grabbed from the van. "I was getting you this. So you can't blame your loss on your goosebumps."

"Loss? In case you haven't noticed, I'm winning now." She took the shirt and slid her arms into the sleeves. They hung past her fingertips, and she rolled them up, then tied the front of the shirt at her waist.

Wow.

He'd never found one of his work shirts attractive before.

"That's so much better. Thank you." Her throaty voice and warm smile drove him to the ball return.

He drew in a couple of deep breaths to steady his heartbeat as he fitted the ball to his hand. There was no reason his nerves should suddenly be popping. He lined up for his approach and swung his arm back.

"Did he buy it?" A man's voice cut through Liam's concentration as he was about to release the ball. It dropped from his hand with a hollow thud and headed straight for the gutter.

"Oh yeah. He totally bought it." Lydia's laugh finally prompted Liam to turn and face the man whose voice he recognized too well.

"Oliver."

"Hey, man. It's been too long." Oliver stepped forward and held out a hand.

Liam shifted his eyes to Lydia, who was still smiling at Oliver. He returned his brother-in-law's handshake. "Sorry, I've been working a lot and . . ."

Who would have thought when they were ten years old, playing basketball together, that one day their relationship would be reduced to awkward small talk? That was what happened when you married your best friend's sister . . . and then that sister died. In the first years after Molly's death, Oliver had checked in often, but after a while, Liam had stopped returning his calls. It was too hard, staying close to anyone connected with Molly.

"I get it, man." Oliver's eyes slid subtly to Lydia, and Liam realized what this must look like. And the fact that Lydia was wearing both his shirt and cap certainly couldn't be helping.

"Uh, this is Lydia. She's—" He didn't know how she wanted to be acknowledged in terms of her relationship to the Calvanos. "She's visiting the Calvanos. She's staying in the carriage house while she's in town, so . . ." He trailed off. So *what*? So he'd decided to take her out for pizza and bowling? What had he been thinking? He knew Molly's family lived here. Knew it would kill them to see him with someone else—even if it was someone he most definitely *was not* dating.

"I'm Oliver. Liam's brother-in-law." Oliver held out a hand to Lydia, who shook it with a smile.

"Nice to officially meet you. Now I don't have to think of you as guy-who-bowled-a-strike-for-me."

"I knew it!" Liam pointed a finger at Lydia. "I knew you didn't suddenly bowl a strike."

"You should have seen your face when you looked up at the scoreboard though." Lydia laughed and opened her eyes wide in what he imagined was supposed to be a—much prettier—impression of him. "I'm offended that you didn't think I could do it."

"You *didn't* do it," Liam pointed out, but he couldn't make himself frown. It was too perfect hearing her laugh.

100

"Sorry. It was my idea. I saw you pummeling her in the last game, so I thought it was only fair." Oliver set a hand on Lydia's arm, and Liam resisted the urge to step between them. His brother-in-law was a notorious flirt—and he always got the girl. Only to dump them soon afterward. Lydia deserved better than that.

"So are you going to help me win this game?" Lydia asked Oliver.

Liam tensed. So she'd already fallen for his charm.

"No, I have to get going. I'm bringing my fiancée a late dinner when she gets off her shift."

"Your fiancée?" Liam did a double-take.

"Don't sound so surprised." Oliver shoved his shoulder. "Time goes by. Things change." He started toward the doors but then turned around. "I know Mom and Dad would love it if you stopped by sometime." He looked at Lydia, then back at Liam. "Both of you."

"Oh we're not— She's not—"

"He's my bowling coach," Lydia filled in.

Liam watched as Oliver's eyes went from the O'Neill Electric hat covering Lydia's hair to the oversized work shirt. "Right. Bowling coach." Oliver winked, and then he was gone.

Liam blew out a long breath, shaking his head, then let himself glance at Lydia.

Her cheeks wore a soft trace of pink, but she turned to him with a smile. "You ready to lose?"

Liam swallowed, his insides hollow.

After seeing Molly's brother, he was pretty sure losing was the only possible outcome of this night.

Chapter 16

Lydia's eyes slid to Liam yet again—to the hands tensed on the steering wheel, the jaw clenched so hard it had to hurt, the shoulders hunched toward his neck. He'd been like this since they'd run into his brother-in-law at the bowling alley, and she wasn't sure why. Maybe because Oliver had jumped to the conclusion that she and Liam were seeing each other? But they weren't. He knew that, and she knew that, and now Oliver knew it. So why did it bother Liam?

She forced her eyes off the hard line of his jaw and to the sky, where the moon had risen, so full and close that she felt like she could open the van window and reach out and touch it.

Liam turned into the driveway and pulled the vehicle up in front of the carriage house. He shifted into park, then just sat, staring at nothing.

Lydia grabbed her door handle, then hesitated. "You sleeping out here tonight?"

"What?" Liam shook his head, as if pulling himself out of a dream. "Sorry." He opened his door and hopped out of the van, and Lydia followed suit, rounding the vehicle to get to the carriage house stairs.

But she hesitated with her foot on the bottom step, glancing at Liam, who was looking up at the sky.

"Are you all right?"

Liam's eyes shifted to her. "Yeah. Sorry. I guess I haven't been very good company tonight."

"Are you kidding? You took me to the best pizza place this side of the Appalachians *and* introduced me to bowling. Best—" She almost said "date" but caught herself. She wasn't interested in dating—and neither was he. "Best night I've had in a long time. You just got kind of quiet after you saw your brother-in-law, that's all."

Liam sighed and rubbed a hand over his head, leaning back against his van. "Yeah. It's hard to see her family, you know?"

Lydia shifted and lowered herself onto the steps, wrapping her arms—warm and cozy in the long sleeves of his shirt—around her knees. "Why's that?"

Liam crossed his arms in front of him, and Lydia averted her eyes from the way his biceps stood out against his shirt. He was talking about his dead wife, for goodness sake. Now was not the time to be thinking about how attractive he was or to notice the way the shadows played off his jaw and made her want to run her fingers over it. She clasped her hands tighter.

"Her parents never thought I was good enough for her."

That couldn't be true. Liam was one of the best men she'd ever met. "I'm sure they—"

But he shook his head, his shoulders tensing. "No, they were right." His eyes flicked to her, then away, but even in the moonlight, she could detect the anguish. "Oliver and I had been friends in grade school, but in high school, I got mixed up with a bad crowd for a while. Ironically, it was Molly who called me out—helped me turn things around. But the way her parents saw it, I held her back from following her dreams."

It was impossible not to ask. "What dreams were those?"

"Molly was a cellist. Her music was . . . incredible." His smile, directed into the distance, told her he was picturing his wife, and Lydia felt an emptiness in her middle. No one had ever loved her the way Liam had obviously loved Molly.

Liam's eyes met hers suddenly, and she sucked in a breath she couldn't release until he looked away.

"Anyway, her parents had spent a lot of money getting her the top private lessons in the country. They wanted her to go to Juilliard. But she ended up going to Tennessee State with me. She got an invitation to play with the Boston Symphony Orchestra after graduation. But by then I'd started my business in Nashville, and I proposed, and she didn't even think twice before turning down the job. Instead, she took a teaching position at a grade school in Nashville." Regret pooled like tar under his words.

"Was she happy?" Lydia couldn't imagine how she wouldn't have been, with a husband like Liam.

He stared up at the moon, a muscle in his jaw working. "I think so," he finally said.

"Then it doesn't matter what her family thought."

A soft sound of dissent puffed from Liam's mouth. "Her relationship with her parents was always strained after that. She missed them so much. In the last year, after she got sick—" He paused to swallow, and Lydia's heart ached for him. "They made up, but I can't help feeling like I stole her from them. Sometimes I wonder . . ." Liam shook his head, as if chasing away a thought.

"What is it?" she whispered. No one had ever opened up to her like this, and even though it hurt to hear what he'd gone through, she also felt . . . connected. Like he was giving her a part of himself.

He turned tormented eyes on her. "If I would have let her go and follow her dream, maybe she'd still be alive."

"But you said she got sick, right?"

"Yeah. But maybe if she'd gone to Julliard or to Boston, she wouldn't have gotten sick." He shook his head again. "I know that doesn't make sense, but . . ." He gave a sad chuckle and slipped into silence.

"My parents died in a helicopter crash." The words whispered out of her, and Liam stared at her for a moment, then nodded. Of course he already knew that. Her parents had been country music royalty. Their deaths on the way to her concert had made headlines everywhere. But he didn't know everything. No one did. Because she'd never told another soul. She'd tried once, with Dallas, but he'd blown her off. Somehow she knew Liam wouldn't. "I bought them the tickets." She couldn't lift her head to him.

The gravel crunched and then his shoes entered her line of sight. He didn't say anything.

She listened to the sigh of the darkness around them, then forced herself to speak: "I bought them out of spite." She covered her face. What must this good man think of her confession? But now that she'd started, she might as well tell him all of it. "They thought it was a bad idea for me to be involved with Dallas romantically. They saw what I hadn't figured out yet, I guess." She directed a disgusted snort at herself. "But I just knew this was our big break. It was our first arena concert—and I wanted to fly them in to show them how wrong they were. How successful I was. Just like them."

She swallowed, shaking her head. "Maybe they'd still be alive if I hadn't been so petty." She watched the moonlight and shadows dance across the cornstalks in the field, blinking away the moisture that had gathered behind her eyelids. "I'm sorry." This wasn't supposed to be about her. It was about Liam. And his wife. She didn't know why she'd thought telling him about her parents would be helpful.

She heard movement but didn't look until she felt Liam settling onto the step next to her.

"I'm sorry." His voice wrapped her up in its warmth, and something inside her cracked open. The tears she'd been fighting were suddenly falling fast and hard onto her cheeks. She looked away, wiping at them, but they refused to stop. It was like the bubble she'd been so careful to keep around herself since her parents' deaths had popped, and all her sorrow had decided to come out in one giant deluge.

"Hey." Now it wasn't only Liam's voice that wrapped around her—his arm circled her shoulders, pulling her gently against his side. "It's okay."

Lydia nodded and gulped, but she couldn't stop the sobs. As Liam tightened his hold, stroking her arm, she couldn't help it—she let her head fall onto his shoulder, let herself give in to the feeling of being protected.

When she finally had herself composed to the point where she was only snuffling, she lifted her head. "I'm so sorry. I didn't mean to— I'm not sure why you're the only person in the world I seem to feel the need to cry in front of."

Liam smiled even as he unwrapped his arm from around her. His warmth lingered.

"As long as I'm not the one making you cry, I can deal with it."

The way his eyes held hers stole her breath, and her heart crackled with anticipation. Was he about to—

"Well." He shifted and stood.

Disappointment dropped Lydia's stomach. Of course he hadn't been about to kiss her.

"I should—" He grasped the back of his neck. "I should get to bed. I have to help set things up for the Fourth of July show tomorrow."

"You do fireworks too?" Not that she was surprised, with the way he'd set fireworks popping in her chest.

But he shook his head. "There are lighting effects too. That's my wheelhouse." He dug a toe into the gravel. "Are you planning to go? To the fireworks?"

"With the Calvanos, yes."

"Okay, well." Liam looked up, hooking his hands in his back pockets. "I guess I'll see you there. Goodnight."

He'd only made it a few steps before she called, "Hey, Liam?"

He turned around, and though his face was in shadow, she was pretty sure he was smiling. "Yeah?"

"Thanks for the pizza. And the bowling. And the . . ." She gestured to the steps. "It was . . ."

"Surreal?" Liam said around a laugh.

"Not so surreal this time. Just really . . . real."

Chapter 17

The coffee tasted extra good this morning. The sun shone extra bright. The day felt extra full of promise.

"So painting went well last night?" Mama's thin eyebrows raised toward her hair, her lips dancing with a smile.

"What makes you say that?" But Liam couldn't dampen his own smile. Mama had been right. He liked Lydia.

A lot.

And the way she'd listened to him last night, the way she'd shared her own heartache—it had strengthened the connection he'd felt that first night in Nashville. He only regretted that he hadn't given in to his impulse to kiss her.

But maybe tonight, after the fireworks . . .

"Are you kidding me, Dad?" Mia stormed into the room, and Liam jumped. There was no way his daughter knew what he'd been thinking. So what was she upset about now?

"About what?" he asked calmly. It'd taken a while for him to learn that things only got worse when he fed into her drama.

With an exaggerated sigh and eye roll worthy of an award, she spun her phone toward him.

Liam stared at the screen, trying to figure out how Mia had gotten a picture of him and Lydia. "What is this?"

"Oh, that's not all." Mia handed him the phone and motioned for him to scroll.

He did, past another dozen pictures, some of him and Lydia making a quick exit from the pizza place, some from the bowling alley, Lydia smiling in his shirt and hat.

"How did you get these?"

Mia rolled her eyes again. "The whole world has them. They're all over social media. Do you know how embarrassing this is?"

Liam blinked at her. Embarrassing? It was an invasion of privacy.

He accidentally caught sight of the comments under one of the pictures. *Good for her. She looks happy.* His heart lifted. Maybe this wasn't so bad.

But then he went to the next comment: *This is her follow-up to Dallas? One star.*

And the next: *Bet this guy thinks he's something special. Wait till she throws a mic at his head.*

And yet another: *I still hope she gets back together with Dallas. They were so perfect for each other.*

That one was followed by a whole bunch of replies in agreement, mixed in with one or two that seemed to be rooting for Liam.

He passed the phone back to Mia, stunned.

All they'd done was go out for pizza and bowling. And the internet had decided it was their business?

"So?" Mia prompted.

Liam raised his shoulders helplessly. What did she think he could do about it? "Ignore it. It'll blow over." As long as he gave Lydia some distance. Which was what the whole world thought he should do anyway.

He rubbed at his jaw. Was that what she would want too?

"Whatever." Mia shoved her phone in her pocket. "Just tell me— Should I prepare for more of these? Or are you going to stop seeing her?"

"I'm not seeing her." Liam fought to keep a grip on his patience. "We're just friends."

"Whatever you say." Mia smirked and pushed past him toward the door. "I won't be home until late."

"Where are you—"

But the door had already slammed shut. Liam let out a long breath and stared at it. It'd be so much easier not to do this right now. But he still had his responsibility as her father.

He yanked the door open and followed her out. "I said, where are you going?" He raised his voice so she'd hear him from across the yard.

"Work. And then Sonia's."

"Are you going to the fireworks tonight?"

She paused at the edge of the driveway. "Are you going to be there?"

"Yeah."

"Then no." She sped toward the car and got in before Liam could respond.

Which was fine. Since he didn't have a response anyway.

He dragged his feet back inside and downed the rest of his coffee, its bitterness biting at his tongue.

"You should go talk to her." Mama sat at the table, calmly sipping her own coffee.

"She left." Liam raked a hand through his hair.

"I don't mean Mia," Mama said patiently.

"Oh." Liam grabbed his keys. "Later. I have to get over to the park. I'm late the way it is."

"Liam—"

But he shook his head. "Not now, Mama." He softened the words with a kiss to her cheek. "I'll be back to pick you up for the fireworks later."

"Oh, didn't I tell you? I'm going to watch from Betty's house. Her son is going to grill for us."

"All right. I guess I'll see you afterward then." So neither his mama nor his daughter wanted to spend the evening with him. He should be happy—it meant he could spend all his time with Lydia. But after what he'd seen on Mia's phone this morning, he wasn't sure that was such a good idea.

He stepped outside, the shadows of the trees providing welcome shade on what promised to be a sweltering day. His gaze locked on the carriage house. Was Lydia awake? Had she seen the photos? Was she embarrassed by them? Happy about them? Did she want him to leave her alone or come knocking on her door and sweep her into a kiss?

He reached the edge of the driveway and hesitated. Two more steps and he could march up those stairs and find out.

With a small laugh at himself, he turned to the van and got in. He might sometimes forget that Lydia was a celebrity, but the rest of the world clearly hadn't.

There was no room for someone like him in her world. And he wasn't about to get in the way of her dreams.

Chapter 18

He was a good kisser. Lydia smiled as her lips met Liam's again—but a blaring noise made her jerk back, and he disappeared.

Her eyes sprang open, and she lunged out of bed toward the phone she must have left on the other side of the room. She didn't remember setting the alarm.

She snatched up the phone, but it took a moment to realize it wasn't the alarm—it was a phone call. She blinked at her manager's name on the screen.

Her eyes fell on the time as she swiped to answer. Was it really 10:30 already? Of course, with dreams like that one about kissing Liam, she couldn't blame herself for sleeping in.

"Hello?" She girded herself for Becca's inevitable question about how the songs were coming. After last night, at least she felt like she could give an optimistic answer.

"Good morning." The voice on the other end of the line sounded downright chipper, and Lydia pulled the phone away from her ear to double-check that it was Becca.

"Good morning," Lydia repeated cautiously. "I started on a song yesterday. I really think it's going to—"

"I thought you might have," Becca interrupted with an out-of-character laugh.

"What?" How could Becca have known? The last time they'd talked, Lydia had admitted that being in River Falls hadn't done much for her songwriting.

"I saw the pictures," Becca said.

Lydia waited for her to clarify.

"They're brilliant," Becca went on, as if Lydia should already know what she was talking about. "You've got the whole world buzzing. And the guy's even kind of cute."

"The guy?" Lydia rubbed her forehead. "Becca, what pictures are you talking about?"

"You didn't see them?" Becca sounded incredulous. "What, have you been under a rock all morning?"

"No, I've been in my nice, comfy bed. Dreaming." She touched her lips. That dream kiss had been so real she could still feel it.

"I suppose that makes sense." Becca laughed again. "You must have been tired from all the pizza and bowling."

"Yeah, I guess. Wait." A rock dropped into her stomach. "How did you—" She yanked the phone away from her ear and put it on speaker, then tapped on her social media accounts.

"Oh no." She dropped to the bed, staring at the pictures of her and Liam that plastered every page. She scrolled through a few of the comments, the rock in her middle growing to a boulder.

"What do you mean, 'oh no'?" Becca sounded giddy. "This is just what we needed. People are going crazy for this."

"Going crazy?" Lydia swallowed. "Someone gave him one star. This one says Dallas should come punch him." She blinked back the sting. Liam was going to hate her. All he'd done was be a nice guy—one Lydia could laugh with and talk to and be herself around. He didn't need to worry about being insulted like this.

"Oh, don't worry about that. At least they're talking about you again. We can really capitalize on this. Try to be seen together in public as often as you can. And don't be afraid to play it up. You know, hold his hand, kiss him. Stuff like that."

"Kiss him?" She was going to be sick. Her manager wanted her to exploit Liam to further her career?

"People love that," Becca said cheerfully. "I gotta fly. Just wanted to check in and say great job. Can't wait to hear that new song." And then she hung up.

Lydia stared at the phone. She'd stopped scrolling on a picture of herself. Liam's hat covered her eyes, but there was no denying the smile on her face. Though he wasn't in this picture, Lydia could imagine exactly where he'd been standing. Because he was the one who had made her smile like this.

The first comment under the picture said, *She looks happy.*

Lydia's mouth curved. She had been happy—happier than she could remember being in years.

She clicked the phone off and set it on the bed. Last night, she'd nearly let herself forget all the reasons she couldn't be in a relationship. And now, this was just one more reason to add to the list.

She stood, the boulder in her stomach making it hard to drag herself to the window. She parted the curtain and peered at the driveway. Her vehicle was the only one there. Which meant Liam must have already left to help set things up for tonight.

Had he seen the pictures before he left? How did he feel about them? Would he want to avoid her now?

She chewed her lip and stared at her phone, still on the bed. With two quick strides, she crossed the room, picked it up, and dialed before she could change her mind. Whether he'd seen the pictures or not, she owed him an apology.

But the phone rang and rang before finally going to voicemail. At the beep, her mind went blank. "Hey, Liam. It's Lydia. St. Peter." She closed her eyes. Using her famous last name wasn't going to help. "I was just calling to apologize about last night. I mean—" She scrambled to correct herself. "Not about last night itself. That was great. About the pictures. Unless you haven't seen them— I mean, I'm still sorry if you haven't seen them, but—" Oh, good grief. She needed to end this call. "I guess what I'm saying is give me a call when you can so we can talk about it. Sorry." She hung up, then threw the phone on the bed as if it were at fault for her inability to think clearly.

Hopefully Liam would call soon, and then she could explain the whole thing. And maybe he'd even forgive her.

She spent the rest of the day trying to work on the song she'd started last night while they were painting, but her words had shriveled up.

She tried calling Liam a few more times, but each time it rang until voicemail picked up. She didn't attempt to leave her long, convoluted message again—she simply asked him to call her when he had a chance. She texted too, in case maybe his phone hadn't rung when she'd called.

But by the time she needed to leave for the barbecue at Abe's, he still hadn't called, and her texts remained unread. She reminded herself that he was working and probably didn't have time to check his phone and make calls to a woman who fell apart whenever he was around.

She'd had no right to dump the burden of her parents' deaths on him last night. He had enough troubles of his own to deal with. But when he'd started talking about his wife and the guilt he lived with, she'd felt so close to him. And the way he'd comforted her and maybe, almost, kissed her, she'd thought maybe he felt it too.

With a sigh, she stepped outside, the thick humidity wrapping itself around her face like a dog's tongue. Sweat trickled down her neck as she made her way through the field, where the cornstalks now brushed the tops of her legs.

"Hey, Lydia." Everyone greeted her with smiles and waves when she reached Abe's backyard, and Benjamin grabbed a paper plate and launched it toward her like a frisbee. "Better get some food."

"Thanks." Lydia stepped through the French doors into the kitchen to fill her plate, then took a seat at the long patio table next to Benjamin. Between the teasing and the laughing, Lydia could almost forget about the unreturned messages to Liam. Thankfully, no one brought up the pictures, though whether that was because they hadn't seen them or because they were too nice, she wasn't sure.

She was going back for seconds of Benjamin's twice-baked potatoes when Simeon entered the front door.

"Hey." She gestured to the food. "We left some for you."

"Thanks." His smile was tight. Had he seen the pictures? He was Liam's best friend. Maybe his reaction signaled Liam's. Should she ask? Was that a sibling type of thing to talk about?

Simeon sighed as he picked up a plate, and it dawned on Lydia that he was alone. "Where's Abigail?"

"She's not feeling well." He plopped a hamburger onto a bun.

"Oh, that's too bad. Tell her I hope she feels better soon."

Simeon concentrated on adding ketchup to his burger but nodded.

Lydia set a potato on her plate, then turned toward the door. But she stopped halfway there. She had to know.

"Have you heard from Liam at all today?"

Simeon looked up, studying her. "No. Why?"

Lydia watched the butter melting into her potato. If Benjamin had asked, she probably wouldn't hesitate to answer. But she hadn't gotten to know Simeon all that well yet. And he was a counselor. So he would probably read all kinds of things into her innocent question.

"No reason." She moved closer to the door. She thought Simeon might stop her, but he had gone back to preparing his hamburger.

"It's just—" The words rushed from her lips. "Someone took pictures of us together last night and they're all over social media, and I've been trying to call him to apologize, but he won't pick up the phone and—" She cut herself off. She was starting to sound desperate.

Simeon frowned. "That doesn't sound like Liam. I'm sure he's just busy."

"Yeah." Lydia swallowed. Somehow Simeon's words didn't bring the reassurance she'd hoped for. "Thanks."

She went outside, but she wasn't hungry for her potato anymore, so she gave it to Benjamin. After they'd cleaned up from dinner, everyone got ready to go over to Founder's Park to watch the fireworks.

Just as Lydia was about to tuck herself into Benjamin's ridiculous little Gremlin—his pride and joy—her phone buzzed with a text. Her heart leaped. Finally, Liam had decided to respond.

But instead of Liam, the text was from Becca.

I'm still waiting to see some pictures of you and your mystery man. Fireworks would be the perfect backdrop. Just saying . . .

Lydia clicked her phone off and shoved it in her pocket. More pictures of her and Liam was the last thing she needed, especially before she'd had a chance to talk to him about yesterday's. But if she went to the fireworks, more pictures were inevitable. Now that people knew she was here, everywhere she went was a photo land mine.

"I think I'm going to go home," she said to Benjamin, closing the car door without getting in.

"What? No, you have to come. If this is about the pictures, I'll be your bodyguard." He held his arms out to his sides, as if he were a bodybuilder.

Lydia grimaced. So he had seen the pictures.

"No, really. I'm starting to get a headache. Maybe I'm coming down with whatever Abigail has."

Benjamin watched her closely, and she rubbed at her temple for effect.

"Fine. I'll give you a ride home."

"It's across the field. I can walk. You go. Tell everyone I'm sorry, but I'll see them soon." She'd leave it up to him whether "everyone" included Liam or not.

Chapter 19

Liam reached for his phone for the six-hundredth time today. And for the six-hundredth time realized he'd forgotten it at home this morning.

The show was about to start, and he wanted to text Lydia to ask if she was here—and if she minded if he sat by her. He told himself that he'd be fine with it if she said she'd prefer they not be seen together again.

He gave a few more last-minute instructions to the technicians running the show, then moved toward the crowds gathering in the large green space along the riverbank. Maybe he could unobtrusively find her and ask how she was doing with everything. How she felt about those pictures, which she must have seen by now.

All day, he'd regretted not talking to her about them before he left home.

He made his way through the sea of people, watching especially for anyone wearing a hat or sunglasses despite the falling darkness.

Finally, he spotted the Calvanos, their blankets and lawn chairs clustered close together. He let out a breath it felt like he'd been holding all day. In the middle of the big family would be the perfect place for her to hide. He dodged around chatting parents and horseplaying kids, his heart already lighting up in anticipation of seeing her.

"Liam!" Someone grabbed his arm from behind, and Liam spun toward them.

"We need you." The technician he'd just left puffed, clearly winded. "Some drunk guy knocked the whole master light board over. It's dead."

"Dead?" Liam glanced once more toward the Calvanos, but their circle was too tight for him to spot Lydia.

"Twenty minutes to showtime," the technician urged.

"Right." Liam tore his eyes away from the Calvanos and jogged behind the tech toward the lighting controls.

A few minutes of fiddling showed that though the light board would power on, it wasn't sending signals to the lights. Liam tried restarting it, praying that this was one of those times that the simplest solution worked the best. He'd spent all day setting this up, and he didn't have time to switch over to another board. He tried not to think about all the work the city might have for him if this job went well—or all the projects he'd miss out on if it didn't.

With the board powered up again, he tested the connection. Still nothing. In frustration, he moved slides he knew would have no effect. He reached around the back of the board to make sure the cables were tight, but his hand found nothing there. Had no one—including him—checked the cable connections? He moved around the back, quickly locating the missing cable on the ground. But one glance at it told him the problem was bigger—the connector pins were all bent at odd angles. They must have been damaged in the fall.

At least a dozen more lights were daisy-chained through this cable. If it didn't work, half the show would be missing. He scanned the extra equipment for a replacement cable. But he'd used his extra cable for a light he'd added at the last minute.

"Be right back." He took off for the parking lot.

"Ten minutes," the tech called behind him.

"I know." The park lights had dimmed as the start of the show grew closer, and Liam could only hope he wouldn't trip over anything as he sprinted past the few people still making their way into the park.

It only took a few seconds to locate another cable in the van, and then he sprinted back toward the lighting booth.

His breaths came hard and fast by the time he reached it, but he worked quickly to replace the cable. The moment he had both ends connected, the park lights went out completely.

"That wasn't us, was it?" the tech whispered.

Liam shook his head, still breathing heavily. He scanned the light board. Thankfully, it indicated a connection with all the lights. Now he just had to hope none of the programming had gotten messed up from the fall.

A giant cheer rang out from the crowd as the first firework lit the sky, followed a beat later by a brilliant play of lights on the water as the tech started the lighting program.

Liam exhaled sharply.

It worked.

He remained close to the board for a few minutes to make sure there were no hiccups, but the tech had everything well in hand, and there wasn't really anything more for Liam to do.

His eyes skimmed the crowd. With everyone focused on the sky and the river, he wouldn't have to worry about anyone taking a picture of him with Lydia.

Slowly, eyes on the ground so he wouldn't fall and end up on someone's lap, he made his way toward the Calvanos.

"Hey." He took a seat on the first blanket in their little encampment, which held a cuddled Asher and Ireland. They both smiled and greeted him, then turned back to the show.

He let his gaze travel over the rest of the Calvanos, anticipation growing by the second. But too quickly, he ran out of Calvanos to scan—without spotting Lydia.

He leaned toward Asher and Ireland. "Do y'all know where Lydia is?"

VALERIE M. BODDEN

Asher shook his head, but Ireland offered a smile that looked a little too sympathetic. "She wasn't feeling well after dinner, so she decided to go home. Abigail's sick too, so maybe they have the same thing." But she didn't look like she believed her own words.

Liam told himself to let it go. If she wasn't feeling well, he should leave her alone. And if she *was* feeling well, then she was probably trying to avoid him. In which case, he should also leave her alone.

He pushed to his feet. Ireland waved, as if she knew exactly what he planned to do. He'd only taken three careful steps when someone grabbed his arm.

Not again.

Liam's eyes went to the water, but the light show continued, its dazzling reds and blues rippling across the river's surface.

He turned to find Simeon next to him. "Hey. Are you blowing Lydia off?" Simeon's voice was low.

"What? Of course not." His friend knew him better than that.

"She said you haven't returned her calls."

"What calls?" Liam reached for his pocket, then remembered. "I forgot my phone at home this morning."

Simeon nodded. "I told her it was probably something like that."

"Thanks, man." Liam knew he could always count on his friend. "Wait. She was asking about me?" He rolled his eyes at himself. Was he a middle schooler?

But Simeon chuckled. "Yeah. Don't ask me why, but I think she might like you." He elbowed Liam in the ribs. "Now you just have to work up the guts to ask her out."

Liam scoffed even as his heart found its way up to the vicinity of the fireworks. "Whatever. Hey, Ireland said Abigail's sick?"

The grin slipped off Simeon's face. "She's—"

"Excuse me," a voice interrupted from the ground. "Can y'all move out of the way? Some of us are trying to watch the fireworks."

"Sorry." Simeon took a step backward. "See you later," he said to Liam, then turned and picked his way back toward his spot among the Calvanos.

Liam watched his friend a moment, concern tugging at him. The way Simeon had looked when Liam asked about Abigail—but Simeon was here, so whatever she had couldn't be too serious.

Liam worked his way through the crowd, reaching his van as the lights on the water dimmed dramatically before bursting into a kaleidoscope of color.

He eased the van out of the parking lot, not switching on the headlights until he was in the street so he wouldn't ruin the effects of the show.

As he pulled away, he could still see the fireworks in his rearview mirror. But maybe it was time for him to stop looking back and start looking forward.

Chapter 20

The sound drew Lydia outside. Though the carriage house was ten minutes from the center of River Falls, she had an almost perfect view of the fireworks from her balcony. She watched the reds and golds and greens sparkling and mingling in the night sky and tried not to feel lonely.

It had been her choice to come back here instead of going to the park with her family. Instead of seeing Liam.

But this was better than risking more photos. Especially when Liam had clearly been avoiding so much as talking to her all day.

She wrapped her arms around herself, despite the warm, muggy air that clung to her skin. She should have known better than to let herself get close to Liam. And she especially should have known better than to be seen in public with him.

She'd allowed her time in River Falls to lull her into a false sense of anonymity. It had just been so nice to feel like a normal person for once in her life. But apparently a normal life was too much to hope for.

A gold firework reached for her before fading into the night, and Lydia sighed. Would it be so bad to disappear like that?

Her phone buzzed, but Lydia ignored it. She didn't need yet another text from Becca exhorting her to exploit Liam for her own gain.

Headlights flashed at the end of the driveway, and the tempo of Lydia's heart jumped. Before she could make a conscious decision, she sprang from her seat and flew down the stairs. Liam was going to hear her apology, whether he wanted to or not.

But before the vehicle was halfway down the driveway, she realized it was too small to be Liam's work van. The car sped toward her, spitting gravel, before Mia slammed on the brakes inches from the carriage house.

"Hi, Mia." Lydia stepped forward as Mia opened the car door. She had no reason to expect a warm reception from the teen, but she wasn't prepared for the sharp glare the girl shot at her. "Glad to see you're wearing your own clothes today," Mia sneered.

"My own . . ." Lydia glanced down at the pink shirt she'd picked out this morning with the thought of seeing Liam in mind.

"My mom used to wear that shirt, you know." Mia's eyes cut right through Lydia's heart.

Oh. Liam's shirt.

"I'm sorry. I didn't think— I was cold, and your dad—" She took a tentative step closer to the girl. She certainly hadn't meant to hurt her.

Mia turned away, and Lydia caught sight of the logo on the paper cup in the girl's hand. "Is that a Curly Q's cup? I didn't know there was one around here. I thought that was only a Nashville thing."

Mia's head whipped up, and she crossed her arm to the other side, so Lydia could no longer see the logo. Her hard glare transformed into a plea.

Lydia stepped around her and wriggled the cup out of her hand. Sure enough, that was the pig with the long, curly tail from the Curly Q's logo. Under the logo were the words, "Nashville, Tennessee."

"Mia, did you go to Nashville?" That was a three-hour drive. Surely, Liam wouldn't have let her go there by herself.

Mia's expression turned defiant, but Lydia could detect the fear behind it.

"So what if I did?"

"Does your dad know?"

Mia shrugged. "It's not like he cares."

"Of course he cares." Lydia may not know how Liam felt about the pictures of them, but she did know how he felt about his daughter.

"Whatever." Mia reached for the cup, but another set of headlights swung into the driveway. The girl pulled her hand back. "You can't tell my dad." Urgency overran her voice. "He wouldn't understand. I had to go, or my boyfriend would have broken up with me." Her eyes glistened. "Please, Lydia."

"Mia, you can't be breaking the rules just for some guy."

"Please." The brokenness in Mia's eyes had stared at Lydia from her own mirror so many times. "He'll ground me forever. It was only a one-time thing. I swear."

Lydia watched the headlights drawing closer. "You promise you won't do it again?"

Mia gave a vigorous nod and made an X over her heart. "Promise."

Lydia gnawed her lip. Liam deserved to know what his daughter had been up to. But Mia was home safe, and she'd promised not to do it again—so what was the point in upsetting both of them? Besides, maybe this was her chance to win the girl's trust. And if she won Mia's trust, maybe she could help her deal with the brokenness that hung tangibly over her. And then Liam wouldn't have to be so worried about her.

The van's engine shut off, and Lydia looked toward the vehicle. But it was too dark in the cab to make out Liam's features.

"Please," Mia whispered.

Lydia turned to her. "Just this once," she warned.

"Thank you." Relief flooded Mia's eyes, and her mouth warmed almost to a smile. Her gaze flicked to the van, where Liam had just opened his door, before she took off for the house.

"Mia," Liam called through the dark.

The girl stopped but didn't turn around. "What?"

"How was your day?"

A firework lit up Mia's shrug. "Fine." She continued her march toward the house.

Though Lydia was a good twenty feet from Liam, his heavy sigh reached her.

Maybe she should tell him about Mia's little trip after all. But his shoulders already hung so heavy that she couldn't bear to add another weight.

Instead, she needed to take some weight off them.

She took a careful step in his direction, and his head turned toward her. Even in the dark he looked exhausted—and uncertain.

"Hi." They said it at the same time, then both laughed the same uncomfortable laugh.

"Are you feeling better?" Liam asked.

"Feeling better?" Lydia tilted her head. When had she not— Oh yeah, she'd told her family she had a headache. They must have told Liam. "Much better. Thanks."

"Good." Liam worked his boot into the gravel. "I hope she was civil to you." He nodded toward the house, where Mia had disappeared inside.

"She was. Mostly." Lydia brushed off the blip of conscience. "Look, I know you don't want to talk to me right now, but you need to know how sorry I am about those pictures. I had no idea anyone—"

"Why wouldn't I want to talk to you?" Liam stepped closer, his voice as warm as the night air.

"Well— I mean, the pictures made it look like—" But she didn't want to finish that sentence. "And the comments people made—" She didn't want to finish that one either. "You didn't return any of my calls or texts."

"I know. I'm sorry." Liam's fingers grazed her elbow. "I forgot my phone this morning."

"Oh." A firework sizzled loudly overhead—but not as loudly as the relief in Lydia's heart. "I thought maybe you were upset about them."

Liam frowned. "When you weren't at the fireworks, I thought maybe *you* were upset about them."

Lydia looked at him in surprise. "Why would I be upset? I'm used to it. One of the prices of being who I am. But you never asked for any of it."

"Yeah, but it's your career at stake, not mine."

"Oh, don't worry about that. My manager says it's good for me to be seen out and about. Keeps people from forgetting who I am." She didn't mention that Becca specifically wanted her to be seen out and about with him.

"I'm sure no one could forget you." The reds and golds of the fireworks above lit up Liam's face. As if suddenly embarrassed, he dropped his gaze. "Is that a Curly Q's cup?"

Lydia had forgotten about the cup she still clutched. "Um. Yeah." She kept her gaze carefully on the ground. Now what did she say? She'd promised Mia, but . . .

"That was always our favorite place. I heard they were building one in Brampton. Was it good?"

"Um." Lydia swallowed weakly. "Yes."

"I'll have to take Mia sometime."

The pop and hiss and thud of fireworks grew to a frenzy, and they both looked up. Sparkles of red, blue, gold, purple, and green danced and jostled over and under and around each other.

"The finale." Liam had to speak loudly over the noise.

Lydia nodded, watching them in wonder. But wait. If this was the finale . . .

She turned her gaze from the sky to Liam, who was still looking up. "Why aren't you there?"

He shrugged, not looking her way. "Because I wanted to be here." The fireworks fell silent halfway through his statement, and his words echoed in Lydia's heart. But he kept his gaze on the sky—now empty aside from the haze of firework smoke that obscured the stars and left a heavy scent in the air. The echo of his words died out.

Maybe he hadn't meant he wanted to be here with her. Maybe he just wanted to be home.

But when he turned slowly toward her, his lips lifted in a light smile. "I think this may have been the best seat in town for the finale."

"We're not sitting," Lydia pointed out.

Liam's soft chuckle added heat to the already warm night. "What are you doing tomorrow?"

The question seemed loud in the suddenly silent night, and Lydia jumped. Was he asking her out? She'd told herself a thousand times that she was done with dating. But she had to admit that Liam made her think . . .

"Because I'm working on the Builder's for the Kingdom house. And we could use some more volunteers."

"Oh." So, not a date. "I don't really know how to build a house."

Liam's smile stretched wider. "You don't have to build the whole thing yourself. And I happen to know you're a great painter."

Lydia's laugh spun through the air between them. "We both know that's not true."

But Liam stepped close enough to nudge her arm. "Come on. It'll be fun. And if you're lucky, you might get to use some power tools."

"How'd you know that was on my bucket list?" Lydia joked.

"Seriously." Liam's eyes came to hers. "I think you'd enjoy it. And maybe you'll get some new song ideas."

She snorted. "Songs about power tools?"

But given that the song she'd been working on last night had stalled, she couldn't say no to any chance for inspiration. And if Liam was going to be there too . . . well, he did seem to bring out her muse.

"Count me in."

"Really?" The surprise in his voice made her second-guess her decision. "I don't know. Are you sure I won't be in the way?"

"I'm sure." Liam's answer was firm. "We leave at 6 a.m."

"Wait. What?" No one had said anything about getting up at the crack of dawn.

But Liam was already on his way toward his house. "Better get some sleep." That warm chuckle floated back to her and settled around her shoulders.

She tried to hold onto her annoyance about the early wake-up time, but she couldn't do it. Not while she watched Liam's energetic footsteps cross the yard—and especially not when he reached his porch and waved, calling, "Go to bed."

She laughed and returned his wave, then climbed the carriage house steps. But instead of going to bed, she grabbed her notebook, needing to capture the melody suddenly singing through her.

Chapter 21

Liam slid his fingers through the handles of the two coffee mugs he'd just filled, walking gingerly to the door so he wouldn't spill. He tugged it open carefully and pulled it shut behind him, breathing deeply of the early morning air. The rising sun colored the sky in variations of peach and purple, and a heavy layer of dew gave everything a fresh, clean scent.

This is the day the Lord has made. If it hadn't been for the coffee in his hands, Liam might have run across the yard. His heart hadn't felt this light in . . . years. Since before Molly had gotten sick.

The thought threatened to derail his joyous mood, but then the door of the carriage house opened, and Lydia stepped outside. Dressed in a pair of faded jeans and a loose t-shirt, with her hair pulled back into a ponytail, she looked both ready to walk the runway and ready to get her hands dirty.

"Good morning," he called. Coffee splashed onto his hand as his pace unintentionally quickened.

She covered a yawn with the back of her hand and made her way down the steps. "It would be with about three more hours of sleep." But she smiled. "I don't know how you get up this early every day."

"I find this helps." He extracted the larger mug from his grip and held it out to her.

Her fingers brushed his as she took it, and he suddenly didn't want to let go.

"I've got it. Thank you."

Right. He made his fingers release the mug, watching as she lifted it to her face, closed her eyes, and inhaled. "Pecan?" Her eyes opened and met his over the rim of the mug.

He shrugged. She'd mentioned in passing that it was her favorite.

Her eyes closed again as she took a sip, and he forced himself to do the same so he wouldn't keep staring at her.

"How come mine is so much bigger than yours?" Lydia wrapped both hands around the mug.

"I figured you'd probably need it more than I do."

"You weren't wrong." She took another sip, then tilted her head toward the sky. "Although for sunrises like this, it might be worth getting up early once in a while."

And suddenly Liam had a vision of the two of them sitting out on the porch, coffee in hand, watching the sunrise together every morning.

He chugged a giant gulp of his coffee, ignoring the burn as it seared his throat. "Should we get going?"

"Absolutely. I was promised power tools, you know."

Liam chuckled and led her to the van. He thought twice about opening the passenger door for her—but just because this wasn't a date didn't mean he shouldn't be a gentleman.

When he got in the vehicle, Lydia was leaning back in her seat with her eyes closed. Just like she had that first night they'd met in Nashville. In his wildest dreams, it had never occurred to him that less than a year later, they would meet again. And become friends. And . . . possibly more?

Lydia's eyes popped open as Liam pulled out of the driveway and onto the road. "So what's wrong with you?"

Liam accidentally pressed his foot to the accelerator harder than he meant to, and the van bucked forward. Apparently Lydia didn't share his *possibly more* sentiment.

"I'm sorry. I don't . . ." How was he supposed to answer that? There were plenty of things wrong with him. But he'd rather not enumerate them all, especially if there was something in particular she had in mind.

"Sorry." Lydia sipped her coffee. "I didn't mean it like that. I just mean, every time I think you couldn't be any more of a saint, you go and do something like build houses for people in need. But there must be *something* wrong with you. Do you have a secret sock obsession or something?"

"Ha." Relief made Liam's laugh louder than necessary. "No sock obsession. But don't worry, there's plenty wrong with me."

"Name one thing." Challenge rang from Lydia's words.

"I'm a terrible songwriter," he shot back, proud of himself for coming up with something so quickly.

"That's true," Lydia conceded a little too easily.

"Hey." He reached across the console to push her shoulder, letting himself enjoy the sparks for a moment before pulling back. "You said the mud puddle song was good."

"I'm not sure 'good' was the word I used," Lydia teased. "But seriously, I think it's great that you give up your time to help others. Mama and Daddy and I volunteered at a soup kitchen every Thanksgiving, but it always felt like it was more for show than to help out."

Liam eyed her pensive expression. He'd been cynical enough to doubt the intentions behind celebrities' charitable acts in the past. And yet— "I'm sure the attention you brought them helped more than you know. We all have gifts we can use to serve the Lord and serve others. Mine just happens to be electricity." His eyes met hers, and a smile played with her lips, and suddenly all he could think about was the electricity pulsing between them.

It took an act of supreme strength to pull his gaze back to the road. Fortunately, they had reached the site of the building project, and he pulled the van to a stop along the curb.

"Wow. It looks like it's almost done." Lydia gaped up the small hill in the front yard to the modest house that they'd framed out a few weeks ago. Siding had started to go on since Liam was here last, and there were doors and windows now.

"Don't worry. There's still plenty to do inside." He opened his door and hopped out, rounding the van to meet up with her. As they walked side-by-side up the path to the front door, Liam just barely caught himself before grasping her hand in his.

"Liam, thank goodness you're here." Harrison Bemis, the project director, swooped down on them the instant they entered the door. In here, things were pretty bare bones yet, the walls framed out but not drywalled, the floor only plywood. "We had guys pulling wire yesterday, but Jake says it's all messed up, and we have our electrical inspection next week. Can you . . ." He gestured over his shoulder.

"Of course." All the visions he'd had of working side-by-side with Lydia all day faded like mist burning off a field. He turned to her. "Lydia, this is Harrison. Harrison, Lydia."

Harrison held out his hand, and Liam had to stop himself from stepping between them. Harrison had graduated from the same high school as Liam but had gone on to sell some sort of software to the government and was now possibly the wealthiest man in River Falls—in addition to being the town's most eligible bachelor. And the worst part was, he wasn't one of those arrogant, standoffish rich guys—he was about the nicest person anyone could meet. If Lydia thought Liam was a saint, what would she think about Harrison, who supported literally every charity in River Falls?

"I was promised power tools," Lydia said as she shook Harrison's hand.

The other man's chuckle grated against Liam's ears.

"Do you know how to use a sander?" Harrison asked.

"Nope," Lydia said cheerfully. "But it sounds fun."

"You'll like it. Come on. I'll teach you." Harrison gestured for Lydia to follow. She smiled at Liam before marching behind Harrison toward the kitchen.

"Hey, Liam." Jake trundled down the unfinished stairs. "Harrison tell you about the mess they made with the wires?"

"Yeah." Liam sighed, raking his fingers through his hair. "Let's see what we've got." He followed Jake up the stairs, allowing himself one more look over his shoulder and then wishing he hadn't as he caught the way Harrison smiled at Lydia. Her back was to Liam, but he was certain she was returning the smile.

The rest of the day passed more slowly than any day should. Liam wasn't sure what was worse: the hours at a time that passed without seeing Lydia, or the fact that every time he did see her, Harrison was at her side—one time he even had his hand on top of hers on the sander. All Liam could do was growl under his breath and get back to the wiring.

That was supposed to be *his* hand on top of hers.

"So how was last night? Did you finally ask her out?" Simeon strode into the room where Liam had been working alone for the past hour.

Liam grunted around the wire nut in his mouth.

"I'll take that as a no."

Though Liam's eyes were locked on his task, he could feel his friend's disapproval.

He pulled the nut out of his mouth. "Is she still working with Harrison?" There was no way Simeon would miss the undercurrent of jealousy in the question, but Liam didn't care.

"Not that I saw. Why? Would it bother you if she was?"

Liam shot a glance at his friend. He didn't need Simeon's counseling right now.

"So ask her out already," Simeon said, as if Liam had answered his question.

"She's out of my league, remember?" Someone like Harrison was much more suited to dating a celebrity.

"True, but for some unfathomable reason, she seems to like you anyway." Simeon's voice was lighthearted, but Liam could tell he was sincere. He only wished he knew if his friend was also correct. Did Lydia like him—or was it that he happened to be a convenient distraction until she returned to her real life in the spotlight?

"How's Abigail?" It was high time they talked about something else. "Feeling better?"

"She's . . ." Simeon sighed, and Liam paused his task to study his friend. Worry hovered on Simeon's brow.

"What's going on?"

But Simeon shook his head. "Nothing. She's on the mend. I'm going to go help with the cabinets."

"Simeon—" But Liam's phone rang, cutting him off, and Simeon disappeared down the stairs.

Liam grabbed the phone out of his pocket. He would get to the bottom of whatever Simeon wasn't saying—whether Simeon wanted him to or not. His friend didn't get to listen to everyone else's problems without sharing his own.

"Hello?" Liam lifted the phone to his ear without looking who was calling but instantly pulled it away as he was bombarded with shouts and curses.

By the time he got the caller—one of his biggest clients in Brampton—calmed down enough to decipher what the problem was, he was already packing up his gear and heading down the stairs.

He beelined for the kitchen, shoving off the annoyance of finding Harrison and Lydia sanding side-by-side.

"I'm sorry." He stopped in front of Lydia. "We have to go."

She looked up in surprise, and Liam worked to sound less brusque. "One of my clients in Brampton lost power, and I have to get over there and figure out what's going on."

"Oh." Lydia set down the sander.

But Harrison offered them both a benevolent smile. "I can give Lydia a ride home later. Then you won't have to go out of your way to drop her off before heading in the other direction."

Liam bit back his sharp retort to Harrison and turned to Lydia. "It's up to you."

She didn't even think about it. "You go ahead and get where you need to go. I'll stay for a while yet."

Liam stared between her and Harrison, then nodded curtly and tramped to the door.

That was that, then.

Harrison had won a battle he hadn't even known they were fighting.

Chapter 22

"Nice job with this." Harrison ran a hand over the cupboard door Lydia was sanding. He'd told her about how he'd salvaged the cabinets from a home that was being remodeled in the wealthier part of town. The wood was still in good shape, and according to Harrison, once everything was sanded and refinished, it'd look as good as new.

"Thanks." Lydia brushed the sawdust off her jeans and pushed her hair off her sticky cheek. After a solid week of work, she was finally on the last one. And then Harrison was going to trust her to paint them. She was still apprehensive about that and dearly hoped Liam would be done spending his days in Brampton by then so he could coach her through it.

Harrison was nice enough, but maybe there was such a thing as too nice. She could have sanded a door right down to the fibers, and he would have told her she was doing a good job. She needed Liam here to ground her—to tell her when it was obvious she didn't know what she was doing. And to teach her with that combination of humor and patience he seemed to have perfected.

She worked for another hour, then pulled out her phone and snapped a selfie with the sanded cupboards. She posted it to her social media accounts, then thought a moment before adding a caption: "A week ago, I had never touched a power tool. Today, I finished sanding all these cupboards. And it feels great."

She'd been hesitant at first to post about what she was doing, but then she'd remembered what Liam had said about using his gifts to serve. She wasn't sure what her gift might be, other than music, which seemed to have largely abandoned her lately. And then she'd thought of his comment about the attention she could bring to a cause. So she'd gotten brave and posted.

And the response had been tremendous, with hundreds and then thousands of people posting about their own volunteer experiences—or pledging to volunteer in their community. It was amazing to think she was making a difference not only in River Falls but maybe even in the world—though it felt presumptuous to think that. She itched to talk to Liam about it—she was sure he'd be able to help her put things in perspective, assuming he ever spent more than a few minutes at home again.

She pushed aside the recurring worry that he was avoiding her.

Just because their limited conversations when he got home from work each night had gotten shorter and shorter, it didn't necessarily mean he didn't want to talk to her. He had to be tired from the long hours he was putting in at work.

Besides, the one morning she'd managed to pull herself out of bed and present him with a steaming mug of coffee before he left, he'd seemed touched—even if he'd taken off without any further conversation.

Lydia's phone vibrated in her pocket, but she ignored it as she swept up the sawdust caked to the floor. She'd reply to the comments on her post later—but not too much later, or Becca would get on her case. At least her new social media activity had gotten her manager off her back about new songs—although Lydia could still feel that deadline pressing closer and closer.

Her phone vibrated again, then rang. Lydia pulled it out, half torn between dread that it was Becca and hope that it was Liam—irrational as that was. But Mia's name flashed across her screen. She tilted her head at the phone. When had she . . . oh right, Liam had asked them to exchange numbers in case either of them needed anything while he was out of town.

Lydia had certainly never expected Mia to use her number though. Maybe the girl had dialed her by accident. She probably didn't even realize it.

Lydia brought the phone to her ear. "Mia?"

"Lydia, you have to help me." Mia's taut voice lifted on the last word.

The hair on the back of Lydia's neck spiked to attention. She tossed the broom aside and hurried for the front door, pulling her keys out of her pocket. "What's wrong? Where are you?"

A shaky breath crackled through the phone. "I got a flat tire."

"Oh." Lydia let out a breath and slowed her footsteps. "Did you call your dad?"

"I can't," Mia answered with a half wail, half plea. "I don't know what to do."

"Why can't you call your dad?"

Mia mumbled something Lydia couldn't make out.

"What?" Lydia pressed the phone tighter to her ear. "I can't hear you."

"I said because he'll be mad."

"Mia, that's absurd." Lydia stopped in the middle of the sidewalk. "Of course your dad won't be mad that you got a flat tire. It happens."

"No." Guilt hung from the word. "He'll be mad about where I am."

"Why?" Lydia squinted down the street, as if she'd be able to see Mia. "Where are you?"

"I'm almost home . . ."

"Mia." Oh brother, that was the tone Lydia's mama had used on her. "Where are you?" she repeated in a less motherly voice.

"Robinsville."

"What are you doing in—" The realization smacked into her. "Were you in Nashville again?"

"No," Mia answered quickly. "I swear I wasn't. I was in Murfreesboro."

Lydia snorted. "That's not better. It's almost as far, and—"

"I know, okay?" Mia snapped. "But I'm stuck here now. Are you going to help me or not?"

Lydia closed her eyes. Maybe she should leave Mia to figure it out on her own. If she thought she was old enough to travel all over the state, then she was old enough to fix her own flat. Or she could call Liam.

And add one more problem to his already long list.

"I'll call roadside assistance for you, all right? And then I'll call you right back and stay on the phone with you until they're done so you don't get abducted or something."

Mia sniffled. "Thank you."

Lydia's heart responded to the softness in the girl's voice. "It's going to be okay." She got the details of Mia's location, then quickly called her own roadside service. They promised to have someone there within thirty minutes, and Lydia called Mia back to wait. Neither of them talked much, but Lydia felt better keeping the connection live. Thankfully, the roadside guy got there faster than expected, and it only took him a few minutes to put on the spare and send Mia on her way.

"You head straight home now," Lydia ordered, that parental tone creeping back in. "And then we can talk."

She jumped into her own car and headed back to the carriage house, then plunked herself on the steps to wait for Mia. Pieces of lyrics floated through her head, and she pulled out her phone to catch them before they waltzed away. She was so focused on recording her ideas that she didn't realize a vehicle had pulled into the driveway until a car door slammed.

She jumped up, the lecture she'd practiced on the drive home readying itself on her lips.

But instead of Mia, it was Helen, with her friend Betty helping her around the car. Lydia pushed to her feet with a smile. She'd never had a friendship like these two ladies shared. An image of Cheyenne the last night they'd stood on the same stage popped into her head, but she pushed it right back out. Cheyenne had never been the kind of friend who would sit and talk for hours or take you to the doctor—or not steal your boyfriend.

"Don't you two look nice. Did y'all get haircuts?"

Both women beamed at her.

"You're such a sweetie," Betty said. "You're single, right? Next time my son is in town, I'm going to have to set you two up."

Lydia laughed. "I am single, yes. But—"

"I'll have him call you." Betty winked at Lydia. "I have to go. My daughter and her husband and my brand-new grandbaby are coming for dinner. You'll help Helen to the door, won't you dear?"

"Of course." How had the tiny, elderly woman managed to give Lydia whiplash so quickly?

Helen offered Lydia a gentle smile as Betty turned her car around. "Don't mind Betty. She's always been a troublemaker."

"I can tell." Lydia chuckled. "How did you two become friends?" She took Helen's elbow and helped her over the path toward the house.

"That's a funny story." Helen's laugh was girlish. "It has to do with a turtle, an Easter bonnet, and a spelling bee."

"A what?" Lydia laughed at the odd combination.

"Come on in for some tea, and I'll tell you all about it." Helen leaned on Lydia as they climbed the porch steps.

142

Lydia hesitated. She absolutely had to talk to Mia when she got home. But she supposed she could intercept the girl as easily from inside as from the carriage house steps. And Helen's company would be a nice distraction from the questions about Liam that continually invaded her thoughts.

She helped Helen inside, then set about making the tea. When it was ready, she carried it to the living room, where she'd settled Helen.

As Helen launched into the story of her friendship with Betty, Lydia kept one ear tuned to the door, listening for Mia. But she and Helen were laughing so hard about the part of Helen's story that involved Betty taking off her Easter bonnet to reveal the turtle hidden under it that she didn't hear the front door open. Mia would have sneaked right past her if she hadn't caught a flash of movement out of the corner of her eye.

"Mia." Lydia sprang from her seat. "Sorry," she murmured to Helen. "There's something I need to talk to Mia about."

"Of course, dear. We're having chili for dinner. You should stay."

Lydia bit her lip. Tonight was Abe's meeting night, and Benjamin had left on a camping trip a few days ago, so she had no plans. "Sure. I'd like that."

She hurried out of the room, flying up the stairs behind Mia. She caught up to the girl just as she was closing her bedroom door.

Lydia grabbed it, and Mia froze, her lip rising.

"You can spare me the lecture. You're not my mom."

Lydia hesitated, but only for a second. She had to say this. "No, I'm not. But I'm the one you called. So you can either listen to my lecture, or we can talk to your dad about it together when he gets home."

Mia rolled her eyes but opened her door wider to let Lydia in.

Lydia took in the white comforter, the sage green pillows, the floral décor. The room was much softer than the girl who inhabited it—or at least softer than she let anyone see.

"You told me you weren't going to go to Nashville again," Lydia started. "You promised."

"I didn't go to Nashville," Mia interrupted. "I went to Murfreesboro." She crossed her arms in front of her—but it looked more like she was giving herself a hug than putting up a wall. Her lower lip trembled, and then a tear plopped onto her cheek.

Lydia could only stare. What was happening here? And what could she do?

"Mia?" She took a step closer, but Mia backed away, swiping a hand over her cheek.

"Are we done?" The girl sniffed and turned her back on Lydia.

"Not really." Lydia stepped gingerly across the space between them and set a hand on Mia's shoulder. "This isn't just about the car. What happened?"

Mia shrugged Lydia's hand off her shoulder. "Nothing. Go away."

"It might help to talk about it." Like the way talking to Liam had helped her. Fortunately, she had enough sense not to mention that to Mia.

"You're not my mom," Mia repeated, her tone nasal—she must be crying harder now. Lydia ached to wrap her arms around the girl in a way she'd never ached before.

But that was likely a recipe for getting punched in the face.

"No, I'm not," she said gently. "But that doesn't mean I can't listen." She moved to sit on Mia's bed.

Mia eyed her but didn't tell her to get up. "Zack dumped me. He said it was too hard never getting to see me. And he already has another girlfriend."

"Oh, sweetie." She didn't mean to use the term of endearment. It just slipped out.

Mia blew out a breath. "I feel so humiliated. And angry. And—"

"Hurt," Lydia filled in.

Mia glanced at her, the disdain returning to her eyes. "Like you'd know."

"Good point. It's not like I caught Dallas making out with my best friend moments before we had to go on stage."

Mia's eyes widened, and Lydia crossed her arms in front of her. Only two people in the world knew what had happened that night—Liam and her manager. And she'd never intended for another soul to find out.

"That's what happened? The night you threw the microphone at him?"

Lydia nodded. There was no point in denying it. "That's what happened."

"Why didn't you ever tell anyone? You could have ruined their career. Instead of—" She cut off.

"My own," Lydia finished for her.

Mia nodded, and Lydia sighed. "I guess I didn't feel like it was anyone's right to know. Plus, it's kind of humiliating. I'm a country music cliché."

Mia snorted. "Me too, I guess."

"Come on." Lydia stood. "Let's go help your grandma with the chili."

"I'll be down in a little bit." Mia grabbed a tissue and wiped at her eyes. "You're not going to tell my dad, are you?"

How had Lydia nearly forgotten what had started this whole conversation? Good thing she wasn't really a parent. She'd be awful at it.

She studied the girl. "You promise you won't do it again? For real this time?"

Mia nodded. "There's no reason to go anymore."

Lydia watched her. This time, instead of defiant, she seemed sincere.

"Okay," Lydia said slowly, fighting against her better judgment. But she'd made so much progress in breaking down Mia's walls—she couldn't risk undoing that now.

"Thank you," Mia breathed.

"You're welcome." Lydia stepped into the hallway but hesitated before closing the door. "It'll turn out for the best."

Mia tilted her head. "Like it did for you?" Her expression was curious, not spiteful.

Lydia shrugged, thinking about the past few weeks in River Falls. "You never know, maybe it did."

Chapter 23

Liam groaned and stretched as he got out of his van. What a mess this week had been, but he had finally finished the emergency job in Brampton. His gaze flicked to the carriage house steps, where Lydia had been waiting for him most evenings lately, Buck curled against her feet.

Empty.

He rubbed at his scraggly cheeks. Apparently she could only take so many nights of his sullenness.

But what was he supposed to do, just talk and laugh with her like normal when it became clearer every day that she'd chosen Harrison Bemis? The guy showed up in every other post she made on social media, always captioned by her gushing terms. *Harrison Bemis, our fearless leader. Harrison Bemis, the man making a difference. Harrison Bemis, second only to God.*

Okay, that last one she hadn't posted. But he wouldn't be surprised if that came next.

And people's comments.

He didn't have to read more than a few to know that America—the world—thought Harrison Bemis a much better fit for Lydia than he was. Hey, even Liam thought it, when he dug right down to the most honest parts of himself.

The only one who didn't seem to think it was Simeon, who had inundated Liam with a string of texts all week urging him to pull himself together and ask her out already.

Liam slid his phone out of his pocket to check his notifications as he strode across the yard.

Sure enough, there was another text from Simeon. *You'll regret it if you wait too long.*

Liam clicked the phone off and stuffed it back in his pocket. Yeah, maybe he'd regret it if he didn't ask her out and Harrison beat him to it. But he'd regret it more if he did ask her out and she turned him down. Wouldn't he?

A scent caught at his nose as he stepped onto the porch, and he sniffed appreciatively.

Chili.

Good. He'd go inside, eat some chili, and focus the rest of his night on not thinking about Lydia.

He opened the door, pausing as the sound of conversation drifted from the kitchen. He tried to remember if Mama had said anything about having her lady friends over tonight. His shoulders grew heavier at the thought. He wasn't much in the mood for socializing. He ran a hand over his hair to smooth it down so Betty wouldn't tease him as she always did.

"It's worth it for chili," he muttered to himself, then forced his feet toward the kitchen.

Three heads swiveled his way from the table. All three were in various stages of smiling, and Liam felt his mouth open, though he had no idea if he'd planned to say anything.

Mama squinted in his direction. "Well, come in and get some chili."

"Right." But he couldn't make his eyes stop swiveling between Mia and Lydia. His daughter was actually *smiling*—he couldn't remember the last time he'd seen that. And Lydia looked . . . incredible. Beautiful. Amazing.

She tilted her head at him, and he realized he was staring.

"I'll get you a bowl." She popped out of her seat before he could say he'd do it himself.

"Thanks." He took the bowl and ladled chili into it, then chose a chair next to Mama, which seemed safest.

"How was work?" Lydia asked, as if they did this every night.

"It was good." He tried to sound just as casual. "Finally got everything squared away with that job in Brampton. How's the Builder's House?"

"It's going great," she gushed. "I got the sanding done today. Harrison said that puts us a couple days ahead of schedule, so he was quite pleased."

"I bet he was." Liam couldn't keep the scowl out of his tone—or off his face.

"Liam," Mama scolded at the same time his daughter shot him a look. Lydia only blinked at him.

"Sorry." Liam rubbed at the back of his neck, and worked his head from shoulder to shoulder. "I'm sure Harrison was pleased with the progress. You did a good job on those cabinets."

"You saw them?" Lydia looked pleasantly surprised, and Liam couldn't help the spark that zapped from his heart to his lips, lifting them in a smile.

"Online, yeah. You've been working hard."

Lydia ducked her head. "It's nice to feel like I'm making a tangible difference in someone's life."

"Speaking of difference," Mia spoke up, and Liam glanced at his daughter in shock. He couldn't remember the last time she'd voluntarily conversed with him.

"The car got a flat tire today. It has the spare on it right now."

Liam coughed around his bite of chili. "*You* changed the tire?" He'd tried a hundred times to convince her that she should learn—but she'd never taken him up on the offer for a lesson.

"No." Mia made a face. "I called Lydia, and she called some guy."

"Not some guy," Lydia jumped in. "Roadside assistance. And I stayed on the phone with her until the guy was done."

Wow. She was not only beautiful but kind and thoughtful and caring and . . . "Thank you." Half of him turned cartwheels that Mia seemed to have warmed up to Lydia. The other half wanted to ask why his daughter hadn't called *him* for help.

"Anyway, the guy said I couldn't drive far on the spare."

Liam should have noticed the spare when he'd gotten home. He blamed his exhaustion for the oversight—not the fact that he'd been distracted by thoughts of Lydia.

"I'll call the shop in the morning," he said. "Where were you when you got the flat?"

"Uh, just . . . a little ways . . ." Mia waved vaguely toward the west, in the direction of the restaurant she worked for.

"Would you like some more bread, Liam?" Lydia passed him the basket that had served Mama's bread for the past fifty years.

"Sure. Thanks." As he took the basket from her, he couldn't help but notice how natural this felt. Almost as natural as sitting across the table from Molly had felt.

A pang went through him. Should he really be comparing the few weeks he'd known Lydia with the lifetime he'd known Molly? Should he really be considering asking her out?

Wait. When had he decided he was considering that?

He stuffed a hunk of bread into his mouth. But say he *were* to consider it—hypothetically. He knew Molly wouldn't begrudge him. How many times had she told him in those last months that she wanted him to find someone to share his life with, to be a mother to Mia?

But his plate was already full, between caring for Mama and Mia and . . . He glanced across the table as Lydia handed Mama her medicines.

There went that argument.

But Mia . . .

Had called Lydia when she needed help.

And there went objection number two.

So what was standing in his way?

He swallowed, knowing the answer Simeon would give him. He was standing in his own way.

Lydia looked up with a smile, and something about it eased the tension coiled in Liam's gut. He let his eyes rest on hers.

Maybe it was okay to want this.

Maybe it was okay to tell her.

His mouth went dry at the thought, and he pulled his eyes off her, dipping his spoon into his bowl even though only a drop of chili remained.

After dinner, he promised himself. After dinner he would finally ask her out—before Harrison could beat him to it.

Chapter 24

"It's a beautiful night." Lydia reclined on the porch swing, rocking it slowly with her leg.

"Yeah." Liam leaned against the porch railing, arms crossed in front of him.

Lydia lifted an eyebrow. He was the one who had suggested they come out here after Helen had retired to the living room and Mia had retreated to her bedroom.

But every conversation she attempted to start, he shut down. Maybe asking her to come outside had been his polite way of asking her to leave. The poor guy did look exhausted.

She edged to the front of the swing. "I should probably head home." The word slipped so easily off her tongue, though she couldn't say when she'd started using it for the carriage house—instead of the giant, empty mansion waiting for her in Nashville.

But she did know that the carriage house felt more like home than that enormous building ever had.

"Wait." Liam straightened, dropping his arms to his sides.

Lydia stilled, but Liam didn't say anything else. She slid back onto the swing, setting it in motion again.

Liam looked out over the yard, then approached the swing and eased down next to her. The air seemed to get ten degrees warmer with his proximity, and Lydia slid a little farther from him, suddenly too aware of how much she'd missed spending time with him this past week. She reminded herself that it was only his friendship she'd missed, but his outdoorsy scent breezed over her, and she was suddenly confused. And alarmed.

"I just wanted to thank you for helping Mia out with her flat today."

"Oh." Lydia let out a breath. What had she thought he was going to say?

Liam's hand rubbed his chin. He must not have shaved for a couple of days, and Lydia found herself wondering what the rough layer of scruff would feel like.

"She shouldn't have bothered you," Liam added. "I don't understand why she didn't call me."

"It was no problem." She touched his knee—just for a second.

He gave her a troubled smile, and a stab of guilt went through Lydia. But if she told him now, he would feel like both she and Mia had betrayed him. And Mia would never forgive her. After the way the girl had finally opened up to her tonight, she couldn't risk that. While they'd set the table, Mia had even mentioned going shopping together sometime.

Besides, she was confident that she'd taken care of it this time. And considering that Zack had broken up with Mia, there really was no risk that she'd go to Nashville again.

"I don't know what happened to us," Liam said.

Lydia's heart jumped—until she realized Liam was talking about him and Mia.

"She used to be my little buddy. She'd come to jobs with me, we'd go to the zoo. But the last couple years . . . It's like I just can't reach her, no matter what I do." He frowned, rubbing at his face again. "I'm glad she has you to talk to." He turned so that she went from watching his profile to staring straight into his eyes.

It was a little too intense, and she let her gaze skate away. "I think she's feeling kind of lost right now. Something I can relate to."

"You can?" Liam sounded skeptical.

She let her eyes travel back to his. "Honestly, I think I've felt lost most of my life."

"You have?" Now Liam didn't sound so much skeptical as compassionate. "Why?"

"I've never really had a place like this before." She gestured to indicate she meant all of it—Liam's house, Abe's house, the whole town. "A place to belong."

"What about that big house in Nashville?"

She shook her head, trying to figure out how to put it into words. She didn't want to seem ungrateful. "It's a nice house. But it was never home. My parents were hardly there when I was little. And then I started touring, so I wasn't either. And then there was always the question of where I was really from . . ."

"Which you know now." Liam's comment wrapped around her.

"Which I know now," she repeated. But the way he was looking at her made her swallow the last word.

"Can I ask you something?" His voice was low, but for some reason it set her heart thudding harder than an electric bass.

She wasn't sure if she'd answered him or not, but he continued. "I was wondering—" He got up and paced away from the swing, then turned abruptly. "Are you and Harrison seeing each other?"

The thudding in her chest fell silent. "Are Harrison and I . . ." She leaned forward. "No."

"Oh." A loud exhale came at her through the dark. And then silence.

"What would make you think that?"

Harrison was a nice enough guy, and she'd certainly heard the rumors that he was the most eligible bachelor in River Falls. But he was a little too smooth for her taste, his words chosen a little too carefully, so that you never knew what he was really thinking.

"I just wondered," Liam said. "All your social media posts about him . . ." Liam ducked his head.

"No," she repeated. "I was just doing what you said. Bringing attention to the cause."

"Oh. That's good." He took a couple steps closer but didn't sit. "Because—"

Lydia couldn't explain why her throat closed and sweat pooled at the back of her neck. But suddenly she found her voice. "I mean, I'm not really looking to date anyone right now. I— I have to focus on my songs and—"

Liam nodded, staring out over the yard.

"And I'll be going back to Nashville soon."

Shut up.

But she couldn't stop. Because if she did, Liam might ask her out. And as much as she might really love going out with him, she couldn't.

Dating meant risk. And risk meant loss. And loss meant heartache. And she couldn't afford any more heartache.

"Plus, I just can't— After Dallas—" She faltered as Liam turned to her with the gentlest smile.

"I understand." The soft rumble of his voice almost made her take back everything she'd just said. "Goodnight, Lydia."

"Wait. Liam." Tears sprang to her eyes as he turned toward the house. Losing his friendship would be worse than discovering Dallas cheating on her.

"Hey." He stepped toward her. "What's wrong?"

"Nothing." She sniffed. The poor man didn't need her falling apart on him again. "I just wanted you to know how much I appreciate your friendship."

"Me too." Liam leaned forward and planted a soft, innocent kiss on her forehead. "Goodnight."

"Goodnight," she whispered. She waited for him to close the door, then headed for the carriage house, her fingers grazing across the still-electrified spot on her forehead.

Chapter 25

"So," Mama said in that oh-so-casual voice that signaled she was about to bring up a topic Liam wouldn't want to discuss.

He pretended to be engrossed in the fishing magazine he'd grabbed off the table in the waiting room, wishing the doctor would call Mama back already.

"You and Lydia . . ." Mama obviously wasn't going to be put off by the fact that he was pretending to read.

"There is no me and Lydia, Mama." He flipped the page harder than he meant to, accidentally tearing a fin off a musky.

"Of course there is," Mama insisted. "If you can't see it, maybe you're the one who needs your eyes examined. Or your head."

With a sigh, Liam closed the magazine, glancing around the nearly empty waiting room. What could possibly be taking them so long to get Mama in? Didn't they know Liam needed to be rescued from this conversation?

"We're friends."

"That's the first step," Mama said. "Friends. Next step, ask her out for dinner."

"She's not interested in dating, Mama. And neither am I." At least, not if it wasn't with her.

"She told you that?" Mama leaned closer and peered into his face, as if he'd be lying about something like this.

157

"Yeah. She did. Just in time to keep me from making a fool of myself." Thank goodness for that.

They'd spent the whole week pretending it had never happened—which seemed to be working perfectly well. They'd even resumed their nightly walks together, though their conversations these days only skimmed the surface. But that was okay. It was better than nothing. Which was what it might have been if he'd gone ahead and asked her out.

Besides, she'd made some good points about why she didn't want to date. Even if she likely had only made them up to spare his feelings. But she was right that she'd be going back to Nashville. And that wasn't an option for him. His life was here now. It had to be. For Mama and for Mia. Plus, he didn't necessarily want the scrutiny that came with dating a celebrity.

"When was this?" Mama gave him a little space.

He shrugged. "Last week. After she came over for dinner that night."

"Ah." Mama looked entirely pleased with herself. "That explains why she's seemed so sad this week."

Liam shook his head with a laugh. "I love you, Mama, but you're crazy as all get out."

Lydia hadn't been sad this week. Maybe a little quiet, but . . .

Something shifted in his chest at the thought of anything making her unhappy.

"You want to know what I think?" Mama asked.

"No. But you're going to tell me anyway."

Mama waved off his snark. "I think she's scared. She's been hurt before. You have to show her it's worth the risk." Mama patted his hand. "But first you have to believe it yourself."

"Mrs. O'Neill."

Oh, hallelujah.

Liam nearly jumped up to give the nurse calling Mama's name a hug.

He needed Mama to get out of here right now. Before she convinced him to do something crazy.

Chapter 26

"Got ya!" Benjamin let out a triumphant yell as he jerked his video game controller, coming close to smacking Lydia in the head with it.

Lydia ducked out of the way and set down her own controller, then stretched her back. She didn't know how her brother managed to sit on the floor for so long without batting an eye. But she was slowly improving at this gaming thing. One of these days, she'd give him a good fight.

"Rematch?" Benjamin nudged her with his elbow.

She shook her head. "I should get back and work on my songs." She couldn't explain why, but things had been flowing this week. Maybe it was the turmoil that had roiled her insides ever since she'd told Liam she appreciated his friendship.

Benjamin jumped to his feet. "Am I in any of them?" He held out a hand to help Lydia up too.

She snorted. "Sure. I wrote a whole song about you. I call it, 'No One Ever Told Me Little Brothers Could Be Such a Pain.'"

Benjamin's laugh was warm, and he gave her arm a brotherly shove. "That's a mouthful. But I think I know who all your songs are about. And it isn't me. When's he ever going to work up the guts to ask you out?"

Lydia's heart jumped, then plunged. Because she'd ensured that would never happen. Rightly so, but still.

"Hold on." Benjamin grabbed her arm and spun her toward him. "He already did, didn't he?"

Lydia concentrated on the pink toenails poking out of her sandals. "No. As a matter of fact, he did not. And he's not going to."

"Yeah right." Amusement colored Benjamin's words. "You want to make a bet?"

"I guarantee it." She'd seen the look on Liam's face when she'd said she wasn't interested in dating anyone.

"Why?" Benjamin squinted at her, moving closer. "What did you do?"

"Nothing. He asked something about me and Harrison, and I told him I wasn't seeing Harrison and that I wasn't interested in dating anyone." Ugh. Saying it out loud made her even less sure than she'd been that night.

"Why would you do that?" Benjamin's stare bored through her, and she looked away.

"Because it's true."

"Bologna." Benjamin pointed at her. "It's because you're the one who's afraid, not Liam."

She pulled her best scoff. "What would I be afraid of?"

"You tell me." Benjamin crossed his arms.

"Aren't you supposed to be all protective and not want your friend to date your sister?"

Benjamin shook his head. "Number one, you're twenty years older than I am, so I don't think I have the right to tell you what to do."

In spite of herself, she laughed.

"And number two, Liam is a good guy."

"I know." The best. That wasn't in dispute. But it was also what made him so dangerous. Because it meant if she surrendered her heart to him, he would have even more power to break it than Dallas had.

"So . . ." Benjamin refused to let it go.

Lydia sighed. She'd been battling with herself about this all week. "Dallas—"

Benjamin cut her off. "Liam isn't Dallas."

"I know that." Lydia didn't mean to snap, but Benjamin didn't understand.

"So, what, you're going to write him off because of something some other guy did?" Benjamin scratched his head. "You know that's dumb, right?"

Lydia snorted. At least she never had to worry that her brother would hold back from telling her what he really thought. "Talk to me when you've lived a little more. Fallen in love, been hurt."

Benjamin crossed his arms in front of him. "Done and done. And you don't see me sitting here having a pity party for myself."

"Is that what you think I'm doing?" Lydia's hands went to her hips. Maybe she'd had enough of Benjamin's honesty for one day. "Because I call it surviving." She picked up the glass of water she'd left on the floor and stormed toward the kitchen.

"Lydia, wait." Benjamin followed her, calm as always. Which only annoyed Lydia more. Shouldn't he be the hot-headed twenty-something and she be the calm and mature older sister?

"I'm sorry." Benjamin stopped at the island. "I know you're not having a pity party. I know you've been through some hard times, with your parents and Dallas and . . . everything. All I'm saying is, if all you think about is your past hurts, you could miss some pretty awesome future possibilities."

Lydia shook her head. He was too young to understand that along with future possibilities could also come future pain.

She made a move toward the front door. But Benjamin skirted in front of her. "We have a rule in this house. You can't leave angry."

Lydia raised an eyebrow. "You do not."

He drew an X over his heart. "Cross my heart, we do. One time, Zeb and Asher missed church because Mama wouldn't let them leave the house until they'd worked out a fight they were having."

"What was the fight about?" Lydia folded her arms in front of her. Surely he was pulling her leg.

"Asher took the baseball Zeb caught at a Smokies game to show off to his friends at school. But he got it confiscated by the teacher."

Lydia couldn't help laughing at that. It didn't sound made up. "I'm not mad. Now will you please move? I have to get home." She froze. She had to stop thinking of the carriage house as home. She couldn't stay there forever.

"Prove it."

Lydia blinked at her brother. "Prove what?"

"That you're not mad." He spread his arms wide and grinned at her.

Lydia rolled her eyes. The Calvanos were a hugging family, that was for sure. Benjamin had told her they got that from their Mama.

"Come on." Benjamin's goofy grin beckoned to her.

"Fine." Lydia took a begrudging step toward him, but before she could take another, he'd swallowed her up in a hug so tight she grunted. Her arms went around his neck just in time for him to pick her up and spin her once.

"Benjamin, put me down," she shrieked.

He obeyed, but they were both still laughing. Until Benjamin suddenly said, "It's funny, isn't it?"

"What?" Lydia wheezed past her laughter. "The fact that you nearly crushed the life out of me?"

"No. The fact that before this summer, I didn't even know I had another sister. And now, I can't imagine you not being part of the family."

"Oh." But her throat was too full to say anything else, so she slugged his shoulder, then gave him another hug.

Chapter 27

Liam couldn't help the sharp intake of breath as he pulled into his driveway after Mama's doctor appointment.

"Is that Lydia?" Mama asked, leaning forward and squinting at the figure seated on the carriage house steps.

Liam glanced at her. There was no way Mama could pick out Lydia from this distance. But it wasn't like it could be anyone else.

"It's Lydia." Why did his throat feel so dry? It was his friend, Lydia.

"Here's what we'll do," Mama whispered, as if she were masterminding some conspiracy. "I'll invite her in for lunch. And then you can start wooing her."

Liam slowed the van. "Wooing? Mama, there will be no wooing. And anyway, I have to get over to Founder's Park to set up the lighting for the weekend concert series."

"Invite her to come with you."

"To work?" Liam shook his head. "You're bonkers."

"Watch it, young man." Mama wagged a finger at him. "I'm still your Mama, you know."

Liam chuckled. "And I love you. But that doesn't make you any less bonkers."

"Just you wait and see. You two will be together before the end of summer." Mama gave him her mother-knows-best look. Trouble was, she tended to be right about everything.

But not this.

He put the van in park, swallowing hard as Lydia looked up with a smile.

"Before the end of summer," Mama repeated.

"Hush, Mama." Liam pushed his door open.

"Hey." He tossed the greeting at Lydia as he rounded the van to help Mama out.

"Hey." Lydia closed her notebook and stood, coming their way. "How was the doctor?"

"It was good, dear," Mama answered. "Liam and I had a nice chat in the waiting room." Mama leaned on Liam's arm as he moved her walker into place. "I told him—"

"Mama." Liam nearly clapped a hand over his mother's mouth. He loved the woman dearly, but who knew what she might say.

Both Mama and Lydia stared at him.

"Do you have the medicine the doctor gave you?" Liam asked meekly.

"In my purse." Mama gave him a look, and he shook his head slightly.

"Let's get you inside. I have to get to work."

"You have to work this afternoon?" The dip in Lydia's voice made Liam's heart swoop. Was that disappointment? Had she hoped they could spend the afternoon together?

For land's sake. He was starting to sound like Mama.

"Over at Founder's Park," Mama jumped in before he could answer with a simple yes. "Weren't you asking me about all the gardens there the other day? You should go with him."

"Mama," Liam warned. He should have gone straight to the park from the doctor's office and made Mama come along. See how fun she found watching him work.

"I'm just setting up the stage lights," he said to Lydia, hoping she could hear his apology for Mama's behavior.

But Lydia was smiling at Mama. "I'd like that."

"It'll be boring," Liam warned. The last thing he wanted was for her to come along out of a sense of obligation.

"I'll bring my notebook." She fanned it in front of her, and he found himself wishing he knew what it held. "A change of scenery is always good."

"If you're sure you want to."

"I'm sure. Just let me know when you're ready to go."

"Let me grab a quick bite, and I'll meet you back out here in twenty minutes." He tugged Mama toward the house.

But Mama didn't budge. "I have a better idea. Why don't you two grab lunch at Murph's on the way?" Her smile was so innocent, Liam almost bought it.

"Oh, that's a great idea." Lydia beamed at Mama, then turned to Liam. "My treat. I still owe you for that night you bought me pizza."

Right. The night he'd started getting crazy notions that there could possibly be something between them.

His stomach soured. But he couldn't back out now. Mama would make it impossible. Anyway, they were friends.

He'd just have to remember that when he was staring at her over a milkshake.

Chapter 28

Lydia sipped the last of her shake from Murph's, leaning back against the bench nestled between beds of purple coneflowers, Shasta daisies, sage, and black-eyed Susans. Butterflies flitted from flower to flower, but Lydia's eyes flitted to Liam. Again.

He'd finished eating quickly and started working on the stage lighting.

He must have been up and down that ladder perched on the outdoor stage a good twenty or thirty times already, his movements agile and fit as he adjusted lights, checked them, changed them. It was clear that he knew what he was doing.

She only wished she did.

He'd obviously been mortified when his mama had invited Lydia to tag along with him to work. Because he didn't want her to come? Or because he was afraid she'd say no?

All she knew was that she'd been sitting on the carriage house steps, thinking about Benjamin's words from that morning: *If all you ever think about is past hurts, you could miss some pretty awesome future possibilities.*

Helen's invitation had felt like a chance to test that theory.

And as she sat here, letting herself explore it, she had to admit that the idea of future possibilities made her heart flutter like a butterfly's wings. But like a butterfly, it couldn't seem to decide if it was safe to land.

On the one hand, she'd never been as comfortable with anyone else in the world. Or as attracted to anyone, she had to admit to herself as her eyes strayed to him again. She forced them to her lap, but the words covering the page of her open notebook were only a testament to the fact that he seemed to be good for her songwriting too.

But that was a problem. She had a career to focus on, and she couldn't rely on being near him to write songs.

And on top of it all, there was still the very real possibility of getting hurt. Not that she thought Liam would ever intentionally hurt anyone, but—

Grr. This circular thinking wasn't getting her anywhere.

She forced herself to get up and walk over a small hill to explore the rose gardens, where trellises covered with thick stems of climbing roses blocked her view of the stage.

When she'd run out of flowers to examine, she found a spot in the shade of a sprawling hickory, laid on her back, and closed her eyes, letting the pleasant warmth lull her into a sort of half-sleep in which Liam's voice kept appearing and receding.

"Lydia." Something brushed her shoulder, and she bolted upright, blinking as Liam's face came into focus.

"Sorry to wake you. But I wasn't sure you'd want to spend the whole night here." Shadows clothed his smile, and Lydia tried to catch her bearings.

"What time is it?"

"Four o'clock." He held out a hand to help her up. "I was about to call Zeb to file a missing person's report. But then I spotted you over here."

"Sorry." Lydia took his hand, the contact sending a ripple through her stomach. "Did you get the job done?" She should pull her hand out of his, now that she was on her feet. But maybe just another second . . .

But he let go, as if suddenly realizing they were still touching. "Yeah. Ready to go?"

"Can I see it?" She told herself she wasn't simply looking for an excuse to spend more time with him. She had always taken the lighting at her shows for granted, and she wanted to appreciate what went into it.

Surprise—and maybe pleasure—lifted Liam's expression. "Sure. It's not much though. It's a small stage and—"

"Liam." She touched her fingers to his forearm. "I'm sure it's great."

He sped up and her hand fell from his arm. She hurried after him, remaining a step behind.

He stopped abruptly when they reached the middle of the green space in front of the stage, and she had to veer at the last second to avoid crashing into him. "Wait here." He jogged toward the stage and vaulted easily onto it. Then he disappeared into the wings.

Her eyes remained fixed on the spot where she'd last seen him, when a cascade of light pulled her attention to the center of the stage. The soft blue light gave off an understated feel. Perfect for an outdoor concert. A few moments later, the lighting shifted hues and split into individual circles of color that drew her forward. Before she knew it, she was standing at center stage, spinning in a slow circle until she was facing the grassy seating area.

She closed her eyes and tipped her head back, imagining the crowd.

It'd been nearly a year since she'd last been on a stage—and being up here now, she felt like she had as a child when she'd stood on stage before her parents' performances, wondering what it would be like to hear all those people cheering and to know it was for you.

"Do you miss it?" She hadn't heard Liam come up behind her, and yet his voice didn't startle her. It was like she'd expected him to be there all along.

She considered his question. "Some parts of it."

"Which parts?" Liam tucked his hands into his pockets, but his gaze was intense, like he was trying to figure her out.

Instead of making her uncomfortable, his interest made her want to open up. "The energy of the crowd." That had always fueled her. "The vibration of the music in my feet." She looked up and gestured at his work. "The atmosphere. When everything is clicking, it's . . . magical." Well, that sounded stupid.

But when she lifted her eyes to Liam, he was nodding, as if she made perfect sense.

"And what parts don't you miss?"

She sighed. "The endless travel. Never getting to sleep in my own bed. Never being in any one city long enough to experience any of the sights. Tabloids reporting on every move I make. Always worrying that the crowd isn't going to like a song."

Liam gave her a thoughtful look. "That's a long list."

"Oh, and the stage fright."

Liam stared at her, as if trying to determine if she was serious. "You do not have stage fright."

"Then why have I thrown up before every single show I've ever done?"

As Liam gave a low whistle, Lydia clapped a hand over her mouth. That had been too much information.

But Liam simply said, "That's pretty impressive."

"I'm glad my ability to vomit impresses you." Ugh. She was not still talking about vomit, was she?

He laughed. "That's not what's impressive. It's the fact that you kept getting on the stage in spite of it."

His smile sent the tingles she'd been feeling all day into a full-out hum.

Maybe Benjamin was smarter than she gave him credit for. Maybe he was right about future possibilities.

"How are the songs coming?" Liam interrupted her line of thought.

"Oh. Good." Self-consciously, she tucked a piece of hair behind her ear. She'd never liked talking about her work before it was ready. But with Liam, it felt different. "I think I have one almost done."

"Really?" His eyes brightened as if she'd told him he'd won the lottery. "Can I hear it?"

Lydia took a step backward. "No way. It's not ready yet." It was one thing to talk about a song in progress, quite another to sing it to anyone.

Liam's not just anyone. The thought came unbidden. But whoever he was, whatever he might be, she was *not* ready to sing this new song yet.

"Please." He stepped closer—so close that she could see green flecks she'd never before noticed in his eyes. So close that she could drown in his warm, outdoorsy scent. So close that she was pretty sure she could hear his heartbeat.

"Okay," she breathed—mostly so there'd be a reason to put some space between them. "But you have to go down there." She gestured toward the grassy area in front of the stage.

"You got it." But he lingered a moment longer, his nearness sending sparks along every one of her nerves.

When he turned away at last to leap off the stage, she let out a long breath. She opened her notebook and paged through it, even though she already knew the song she wanted to sing.

"Only one verse," she called down to him.

He offered a silent thumbs-up, his gaze more intense than the casual gesture suggested. She glanced at the page again, then closed her eyes. She'd sung these words in her head enough times that she knew them by heart. And if she was going to do this, she couldn't look at him.

All my life I've been hiding right here in sight.

A shiver went up her spine as her voice swelled into the breeze. The melody caught at her in a way no song had in years, and her heart surged.

I didn't even realize, didn't put up a fight.
Wore my mask of glitter. My mask of gold.
Hid right there behind my microphone.
A thousand I love yous shouted from the front row,
But no one could see me, no one could know.

Lydia pulled in a deep breath, so caught up in the song that the words of the chorus flowed out.

Didn't know it could be like this,
Didn't know there was so much I had missed.
Open my heart, open my mind,
Let you in to see a little piece of my life.
Didn't know it could be like this.

The last note trailed off, and she opened her eyes to find Liam pressed up against the front of the stage, his eyes wide, mouth open. "Keep going."

"That's all I have so far." Okay, that wasn't the complete truth. But that was all she was willing to share right now. Because the next verse was way too vulnerable to sing to the person who had inspired it.

"Well." Liam vaulted back onto the stage. "It was amazing."

"You think so?" She'd never felt so uncertain about her music before. But she'd never put so much of herself into her songs before either.

"Ask me that again when you're singing at the Country Music Awards next year."

"Ha." Lydia waved off the obvious exaggeration.

Liam peered at her. "You don't want to win a CMA?"

"No. It's not that." Of course she wanted to win a CMA. She wanted to win six CMAs, like Mama and Daddy had.

"What then?" His expression went serious, and Lydia had to look away before he read it in her eyes. If she wanted to win a CMA, if she wanted to get her career back on track, she'd have to go back to Nashville. Soon.

"Nothing." She brushed off the question. "The song's just nowhere near ready yet."

"Sounded ready to me. I'll be right back." He disappeared into the wings, and after a moment, the stage lights went out, the late afternoon sun now the only spotlight.

Liam returned, leading her to the edge of the stage. He jumped down, then held up a hand to help her. Their fingers remained locked for a second after her feet touched the ground.

Until something soft and powerful rammed into Lydia's leg, making her stumble backward. Liam's fingers slipped out of her hand but landed on her arm to steady her.

"Princess." Ava ran up to them, grabbing the feisty white and brown puppy's collar. "Sorry. She's still in training."

"Didn't you hear us calling?" Joseph came up behind his wife, walking their big white Samoyed Tasha and the dog that looked like a lab but wasn't—Lydia couldn't remember what breed they'd said he was, but she did remember that his name was Griffin.

"No. Sorry. We were . . ." Lydia noticed Ava grinning toward her arm, where Liam's hand still rested.

He pulled it away.

"How was your honeymoon?" Lydia hadn't seen them since they'd gotten back a few days ago.

"Incredible." Ava still wore that knowing grin. "But I think these three are glad we're home."

"Have either of you talked to Simeon lately?" Joseph asked abruptly.

"Not in a week or so," Liam answered.

Lydia shook her head. "Not since church on Sunday. Why?"

Joseph shrugged. "I don't know. We called to invite them over, but he said Abigail wasn't feeling well. But that's been the excuse for weeks now."

"Oh my goodness." Ava's eyes widened, and she clapped a hand over her mouth. "How did I not put it together sooner? I bet she's pregnant!"

"What?" Joseph stared at his wife. "Wouldn't they have told us?"

"Not necessarily." Lydia nodded at Ava. It made sense. "A lot of people don't tell anyone until after their first trimester." Not that she had any personal experience with it.

"Really? I wouldn't be able to wait that long." Joseph bent to scratch behind Princess's ears.

Ava rolled her eyes. "You waited *eight years* for me, you know."

"That's what I mean." Joseph straightened and kissed the top of Ava's head. "I used up all my patience waiting for you. Sorry, but everyone's going to know the moment we're expecting."

Lydia pressed a hand to her own middle. She didn't suppose she was likely to ever become a mother. But she suddenly realized that having siblings meant she'd be an aunt. "You'd better," she told Joseph. "Because their aunt Lydia is going to spoil those kids."

They spoke for a few minutes more, agreeing to let Simeon and Abigail tell them about the baby in their own time. Then Ava and Joseph continued on their walk, while Lydia and Liam headed for his van.

A contented silence rode home with them.

When they got there, Liam shut off the engine, and Lydia sighed.

Liam paused in opening his door. "Everything good?"

She smiled at him. "Yeah. Everything is great, actually. Thanks for letting me tag along."

"Anytime." Liam hopped out of the van, and Lydia did the same. She shuffled reluctantly toward the carriage house steps. She should let him get to whatever else he had going on tonight.

"Taking off again?" Liam's question startled her, until she looked up and discovered it hadn't been directed at her.

"Yeah." Mia adjusted the backpack on her shoulder. "I have to work, and then I'm going to spend the night at Katie's."

"Well, be home early tomorrow morning. I thought maybe we could go to Chattanooga. We always said we'd go back."

Mia's gaze flicked to Lydia, then back to Liam. "Sorry. I have to work tomorrow too."

"No you don't. I checked the calendar." Liam's frown creased his forehead into rough lines.

"I picked up an extra shift." Mia jangled her keychain, impatience clicking in time with the keys.

"Can't someone else take it? I feel like I've hardly seen you all summer."

Lydia watched the girl. Surely she wouldn't be able to say no to that plea. But Mia turned toward the car. "Sorry. Why don't you take Lydia?"

Lydia lifted her head sharply, her insides giving a hard lurch at the thought of spending a whole day with Liam.

"Mia—"

But the teen was already tossing her backpack into the car. "I'll be home sometime tomorrow night." Her door had barely closed before she backed the car into a quick turn, then sped down the driveway, dust devils kicking up in the gravel behind her.

Liam's long exhale nearly broke Lydia's heart.

"I'm sure she'll go with you another time."

"Yeah." But disappointment thick enough to taste hung on the word.

"Do you still want to go?" She fiddled with the charm bracelet on her wrist, not quite sure she could look at him.

"No. That's okay."

"Oh." Now she was the one sounding disappointed.

"Why?" He paused, and she let herself look up. "Do you?"

She bit her lip. Was this taking things too far? Was it too big of a risk?

If all you think about is past hurts, you could miss some pretty awesome future possibilities.

"I mean, I've never been there."

Liam's smile was slow, but it was sure. "I'll pick you up right here at eight o'clock. We'll have to take the van."

Lydia grinned at him. "I like the van. And make it seven."

Chapter 29

This isn't a date.

But it was hard to convince himself of that with Lydia's fingers locked in his. It was only because they were currently riding the world's steepest incline railway—and it turned out she was afraid of heights as well as stages—but still, his heart refused to acknowledge that there was nothing more to it.

The way she'd sung to him at the park yesterday, the way she'd nudged him to invite her here today. Was it possible that Mama had been right about wooing her?

"I have no idea how you talked me into this," Lydia muttered. She closed her eyes as the track steepened beneath the train. The seats in the sloped car faced down the mountain, and at this steep angle, the best view was through the window on the roof.

"You're the one who wanted to come," Liam reminded her, letting himself wrap his other hand around hers too.

"That was before I knew it involved getting in this death trap."

Liam chuckled. "It's not a death trap. It's been going up and down this mountain for over a hundred years."

"Not helping," Lydia murmured.

"Open your eyes," Liam urged.

She shook her head against the seat. "No thanks. Just tell me when it's over."

"Come on." He considered reaching over and prying her eyes open, but that would probably be unwise. "Trust me," he coaxed when her lids remained scrunched shut. "You don't want to miss out just because you're afraid."

Lydia's eyes popped open suddenly. "What'd you say?"

"I said you don't want to miss this. Look." He nodded toward the window in front of them.

Lydia kept her gaze on him for a moment, then slowly turned her head toward the front of the train.

Her grip on his fingers tightened, and he strengthened his hold on her.

"Wow," she breathed.

"Told you." Below them, the world fell away, but in front of them, it seemed to stretch forever, until the sky and the earth melded into one far in the distance.

"I imagine a view like this could inspire a song or two." Liam rather hoped she'd break into one right here and now. Or maybe he would.

Lydia's head swiveled toward him. "Yeah." Her lips curved, and her eyes softened, though her grip didn't loosen. "I imagine it could."

When the train came to a stop, Liam debated whether to let go of Lydia's hand. But the steps in the car were steep, and he didn't want her to fall. And then once they disembarked and stood on the mountaintop, he figured he'd better hold on to help with that fear of heights.

He tugged her toward a stony lookout, but she pulled back.

"You don't think I'm going over there, do you?"

"Yep." He tugged again. "Come on. It'll be totally worth it. And I promise not to let go."

Lydia eyed him, and he wondered if he'd gone too far, if it had sounded too much like something a boyfriend would say.

But she let him pull her along. "You'd better not."

Her steps slowed as they neared the railing at the edge of the cliff.

"See?" He spread his free arm in front of them. "It's worth it, right?"

Lydia didn't respond, but when he turned to her, she looked awestruck.

"Yes," she finally murmured. "Totally worth it."

"Aww. Y'all are so cute. Let me get a picture for you." An older woman scurried up next to them. "You don't want to take a selfie. People have fallen off cliffs doing that."

"Uh." Liam looked to Lydia. The last time their picture had been snapped together, things had gotten all kinds of awkward.

"I'm game if you are." Lydia pulled her phone out of her pocket and passed it to the woman.

"You sure?"

Lydia nodded and slid her sunglasses up into her hair.

He passed his phone to the woman as well, then they both turned to face her, with their backs to the overlook.

But in the process their hands had come unlinked. Liam tried to decide whether it would be appropriate to grab her hand again now.

The woman lifted the first phone. "Put your arm around her."

Liam didn't need to be told twice. He wrapped his arm around Lydia's back, letting his hand rest lightly on her bare shoulder. Sparks of hope shot straight through his fingers when she leaned into him. He only hoped he wasn't smiling *too* big for the picture.

"Perfect. Stay right there," the woman called.

No problem. He might just stay right here forever.

But too quickly the woman was done and approaching them with their phones held out in front of her.

"Thank you so much." Lydia stepped forward, out of his arm, to take the phones. She passed him his.

"No. Thank you," the woman said. "It does this old heart good to see a young couple so in love. Reminds me of my husband and me. He was called home to the Lord last year."

There was so much to unpack in her statement that Liam didn't know where to start. "We're not—"

"I'm so sorry." Lydia pressed a hand to the woman's shoulder.

Okay, yeah, that was probably the better response.

"Thank you, dear." The woman patted Lydia's hand. "Y'all cherish the time you have together."

"Oh we—" Liam tried to correct her again.

"We will," Lydia interrupted.

Liam's head jerked to her. But she was smiling serenely at the woman, as if she hadn't just said something earth-shattering. Then she linked her fingers through Liam's and pulled him toward the path.

He was sure she'd let go once they were out of the woman's line of sight, but she kept her fingers curled around his. He considered asking why she hadn't corrected the woman, but he didn't want to ruin this. Whatever *this* was.

They spent the rest of the afternoon wandering the top of the mountain, ordering ice cream cones, talking. And holding hands. Every time they had to use their hands for something else—like eating their ice cream—his heart dipped. But her hand always found its way back to his. And he wasn't about to let go.

Chapter 30

She should let go of his hand. But his fingers felt so perfect around hers, their arms resting together on the console between them in his van. She'd noticed the questioning looks he'd been giving her all day. But he hadn't asked what this was—and she hadn't said. Mostly because she didn't know.

She only knew that the idea of future possibilities felt more real today than it ever had before.

Liam eased the car toward downtown River Falls.

"Do you want to get some pie?" He glanced at her, his eyes shining with that light they'd worn all day.

They'd had dinner at a delicious seafood place in Chattanooga after descending the mountain, and she was still stuffed. But she wasn't ready to say goodnight. "There's always room for pie."

"That's what I say." He pulled into the parking lot at Daisy's. "Do you want a hat or something?"

She considered. She'd worn her sunglasses most of the day, but she hadn't worried much about what would happen if anyone recognized her. Besides, most people in River Falls seemed to think of her as just another neighbor now. "That's okay. Unless my hair's a mess." It *had* been pretty windy on top of that mountain.

Liam let go of her hand and tucked a strand behind her ear. Electric tingles worked their way up her scalp.

"There." He cleared his throat and dropped his hand. "Perfect."

He opened his car door and hopped out, making it to her door before the tingles from his touch had passed.

He took her hand to help her out of the vehicle, and she threaded her fingers through his so he wouldn't let go.

But as they stepped inside, his hand shifted to the small of her back, and Lydia couldn't decide which was better.

"Is this okay?" He leaned close to whisper the question, and now the feel of his breath on her shoulder was all she could think about.

She managed to nod as they stepped forward to place their order—triple chocolate for her and peach for him.

She wrinkled her nose.

"You don't like peaches?" He had to take his hand off her back to pull out his credit card.

"They're too fuzzy."

He laughed. "Not in pie. Come on." He picked up the slices. "You have to taste it."

They slid into seats at a table overlooking the river.

"Should we pray again, or does our prayer from dinner still count?" Lydia joked. Eating with the Calvanos so often, she'd become accustomed to praying before meals. She even enjoyed it, if she was being honest, as it gave her such a beautiful picture of their hearts. And it helped fan the fire of the faith she'd begun to notice flaring in her heart again as she continued to go to church with them week after week. She'd even started reading her Bible again—and had a few songs in progress based on Scripture.

"We can pray again if you want." Liam's smile was brighter than any stage lights she'd ever seen. "Would you like to do it this time?" He'd prayed at dinner, an almost poetic prayer thanking God for the majesty of his creation and for the care he had put into forming and caring for each one of his people. Afterward, she'd told him maybe he should be a songwriter after all.

There was no way Lydia's prayer would match that. It took her weeks of writing and revising to come up with something as poetic. But she nodded. This was part of her heart she wanted to share with him.

Liam's smile grew as he closed his eyes and reached for her hands across the table.

"Heavenly Father." She began her prayer the same way Liam had, though in a whisper. She didn't necessarily need everyone else in the pie shop knowing her heart too. "A year ago, I had no idea it would be possible for my heart to overflow like this. Thank you for bringing me to River Falls. For bringing me to my family. And new friends. And . . . Liam." His hands twitched, and she squeezed them tighter. "Thank you for a wonderful day. And please bring your comfort to the sweet woman who took our picture today. Oh, and please bless Abigail and Simeon and their . . ." She opened her eyes and took a quick, furtive glance around the restaurant. "You-know-what," she barely whispered, just to be safe, though no one seemed to be paying attention to them. "In Jesus' name we pray. Amen."

"Amen." Liam lifted his head, his eyes coming straight to hers. "Lydia—"

"Are you going to let me taste that peach pie, or what?" She hated herself for cutting him off. She wanted to explore the possibility of being more than friends, didn't she?

"Yes, ma'am." He let go of her hands, his eyes dropping to his plate as he stabbed a big bite onto his fork.

He lifted it with one hand, holding the other hand under it like a safety net, and leaned toward her.

Lydia opened her mouth and let it close around the fork, moaning as the sweetness of the fruit hit her taste buds.

"Told you." Liam's chuckle was warm, and if he was disappointed that she'd cut him off a moment ago, he didn't let it show.

"Now you have to taste a piece of mine." She cut off a large bite of the three-toned chocolate. She lifted it toward his mouth, concentrating on his lips.

"Hello, Liam."

Liam jerked back, making Lydia jump. The pie tumbled off her fork and splattered on the table. "Liam, what—"

But he shoved his chair back and scrambled to his feet. "George. Meredith," he said to the older couple hovering at the edge of their table. He shook the man's hand woodenly, then gave the woman a stiff hug.

"We've been hoping you'd stop by," the woman said softly.

"I'm sorry. I've been . . ." Liam ran a hand through his hair, and Lydia looked back and forth between him and the couple. They clearly cared about him—and made him super uncomfortable.

"And you're Lydia St. Peter." The woman turned to address Lydia.

"I am." Lydia gave Liam an uncertain look, and he failed in his attempt at a smile.

"Sorry. George, Meredith, this is Lydia St. Peter. Lydia, this is George and Meredith Hopewell. Molly's parents."

"Oh." Lydia had not been prepared for that. "It's so nice to meet y'all."

"I have to tell you." Meredith leaned closer to Lydia. "We're big fans."

"Thank you." She rubbed at her wrist. What else could she say to the in-laws of the man she'd just realized she wanted to date?

"Do you like barbecue?" Meredith asked.

"Of course she does," George said to his wife. "What kind of Southerner doesn't like barbecue?"

"Some people are vegans," Meredith said in an undertone.

Lydia laughed. "Don't worry. I've never met a barbecue I didn't like."

"Oh good." Meredith sounded relieved. "Y'all have to come over tomorrow after church for some barbecue."

"Oh, uh, we're not together. I mean, we're friends," Liam jumped in.

The word shouldn't have hurt. It was what she'd told Liam they were. But she'd thought—hoped—that maybe after today . . .

"Of course." Meredith's eyes flicked to Lydia, who tried to make her expression confirm what Liam had said. "So you'll come? Both of you?"

"I don't think . . ." Liam tucked his hands into his pockets and looked out the window.

"Please, Liam. We miss y'all." Meredith's eyes shimmered.

Lydia couldn't take it anymore. "Of course we'll be there."

Liam shot her a look she couldn't read, but Meredith squeezed her arm. "Thank you, dear."

She turned to Liam. "And be sure to bring Mia. That granddaughter of ours is growing up way too fast."

George and Meredith left them to go order their pie, then took a seat on the other side of the small restaurant. Lydia and Liam finished their pie in silence. She didn't try again to offer him a bite of hers, and he didn't offer her another bite of his.

She considered attempting to make conversation, but Liam's eyes were fixed on his plate, his shoulders pulled tight toward his ears.

Whatever future possibilities she'd let herself fantasize about earlier today disappeared faster than the chocolate on her plate.

Chapter 31

"Dad!" Mia elbowed him in the side.

"Sorry. What?" Liam blinked at the church pew in front of him.

"Church is done. We can go." Mia gestured to the nearly empty rows around them.

On his other side, Lydia looked over from chatting with Asher and Ireland. "I'm ready when you are." Her small smile didn't cover the hurt that hovered in her eyes.

Liam dropped his gaze and pushed to his feet. The ball of emotion still rolling inside him from yesterday had made it impossible to concentrate on Pastor Calvano's sermon this morning.

When they'd gotten to Daisy's yesterday, he'd been letting himself imagine kissing Lydia goodnight. But after seeing George and Meredith, he'd barely even mumbled the word to her. The worst part was, he'd seen the confusion all over her face. But there was nothing he could do about it. He'd already hurt George and Meredith enough. They shouldn't have to watch him moving on with his life when their daughter never would.

And now he had to sit through the next few hours at their house, trying to convince himself this was for the best. That Lydia was better off without him holding her back from her career. And if the rest of her new songs were anything like the one she'd sung for him at the park the other night, her career was going big places.

186

"There's Grandma and Grandpa." Mia pointed toward the lobby. She hadn't been thrilled when Liam had told her they'd be going to her grandparents' for lunch, but at least she hadn't put up a fight. Liam supposed he should thank God for small miracles.

"Where's Gran?" He looked around for his mother.

"She went to lunch with Betty. Remember?" Mia gave him an odd look.

"Right. Let's go then." He followed his daughter down the church aisle, glancing over his shoulder to make sure Lydia was coming as well. She was closer behind him than he expected, and he sped up to stay a step in front of her. How would George and Meredith feel if they saw them walking down a church aisle together?

George and Meredith beamed as they pulled Mia into a hug. Then Meredith hugged Liam, followed by Lydia, who smiled at him over his mother-in-law's shoulder.

"I hope y'all are hungry." Meredith led the way out the doors. "Grandpa made enough barbecue to feed the whole town. You remember the way to our house?"

Liam laughed. George and Meredith had lived in the same house since he'd known them. "I remember."

He, Lydia, and Mia continued past George and Meredith's vehicle toward his van and Mia's car. They'd driven separately since Mia had to work later.

"Why don't I ride with Mia?" Lydia suggested.

Liam's heart skipped a step, but he nodded. She'd ridden with him to church, and he didn't blame her for not wanting a repeat of that silent trip, so different from the journey home from Chattanooga yesterday.

He'd tried, on the way to church, to come up with an apology, an explanation of what had changed. But he'd never managed to open his mouth. At least if she went with Mia, he wouldn't have to try again.

"Drive carefully," he said to Mia as she and Lydia moved toward the car doors.

"Obviously," Mia said dryly.

Liam worked up a chuckle and continued to his van. He waited for Mia to pull out, then followed her.

From what he could tell, Mia and Lydia must be having a good conversation—both of them kept making big gestures with their hands, and Lydia's head bobbed up and down every once in a while. He could almost hear the laughter from here.

A sigh creaked out of him. Lydia had been good for Mia.

And for him.

"What do I do here, Lord?"

The prayer hung unanswered in the empty van, and Liam pulled to a stop next to Mia's car in George and Meredith's large driveway.

Lydia was still in her seat, and Liam got out and opened her door for her.

"Thanks." She was still chuckling about whatever she and Mia had been discussing, and her smile flooded him with relief. Her pomegranate scent swept over him as she stood.

"You're welcome." He let his fingertips brush her forearm, only for a second.

But that was a mistake. Because now he wanted to wrap her whole hand in his. Or better yet, wrap all of her in his arms.

"Come on in," Meredith called from the front door. Liam gestured for Lydia to go ahead of him, then let Mia step between them. He needed that buffer right now.

In the house, Lydia paused to look at the same picture of Liam and Molly's wedding day that hung in Mama's house.

Mia continued past her, but Lydia turned to Liam with a sad smile. "She was beautiful." She squeezed his hand, then followed Mia, who disappeared into the kitchen.

Liam blew out a breath, examining the photo. Molly certainly had been beautiful. And caring. And talented. And he would never stop loving her. But as much as he wanted her to be, she wasn't here anymore.

Lydia was. And she was also beautiful. And caring. And talented. And—

"Help me with the grill?" George's gruff call from the patio door across the house made Liam jump, as if his father-in-law had caught him doing something wrong.

"Uh. Yeah. Yes, sir." Spine rigid, he crossed through the living room and dining room to the patio door and followed George onto the deck. George went straight to the grill and started flipping meat. Liam shoved his hands in his pockets and watched.

He'd never been able to talk to his father-in-law—and even less so now.

"How's work?" he made himself ask.

"Retired last May," George grunted.

"Oh. Congratulations." And that totally expended the one topic of conversation Liam had come up with. He took a step toward the house. Maybe the women needed help carrying things outside.

But George turned from the grill and cleared his throat as if he was about to make an announcement.

Liam froze, his escape foiled.

"She was happy, you know." George looked out over the yard, not at him. "Molly. She told us she was happy a thousand times. We just . . ." George waved the spatula he still held, letting his eyes come to Liam. "And when it comes down to it, that means more to us than any job she could have gotten or awards she could have won. You gave her a good life."

"I— Uh—" Liam rubbed at his chest, trying to loosen the tightness. "Thank you." He needed some water to ease the burning in his throat. But there was none out here.

George glanced over his shoulder toward the house. "Meredith is pretty excited about your new lady friend. Couldn't stop talking about her all night. She said she thinks Molly would like her."

"Oh." Why had he not brought a water bottle with him? He could barely get his tongue to shape the words. "We're not— She's not my—"

George held up a hand. "You don't owe us any explanations." He scratched his eyebrow. "You know what Molly said to me in one of our last conversations?"

Liam shook his head. He'd stayed away from the house when George and Meredith came to see Molly so he wouldn't ruin their visits.

"She said, 'Make sure he's happy, Daddy.'" George's eyes watered, and Liam had to look away. He'd never seen his stoic father-in-law get emotional before, aside from at Molly's funeral.

George cleared his throat, and when Liam looked back to him, his eyes were dry. "And we've failed her."

"I didn't exactly make it easy." Liam's fists tightened. Molly would have been ashamed of the way he'd avoided her parents when he knew they were hurting. "You were here and we were in Nashville and . . ."

George shook his head. "I want to do better by you, Liam. Molly would want that. So please know that you have our blessing to date or marry or . . . whatever you want to do. We want you to be happy, just like Molly did. You know we've always thought of you as a son."

This time, it was Liam who had to blink and clear his throat. No, actually—he'd had no idea they thought of him like that.

The patio door opened, and Mia spilled out, followed by Meredith. Liam stepped forward to help her with the bowl of fruit salad she carried. But his eyes didn't leave the door.

And the moment Lydia stepped through, meeting his gaze with a questioning smile, he knew.

He did want to date her. Marry her, even, someday.

But right now, what he really wanted to do was kiss her. Just as soon as he could get her away from his daughter and his in-laws.

Chapter 32

"Thank you so much. This was fun." Lydia bent to embrace Meredith. "And delicious." She gave the gruff George a quick hug too.

"Y'all don't be strangers now." Meredith waved as Liam opened the van door for Lydia. Mia had left for work an hour ago, so Liam was her only option for a ride home.

Fortunately, he seemed to be in a much better mood than he had been last night and this morning. Lydia didn't know what had shifted, but it was like she could feel the weight that had been lifted from him.

"You really had fun?" he asked as he backed the van out of the driveway.

"Of course. Didn't you?"

"I did." He turned to her—and that was another thing that had changed: the way he looked at her. Like he wanted to know everything about her. It was a little unnerving, but it also made her heart jump up and take notice.

"So what did you and George talk about while you were grilling?" She'd first noticed the change when she'd come outside for lunch, so maybe their conversation could shed some light on it.

"Not much." But his Adam's apple bobbed with his swallow. "I asked how work was going for him, and he told me he retired."

"Oh." That didn't explain the change.

Lydia watched the now-familiar sights go by: Joseph's vet office. Daisy's. The park.

All of them held so much of her heart now.

"He told me about his last conversation with Molly too," Liam said quietly as they crossed the bridge that led away from downtown. "She told him to make sure I was happy." Liam's voice cracked, and her hand was suddenly in his.

"That's really sweet."

Liam tightened his grip on her hand but didn't say anything else until he turned into the driveway in front of the carriage house. "He wanted me to know I have their blessing to—uh—to date again."

"Oh." Lydia's pulse made a drastic tempo jump. "Do you want to date again?"

Liam stopped the car and reached across the steering wheel to put it in park with his left hand, not taking his right hand off of hers.

"That depends." He turned so that he faced her.

"On what?" Her words felt wispy, and she couldn't catch her breath.

"On you." His hand brushed her cheek, and her eyes went to his.

She leaned toward him. "On me?"

"Lydia." His breath brushed over her lips a moment before she found his with her own. Her hands slid up his arms to his shoulders, and his wrapped around her back and into her hair. She tried to move closer, but her leg bumped the console, and she remembered that they were in his work van.

A giggle slipped out of her, and Liam pulled back.

"Sorry." She caught her breath. "I was just thinking this was the perfect place for our first kiss."

"I'm glad you think so." He tugged her closer. "Because I think it's perfect for our second kiss too."

Chapter 33

"Do you have to be so happy this early in the morning?" Mia groused, shuffling into the kitchen with her eyes still half closed. "It's disgusting."

"Sorry." Liam stopped whistling but couldn't tame his smile.

"Never apologize for being happy," Mama said from her seat at the table. "It's a gift from the Lord."

"You're right, Mama. It is." He pulled another coffee cup from the cupboard, filled it, and passed it to Mia. "Maybe this will help."

But coffee wasn't the reason for his own joy. It had been an incredible week. Though he'd been busy with work, he'd spent nearly every extra moment with Lydia—walking Buck, talking, stealing kisses. He and Molly had been teenagers when they'd gone through the new relationship phase—and though he was twenty-some years older now, the excitement and newness felt much the same, even if tempered by their adult responsibilities.

"Lydia and I are going to work on the Builder's House today. But I thought we could all have dinner together tonight."

"Lydia too?" Mia eyed him over her mug.

"Yeah. Is that okay?" Not that he needed his daughter's permission, but he'd feel much better if he had her blessing.

Mia shrugged. "She's actually pretty cool."

Liam chuckled. "I think so too. Actually, I think she's really cool. Actually, I think she's super—"

"Ew. Dad. Don't."

"What?" Liam grinned at his daughter. "I was agreeing with you."

"Well, don't." But Mia was smiling as she left the room.

"I think that might have qualified as an actual conversation." Liam lifted his eyebrows at Mama. "Will wonders never cease?"

Mama's laugh was gentle. "God is faithful. Just like I told you."

Liam dropped a kiss on top of her head. "Right again. I think having Lydia to talk to has been good for her."

"And for you."

He couldn't argue with that.

He stepped out the front door, his eyes instantly going to the carriage house. Lydia wasn't outside yet, and his feet kicked into a jog as the anticipation of seeing her built in his chest.

He took the carriage house steps two at a time and knocked impatiently on the door.

It only took a second for Lydia to answer it. "Hey, I was just about to—"

He pulled her into his arms, dropping his face into her hair and soaking in a deep breath of her pomegranate shampoo. "I missed you."

Lydia's soft shoulders lifted with her laugh. "It's only been seven hours." That was true. They'd sat outside talking until midnight last night.

"That's seven hours too long." He loosened his grip just enough to lower his lips to hers.

She inhaled, her hands splaying on his back as she pulled him closer. Liam let his fingers trail over the soft skin of her shoulders. Maybe they should skip going to the Builder's House and kiss all day instead.

But Lydia pulled back gently, her eyes bright and cheeks flushed. "We should do that some more later."

"Why wait?" Liam tugged her closer and brought his lips to hers again.

This time Lydia pulled back after only a moment, still smiling. "Come on, we promised we'd be there."

"That was dumb of us."

Lydia laughed. "Nice try, but you can't fool me, Liam O'Neill. I already know what a good guy you are." She stepped through the door, slipping her hand into his.

"I knew it was a mistake to let you see that." But he pulled the door closed behind her and let her lead him down the steps.

Fifteen minutes later, Liam parked the van on the street in front of the Builder's House. Lydia reached for the door handle, but he grabbed her arm. "Hold on."

She turned to him with a curious look.

"Are we . . . Do we want people to know . . ."

Lydia's smile started slow but grew quickly. "About us?"

"Yeah. Would you rather I didn't hold your hand or—"

"Or do this?" Lydia grinned and leaned forward, dropping a quick kiss onto his lips.

He grinned right back at her. "I guess I have my answer." He reached for his door handle, but this time Lydia grabbed his arm.

"Unless— Are you sure you're okay with it? Pictures of us could end up getting posted, and people might say things."

"Let them say whatever they want. I only care about what you think." He leaned over for another kiss, only allowing his lips to linger for a second so he wouldn't be tempted to stay right here.

They got out of the van, and Liam grabbed his tools from the back, popping an O'Neill Electric hat onto Lydia's head just for fun.

She pulled her hair through the back of it. "How do I look?"

Liam could only make an unintelligible noise in the back of his throat.

"That bad?" Lydia laughed and pulled the hat off.

Liam shook his head. "That good." He let himself slide his hand through her hair, down her shoulder, and into her hand.

The first person they met on the way into the house was Simeon, carrying a large potted bush in front of him.

As if of one mind, both Lydia and Liam stopped.

"Hey, man. Haven't seen you around in a while," Liam called.

Simeon frowned. "I've been— Well, look at you two." His expression brightened. "About time."

"You know what they say, 'Good things come to those who wait.'" Liam let go of Lydia's hand to wrap his arm around her instead.

"I guess so." But Simeon's smile had already fallen away.

"How's Abigail?" Lydia asked.

"She's good. I'd better get this planted. As soon as I'm done here, we're heading out of town for a few days."

"Oh, that'll be fun. Y'all have a good vacation." Lydia waved to her brother as he traipsed off with his shrub.

"Maybe they'll make their big announcement when they get back," she leaned into Liam to whisper.

"Maybe." But Liam watched Simeon set the shrub down and attack the soil with a shovel. He couldn't shake the feeling that whatever his friend was hiding, it wasn't good news.

When they got inside, Liam was called to help finish installing the ceiling fans in the upstairs bedrooms, while Lydia was needed to help paint in the family room.

"Have fun." Lydia gave a cheerful wave, and Liam made his way upstairs, telling himself to ignore the flare of jealousy as he spotted Harrison approaching Lydia.

There was no reason to think she would be interested in the other man when she'd just been kissing Liam.

Right, other than Harrison's good looks, charm, money. The fact that he made a much better match for her. The fact that the internet had already made it known that they preferred Harrison.

Liam pushed the thoughts out. He didn't care what the internet thought.

But what if Lydia did?

"Hey, Liam. Can you figure out why this fan won't turn on?" The voice from atop the ladder in the middle of the bedroom was a welcome distraction, and Liam spent the next couple of hours troubleshooting and installing fixtures.

By the time he was ready for a break, the doubts he'd been feeling about Lydia and Harrison had all but disappeared. Until he went downstairs and found Harrison at Lydia's side again—or maybe still. Harrison was watching Lydia intently, though she seemed to be staring at the floor. Did she want Harrison to leave her alone?

Liam strode toward them, keeping one eye on Harrison and holding himself as tall as possible—which was a good three inches taller than the other man.

But Harrison seemed completely unperturbed by his approach. "Hey, Liam."

Lydia looked up, her smile instantly pulling his own lips up in response, though he wasn't ready to let his guard down with Harrison.

"How's it going upstairs?" Lydia stepped to his side and slipped an arm around his back. Liam's heart just about jumped out of his chest.

Take that, Harrison.

Lydia had spent the morning with him, and still she'd chosen Liam.

But Harrison smiled politely at them, no trace of surprise or jealousy in his expression.

Liam let himself relax a little. "Good. Fans and fixtures are all installed and working. How's it going down here? The paint looks great." He kissed the side of Lydia's head, then eyed Harrison again.

"Thanks." Lydia snuggled closer to him. "And I'm not even covered in paint this time."

"Harrison," someone yelled from the front door. "We need you outside."

"Be right there," Harrison called over his shoulder, then turned back to Lydia. "Just promise you'll think about it, okay?"

Liam stiffened. "Think about what?" He pulled himself up taller again.

Harrison didn't bat an eye. "I was just telling Lydia about the benefit concert to dedicate the house. We already have a band scheduled, but they're a small local group, and we thought Lydia might be willing to play a song or two. Maybe raise a little more awareness."

Liam's shoulders relaxed, and he took back every unkind thing he'd thought about Harrison. The man was a genius.

They both turned to Lydia.

"You know it felt good to be back up on that stage the other night," Liam encouraged.

Lydia chewed her lip, but Liam could see the smile hovering under the worry.

"And I really want to know how that song ends," he wheedled.

She laughed, but he could see her wavering. He folded his hands in front of him in a plea.

"Fine. I'll do it. But I'm not promising to sing that song."

Liam let out a cheer, and Harrison gave them both a thumbs-up as his name was called from outside again. "That's awesome. Thanks so much. Excuse me. I'd better . . ."

But neither of them looked at him.

"I'm not sure about this," Lydia mumbled.

"I am." Liam brushed a kiss across her lips. "You're going to be amazing." Then he thought again. "I take that back. You're not going to be amazing."

"I'm not?" Lydia tried to wiggle out of his arms.

"Nope. Because you're *already* amazing."

"Oh, I'm going to throw up." Lydia pressed a hand to her stomach.

"Now?" Liam took a slight step backward.

"No." Lydia's laugh was nervous. "Before the concert."

"Well then." Liam stepped closer. "I'll be there to hold your hair."

"Really? You would do that?" Lydia looked at him as if he'd promised her a private island.

"Of course I would." He brushed a strand of hair off her forehead. "I'll do anything for you."

Chapter 34

Lydia paced behind the outdoor stage at Founder's Park, running through the lyrics of the song she'd just finished yesterday. She'd spent the past two weeks working almost constantly on her music—with breaks to hang out with Liam and her family—and she was feeling surprisingly good about it.

Good thing, too, since she was supposed to be on stage in five minutes.

When she'd peeked half an hour ago, the seating area had been more packed than she'd expected for the small town. She pressed a hand to her stomach.

"You okay?" Liam strode toward her from the spot where he'd been manning the lights. "Need to throw up?"

She considered his question. "You know what? I don't think so." Nerves zipped through her like lightning, and her legs felt unsteady, but at least she wasn't queasy.

"Oh good."

"You were afraid you'd have to hold my hair, weren't you?" Lydia teased.

"No. I was afraid I wouldn't be able to do this." Liam bent close and gave her a long, lingering kiss that made her forget the stage, the crowd, even her songs.

"Two minutes, Lydia," a voice cut into their kiss. "Harrison wants you in the wings."

A low growl came from Liam's throat as he pulled her closer. She let herself enjoy his lips a second longer, then pulled back. "Come on. You're the one who got me into this."

She clutched his hand and led the way to the wings, where he kissed the top of her head, then moved to the lighting controls.

"I'll be right here."

A sense of dread rolled over her. The last time she'd performed in public, her whole world had fallen apart—in front of everyone.

From the stage, she heard Harrison introducing her.

"You can do it." Liam gave her a small nudge. "You're amazing, remember?"

Lydia shook her head but let the applause pull her forward.

A single, dim spotlight created a small circle of purple-hued light on the stage floor. Lydia made her way toward it, offering up a prayer as she walked.

When she reached her mark, she bowed her head for a moment, pulled in a shaky breath, then let herself look up. The crowd had grown even larger than when she'd looked earlier, but she focused on the front row, where Abe sat with Asher and Ireland, Joseph and Ava, Zeb and Carly, Simeon, and Benjamin. Even Grace and Levi had come to town for this.

Lydia pressed a hand to her heart, its rhythm matching that of the thunderous applause. She moved her mouth closer to the mic. "Thank you so much for that warm welcome. I want to sing you a new piece I call 'Songs of Home.'"

She let herself look to the wings. Liam was standing at the light board, but his eyes were on her. His smile gave her the courage to nod to the guitarist Harrison had found to accompany her.

Music filtered from behind her, and she closed her eyes, letting the words rise from her soul.

There wasn't no fanfare, wasn't a crowd,
The day she rode into that quiet little town.
There wasn't no announcement, no blinding lights,
Just a sweet little room and soft summer nights.
She was looking for peace, she was looking for hope,
She was looking for somewhere that might feel like home.

She opened her eyes, taking a breath as her gaze swept the crowd.
Some people were smiling, some were swaying to the music. Some
had their phones lifted in front of them. Joseph and Asher and Zeb
had their arms around their wives. Grace clutched Levi's arm, leaning
forward with a huge smile. Benjamin shot her a quick thumbs-up, and
even Simeon was smiling.

Lydia moved into the chorus, drawing strength from the energy of
the crowd.

It happened in a flash, yet it happened so slow.
One day, she started singin', singin' those songs of home.
Now they light up her fingers, she feels 'em in her toes.
Her heart beats the rhythm of those songs of home.

The guitar took over, and this time when she took a breath, it felt
like something had been set free inside her. She let her eyes go to Liam,
who looked entranced. At the cue for the second verse, she turned back
to the crowd.

There wasn't no neon sign, no lightning strikes.
Just sweet church picnics and talking all night.
Family and friends gathered round every table.
Bowling and pizza and lives that were faithful.
Oh, she found her peace, yeah, she found her hope.
She found that sweet little place she calls home.

By the time she finished the song, the crowd was on its feet, cheering. Lydia couldn't help the giddy giggle that escaped. She had done it. She'd performed again. More than that, she'd *felt* the music in a way she hadn't in years.

She returned the microphone to its stand, waved to the crowd, and hurried off the stage, her heart still throbbing with the exhilaration of it all.

She'd only taken two steps into the wings when she was swept up in a pair of strong arms.

Liam pressed his lips to hers before setting her down and resting his forehead on hers. "So I guess you took my advice and wrote a church picnic song after all."

Chapter 35

Lydia cracked an eye open, her blankets cozy around her, trying to place the annoying buzzing sound. Her gaze landed on her phone. But she hadn't set an alarm for today. It was her birthday, and she had decided to use the excuse to sleep in, mostly because Liam had taken the day off, so she didn't have to get up early to get outside and say goodbye to him before he left. He was all hers for the day.

The thought made her smile as she reached for her phone. If this was Liam, she'd forgive him. If it was anyone else . . .

She groaned as her eyes fell on her manager's name and then the time.

"You do own a clock, don't you?" she said as she lifted the phone to her ear.

"You need to get on a plane right now." Becca's urgency pulsed through the phone.

"I— What? Why?"

"Bryce Parker heard your new song. He wants you to open for his tour." Barely contained giddiness bounced off Becca's words.

"Slow down." Six in the morning was way too early to process what Becca was saying. "Bryce Parker heard my song? How?"

Becca gave an impatient click of the tongue. "Someone who was at that building thing-a-ma-bob you did last week posted it online."

"The Builders for the Kingdom benefit?"

"Sure. Yeah." Becca clicked her tongue again.

"Who posted it?"

"I don't know." Becca sounded about ready to strangle her for all the questions. "It doesn't matter. What matters is, Bryce loved it. And he's in Memphis, but only for today. You need to get on a plane and get over there. I've already got my ticket. I'll meet you there."

"Today?" Lydia finally managed to push herself into a seated position, her legs crossed in front of her on the bed. "I have plans today."

"Lydia!" From the sound of it, Becca must be barely restraining herself from throwing the phone across the room. "We're talking about Bryce Parker. He's right behind Dallas and Cheyenne on the charts. Working with him could catapult your career. This is the biggest opportunity you're ever going to get."

"I know." Lydia rubbed her temples. This was what she'd been waiting and working for. But Liam had been hinting about his big plans for her birthday all week. She couldn't just take off on him. "Isn't there any way we could reschedule?"

"Oh sure." Becca's voice dripped with sarcasm. "I'll call him up and be like—" Her voice switched to a simper. "'Thanks for offering my client the opportunity of a lifetime, but today's not convenient for her. Could you please rearrange your tour schedule to fit her needs?'" Becca's usual, hard voice returned. "What could you possibly have going on today that's more important than meeting with Bryce Parker?"

There was no way Becca would understand, but Lydia might as well be honest. "Liam planned something for my birthday. I'm not sure what, but he put a lot of work into it, and . . ."

"Look, Lydia, I'm happy for you. I really am. You're finally out of your funk. But now you have to ask yourself what it was all for. It was so you could write music again. Which you're doing. Now you need to take the next step. Get on a plane."

"But—" Lydia chewed her lip. Did she really have to choose between Liam and her career?

You knew this was coming.

Hadn't her head been warning her for weeks that this was a bad idea? That eventually she'd have to leave River Falls. But the argument had been weakening day by day, until she'd nearly convinced herself that maybe she *could* stay here forever. Maybe this really could be her home.

"Look." Becca's voice took on that gentle quality that weirded Lydia out every time because it was so un-Becca-like. "I know this relationship is new and exciting. But are you really going to give up this once-in-a-lifetime opportunity for something that may not last? I mean, you thought Dallas was going to be forever, right? And look how that turned out."

Lydia fingered her bracelet. So many things in her life hadn't lasted. Maybe Becca was right. Maybe this would be another one of them.

But she wouldn't know unless she gave it a chance.

"I'm sorry," she said again. "I can't meet Bryce today."

Chapter 36

"I hope you're having a good birthday." Liam nuzzled his lips into Lydia's neck, her hair tickling his cheek.

"Hey, man, don't forget that's my sister." Simeon smacked the back of Liam's head lightly.

"I know." Liam straightened, still smiling at Lydia. "And you're the one who told me to ask her out."

"You can thank me later." Simeon lifted his full plate of food, then continued toward the tables Liam had set up under the trees in the backyard.

"He seems to be in a better place lately," Liam muttered to Lydia.

"Hmm? Yeah." Lydia glanced toward Simeon, then touched a hand to her forehead.

"You're sure everything's okay?"

She'd been distracted all day, though she kept insisting it was nothing. But she'd barely seemed to notice that he'd taken her to all the places they'd made memories together in River Falls. At the bowling alley, she hadn't even reacted when she'd bowled her first strike ever.

"Of course." There she went again. Her strained smile made uneasiness shift in his stomach. Was she changing her mind about them? About him?

"Hey, Lydia," Benjamin called. "You gonna sing us something or what?"

"Let her eat first," Liam called back, pointing to Benjamin's heaping plate. Grace hadn't been wrong when she'd said you had to put up a fight to get food when the Calvano boys were around.

But Lydia shook her head. "That's okay. I'm not hungry." She slid her hand out of his.

Closing her eyes, she hummed a few bars before opening her mouth to unleash her full, rich alto:

I was wandering around, all on my own,

So, so lost, and I didn't even know.

But then you came along, swept into my heart.

And I had to wonder—what had kept us apart.

Because without you, oh,

I was a river without the rain,

Fire without the heat,

Lightning without the crash,

Bitter without the sweet.

Without you, I was all alone.

But now I know—I know you hold my soul.

The tempo was upbeat, and Liam let her words carry him away. She had shared the song with him last night, so he knew that though on the surface people might hear it as a song about a relationship, it was more about her walk of faith. Which gave him more joy than any song she might write about him ever could.

When the song was done, he let out a wolf whistle that made Lydia laugh the low laugh that drove him wild.

That was better.

"Well, darling. That was worth getting on a plane for." The deep voice from near the house made them all turn. A man in jeans and a white t-shirt clearly meant to show off the fact that he spent hours a day in the gym stood there, holding a bouquet of flowers that dwarfed the one Liam had given Lydia earlier.

Liam tensed at the way the guy's eyes traveled over Lydia.

"Oh my goodness. Bryce Parker." Lydia pressed a hand to her chest, her face flushing. "What are you doing here?"

Liam stared from Lydia to the stranger. She knew him? Had she invited him? To Liam's house?

"I heard you couldn't get away from your birthday party. So I decided to crash it." He stepped forward with a smooth smile that filled Liam with the sudden urge to throw a punch. "I brought these to make up for it."

"Oh. Um. Wow. Okay." Lydia took the flowers and lifted them to her nose, the same way she had with Liam's. "Thank you."

Liam had never seen her so tongue-tied, and it made his insides go numb.

He took a step forward and held out a hand, telling himself it didn't matter that he couldn't remember the last time he'd seen the inside of a gym. "Liam O'Neill."

"Sorry." Lydia looked at him as if she'd completely forgotten his existence. "Liam, this is Bryce Parker. He just won a CMA for album of the year."

"Ah."

Lydia was still staring at Bryce as if she couldn't believe he would grace her with his presence.

"Is there somewhere we can talk?" Bryce glanced over his shoulder at Liam's house. "I promise I won't take up too much of your time."

"Um." Lydia gave Liam a questioning look. "Do you mind?"

"Of course not." He was even gentleman enough to open the door and gesture them through.

And he didn't slam it behind them.

Chapter 37

Lydia didn't know if she should pinch herself or jump up and run from the room.

Here was Bryce Parker, sitting across the table from her in Liam's kitchen, offering her everything she'd ever dreamed of.

And she wasn't sure if she should take it.

"So what do you think?" Bryce's expression was at once hopeful and charming and pleading. He'd spent the past twenty minutes outlining his plans for the year-long worldwide tour, for a couple of collaborations, for a possible album produced by his label; in short, for everything she'd had before, but better.

"I—" She flipped vacantly through the contract he'd set in front of her. If she agreed to this, he wanted her in Nashville by the end of the month—which was only two weeks away.

She pushed up from the table and grabbed a glass out of Liam's cupboard, filling it at the sink.

"What else can I say to convince you?" Bryce's chair scraped back, and then he was standing there too, watching her earnestly. "I really want you on board. Think what it could do for your career."

She didn't have to think about that part. It was obviously the opportunity of a lifetime.

"And it's not like I'm being completely altruistic here." Bryce hit her with that charming smile. "It'll be good for my career too. Especially when we top Dallas and Cheyenne in the charts." He winked at her.

Lydia pressed a hand to her stomach. She'd just been getting used to the idea of staying in River Falls, of living a regular life . . . of being with Liam.

But was any of that feasible? It had been a nice vacation. But maybe it was time to get back to the real world.

"I'm sorry. I'm going to need— Could I have a few days to think about this?"

Bryce's smooth expression faltered for only a second. "Of course. But only a few. My manager has someone else in mind, but I told her I wanted you. If we don't move fast though . . ." He pulled out a money clip, riffling through a stack of bills to pass her a card.

"Three days, tops." Lydia tucked the card into her pocket.

"Deal." He held out a hand to shake hers, wrapping his other hand around hers as well. "I'd better fly. My manager about had a fit when I told her I was taking off so close to our next stop. But I really wanted to ask you in person."

Lydia had no idea how to respond to that, so she simply nodded and led him toward the back door.

The moment she opened it, the low babble of conversation stopped and all eyes swept to them. She tried to lock onto Liam's, but his skipped from her to Bryce, and his mouth flattened.

"Can I get you some cake, Mr. Parker?" Ireland stepped forward with a friendly smile.

"It'll have to be for the road, but I never could resist anything sweet."

Lydia was pretty sure a snort came from Liam's direction, but when she glanced his way, he was staring at the ground.

"We were hoping you'd sing something for us," Benjamin piped up.

"Sorry." Bryce took a forkful of the cake Ireland handed him. "I have to go. But next time, Lydia and I will sing something together for y'all. All right?"

Though Liam didn't look up, a thundercloud may as well have covered his face.

"I'll talk to you soon." Bryce squeezed her arm. "I hope it'll be good news." He strode across the lawn, toward the driveway, where, Lydia now noticed, a limo waited for him.

As soon as it had pulled away, a dozen voices bombarded her with questions.

"You know Bryce Parker and you didn't tell us?"

"What did he want?"

"What did he mean, 'next time'?"

Lydia's legs suddenly refused to support her, and she fell into the nearest Adirondack chair. She told everyone about Bryce's offer—the travel it would entail, the success it could bring—and answered every one of their questions as patiently as she could. But the one person she most wanted to talk to remained silent, staring at his hands clasped between his knees.

"So what are you going to do?" Leave it to Benjamin to ask the one question she couldn't answer.

She swallowed, unable to look at Liam. "I told him I need a few days to think about it."

"Whatever you decide, we'll support you. But for now, we have to get home to let the beasts out." Joseph got up and squeezed her shoulder, and Ava bent to hug her.

One by one, the rest of her family headed out as well, trailing their congratulations and birthday wishes. Mia left for work, and Liam helped his mama back into the house.

Alone in the yard, Lydia spun in a slow circle, taking in the wide open lawn, the river, Liam's welcoming home, her cozy carriage house, the field she'd walked across a hundred times to see her family. The place had started to feel like home, she couldn't deny that. But what if Becca was right? What if it was all only temporary? That had been her plan from the beginning. Meet her family, rest, write some songs. She'd accomplished all three. So maybe it was time to move on.

She sniffed and stacked the gifts from her family onto a pile. A River Falls t-shirt from Asher and Ireland, a gift card to Daisy's from Joseph and Ava, a journal from Zeb and Carly, a flowering plant from Simeon and Abigail—who had sent her apologies through Simeon—a handheld video game of some sort from Benjamin, a framed picture of her birth mama from Abe, and a box of fudge and cherries sent from Grace and Levi in Hope Springs.

She eyed the pile—she was going to have to take multiple trips if she didn't want to leave a trail of gifts across the yard.

But before she could load anything into her arms, the back door banged open. Liam hesitated at the top of the steps, then started slowly toward her, one hand behind his back.

She wanted to ask what he thought about the Bryce Parker offer, but her vocal cords stretched tighter than guitar strings, and she was afraid they might snap if she said anything.

"Happy birthday." He pulled his hand slowly from behind his back and passed her a small box wrapped in gold and pink paper.

"You didn't have to . . ." But she was already pulling the wrapping paper off.

Inside was a small, velvety box. Lydia glanced at Liam, but his eyes were on her hands. Slowly, she lifted the lid.

"Oh, Liam."

"It's for your charm bracelet." He fingered the bracelet on her wrist, then took the cross charm out of the box and attached it next to the music note from her parents.

"Thank you," she whispered. This was not going to make it any easier to decide.

"You're welcome." He leaned forward, as if to kiss her, but then pulled back. "I'll help you carry this stuff home. I mean, to the carriage house."

"Oh. Okay." Hurt and confusion collided against her ribs. Were they not going to talk about it at all?

Silently, Liam gathered up most of the stuff, though Lydia grabbed the plant. They trooped across the yard and up the steps to the carriage house.

She opened the door and moved inside to set the plant on the table. Liam deposited his items there as well.

Then they just stared at each other.

"I guess I should—" Liam thumbed toward the door.

"Wait." She grabbed for his arm but couldn't quite reach it.

He stopped anyway, his expression unreadable.

"You never said what you thought of Bryce Parker's offer."

Liam looked toward the door as if seeking an escape hatch. "It's a good offer," he said finally, his tone flat. "A really good opportunity for you."

Lydia's heart tumbled toward her feet. "So you think I should take it?"

He stepped forward, his expression pained, and took her hand in his. "It has to be your decision. Whatever you decide, I'll support you." He brushed a kiss across her knuckles, then let go of her hand and disappeared out the door.

Lydia stared after him. He'd support her. Did that mean he'd buy her album and tell his grandkids that he'd known her once? Or did it mean he'd be there, holding her hand, at her side, through it all?

215

Chapter 38

Liam's arm rested on the console between his seat and Lydia's. He wanted to reach the rest of the way for her hand, but he wasn't sure she'd welcome the touch. He'd been trying to give her space to make her decision—and it was killing him.

As much as he wanted to beg and plead with her to stay, he wouldn't. He'd already destroyed Molly's dreams. He refused to do that to Lydia too. If she chose not to take Bryce Parker's offer, it had to be because she didn't want to take it—not because Liam had held her back.

What was he thinking?

Of course she'd take the offer. Liam may not be a country music expert, but when one of the biggest stars in the industry flew out to ask you personally to sing with him—well, only a fool would turn that down.

He tried hard not to wish Lydia were a fool.

"It's too bad your mama has a headache today," Lydia said as Liam pulled into the parking lot of Beautiful Savior.

"Yeah." He wished he could offer her more than grunts for answers, but he was afraid if he said too much, his feelings would be too easy for her to read.

"Maybe I should have stayed home with her. Made her some tea."

Oh man, if Liam's heart squeezed any tighter, it was going to go right ahead and snap. The way this woman cared for his family—the way he cared for her. How could he not ask her to stay?

But he refused to give in to his own selfishness. Lydia had to decide by tomorrow, and he wasn't going to do anything to make that decision harder. "She'll be fine. We can pick her up something from Daisy's on the way home if you want." He swung the car into a parking spot.

"That's a great idea." Lydia's face brightened, and he nearly pushed her curls behind her ear and pulled her closer for a kiss. But that wouldn't exactly count as not trying to influence her decision.

He got out of the van, intending to open her door as well, but she'd already hopped out by the time he reached her.

She gave him that same tentative smile she'd adopted ever since Bryce Parker had shown up uninvited but then slid her hand into his.

He exhaled, as if he'd been swimming underwater for the past two days. Maybe holding her hand meant the ache would be even worse if she left, but for right now, this was exactly what he needed.

They started toward the church but were intercepted by Cole Davenport. "Hey, Mr. O'Neill. Is Mia coming this morning?" The teen looked so hopeful that Liam almost couldn't be upset by the amount of attention he'd been paying to Mia lately. Much as he wished Mia still thought all boys except her daddy had cooties, if she was going to date, Cole was the kind of kid he wanted her with.

"Sorry, no. She was called into work at the last minute. I guess a bunch of people called in sick today." Liam probably should have insisted that she come to church with them instead, but her boss was a good guy, and Liam didn't want to leave him in the lurch.

"Oh. Okay." Cole stepped ahead and opened the door for them.

"Thank you, Cole." Lydia offered the teen the real smile Liam had missed so much.

"Thanks, Cole." Liam shook the young man's hand and followed Lydia inside to find that she'd already been swept into conversation by Joseph and Ava.

He was about to join them when he caught sight of Simeon standing outside the building. When his friend didn't move after a moment, Liam pushed the door open.

"Hey, man. You coming in or what?"

Simeon either didn't hear him or chose not to answer.

Liam stepped outside, shutting the comfortable air conditioning in behind him and moving into the thick humidity. "What's going on?"

Simeon finally looked over, his eyes red-rimmed and bloodshot.

Liam sucked in a sharp breath. "Have you—" He'd known Simeon for the better part of forty years, and never once had he asked this question—but he had to ask it now. "Have you been drinking?"

Simeon's laugh rang with irony. "I'm usually the one asking that question to clients. But no." He rubbed at his eyes. "Just not sleeping well."

"Do you want to talk about it?" Not that Liam could be much help when Simeon was the counselor here. But his friend had lent him a shoulder more than once. The least Liam could do was attempt to offer the same.

"I'm fine. Let's go inside."

"Don't they call that avoidance or something?"

Simeon let out a soft pft of air.

"So?" Liam crossed his arms, then remembered hearing a long time ago that the posture indicated you were closed to others. He dropped his arms to his sides. "What's going on?"

Simeon opened his mouth, but the church bells clanged from the steeple above them. He shrugged and turned toward the door, but Liam caught his arm.

After another few seconds, the church bells stopped, although their tones echoed off the surrounding hills.

"Is it Abigail?" Liam asked quietly, pulling Simeon a few steps from the door.

Simeon shook his head but then seemed to crumple. "She's had—" He cleared his throat and shook his head again.

But Liam wasn't going anywhere until Simeon spit out whatever it was. He couldn't help if he didn't know. Wasn't that what Simeon always said?

"She's had a few miscarriages over the past couple of years. This last one . . . She's having a really hard time dealing with it. And I don't know how—" He pinched his nose. "I feel like I'm losing her too."

Liam could only stare at his friend. He hadn't expected a single one of those sentences. "A few? I didn't— Why didn't you ever say anything?" He didn't mean to sound offended. But he'd been Simeon's best friend for decades. How could his friend not have told him?

"She didn't want anyone to know." Simeon tipped his head back and watched the gray clouds that had begun to gather overhead. "We've prayed so hard for this." He brought his gaze back down. "I've prayed so hard for her. I'm trying to help her, but she keeps pushing me away."

"I am so sorry." Liam clapped a hand on his friend's shoulder. "I'll pray for you both too. Is there someone else she can talk to? I know you're a counselor, but—"

But Simeon was already shaking his head. "I tried to suggest that. But she won't."

"Okay." Liam blew out a breath. He wished there was a way he could fix this for his friend. "Is there anything else I can do?"

"Nah." Simeon shrugged Liam's hand off his shoulder. "Thanks. But I'm sure it will all be fine." He put on a smile that Liam knew better than to believe. "Come on, let's get inside. The service already started."

Liam studied his friend. Maybe he should insist on talking about it some more. But what else was there to say? He could only imagine the pain his friends were going through. If anything had ever happened to Mia . . .

"Hey." Simeon stopped in front of the church doors. "Don't say anything to anyone, okay? I promised Abigail."

Liam frowned. The Calvanos would be an excellent support system for Simeon and Abigail if they knew. "It's nothing to be ashamed of. It's no one's fault."

"I know that," Simeon snapped.

Liam held up a hand in surrender.

"Sorry." Simeon ran a fist down his face. "I need to help her understand that. Then we'll tell everyone."

"Your call." Liam followed Simeon into the building, trying to figure out how he was supposed to keep this from Lydia.

Then again, if she decided to leave, he supposed it wouldn't be too hard. He swallowed down the queasiness brought on by Simeon's revelation and the thought of Lydia leaving and tried to find peace in the words of the hymn that already filled the church.

Chapter 39

Lydia closed her eyes as the hymn ended. Peace had eluded her ever since the moment Bryce Parker had made his offer. She'd hoped to find it here, but so far, all she'd found was more questions. Like why hadn't Liam held her hand in the van? And where had he gone?

She glanced over her shoulder just in time to spot him entering the sanctuary behind Simeon. When they reached the pew, Simeon stepped aside to let Liam enter first, and Lydia slid over to make room.

"Where'd y'all disappear to?" she leaned close to whisper, letting her arm press against his.

He shook his head and gave her a tight, worried smile. For a moment, she thought he was going to press a kiss to her head in that way that made her feel cherished, but Pastor Cooper—the youth pastor who served with Abe—started speaking, and Liam's head swiveled to the front. Beyond him, Simeon seemed completely focused on the service as well.

Lydia sighed and attempted to pay attention too.

"Have y'all ever been in the pitch dark?" Pastor Cooper started his sermon. "I don't mean like going to bed in your house at night. I mean like in the woods in the middle of the night with a blindfold on. That kind of dark."

Lydia nodded, as did most of the people around her. But she hadn't been in the woods. She'd been on tour, in the dressing room of some arena—maybe in Denver—and the power had gone out. The room had no windows, so though it was the middle of the day, Lydia suddenly couldn't see the lipstick she'd been holding in front of her face. Fortunately, the power had come back on a minute later, but Lydia had never forgotten that disembodied sensation. It was the same sensation she'd felt after Mama and Daddy died. The same as after Dallas and Cheyenne had betrayed her.

"Some of y'all know that my parents used to serve at a Bible camp with Pastor Calvano and his wife when I was a little kid," Pastor Cooper continued.

Grace had told Lydia about that. And about how her mama had desperately wanted Grace to marry Pastor Cooper—even though they hadn't seen each other since they were eleven.

Pastor Cooper pointed to the pew filled with Calvanos. "Y'all remember that time the power went out, right?" Around Lydia, her siblings bobbed their heads, some of them chuckling already.

Pastor Cooper looked to the rest of the congregation, leaning forward as if to let them in on the joke. "I started crying," he admitted. "And I said, 'Somebody help me open my eyes.'"

A laugh went through the congregation, and next to her, Lydia felt Liam relax a little. She let her eyes go to him. He wasn't laughing, but the hint of a smile touched his lips.

"Darkness like that—" Pastor Cooper pursed his lips into a low whistle. "It's scary. It's impossible to navigate on your own. It can make you think you're all alone. I knew my parents were in the next room. But I started bawling because I thought maybe the darkness had swallowed them up. And maybe it was going to swallow me up too." Pastor Cooper shook his head. "To be fair, I was five at the time."

He smiled but then grew serious. "Living in this world can sometimes feel like being plunged into that kind of darkness." He flipped through his Bible. "God tells us in Isaiah, 'We look for light, but all is darkness;

for brightness, but we walk in deep shadows.'" Pastor Cooper looked up. "That's a scary place to be. A place where all you can do is stumble. A place where you feel all alone. A place where you feel like you can't even open your eyes."

Lydia swallowed. She'd felt like that so many times in her life.

As Pastor Cooper paused, Liam leaned away from her, and she had to concentrate on the front of the church so the darkness didn't fight its way back. But then Liam's arm was around her shoulders, and he was snugging her tight against his side.

She looked up. His eyes were on Pastor Cooper, his mouth in a straight line, but his arm was warm and secure around her shoulder. She let herself rest her head on his arm for a second.

"So where do you turn when it's dark like that?" Pastor Cooper asked. "I'll never forget the way I felt in that power outage when I saw my daddy's flashlight cutting through the dark to come save me. I think I said something like, 'You're back.' And my dad, of course, said, 'I've been here the whole time. I never went anywhere.' Obviously he hadn't. Just because I couldn't see him didn't mean he wasn't there. Y'all see what I'm saying, right?" Pastor Cooper paused as if making sure everyone got it. "Over and over, the Bible tells us that Jesus is our light. He's not some puny little flashlight, either. He's not just a spotlight, not even the moon or the sun. He's greater than them all. He's the Light of the World. 'The light shines in the darkness, and the darkness has not overcome it.' And even when we can't see him, he's still there." Pastor Cooper paused, as if to let the words sink in. "I know it can be hard to believe it, when we're in the middle of those dark times. But listen to what he tells us." He picked up his Bible. "'Do not fear, for I have redeemed you; I have summoned you by name; you are mine.'"

VALERIE M. BODDEN

He set the Bible down and scanned the congregation. "You know what that means, right? 'You are *mine*,'" he repeated. "So many people in this world are searching for a place to belong. But here God is saying that belonging isn't about a *where*, it's about a *who*. He is saying you belong to *him*."

The words swept over Lydia, and she had to close her eyes and catch her breath. All that wondering she'd done about who she was, where she belonged. Was this the answer?

"And do you know *why* you are God's?" Pastor Cooper continued. "Do you know what you did to earn your place in his family?" Lydia pressed her lips together. She couldn't think of a single thing she might have done that would make God want her.

"Nothing," Pastor Cooper answered exuberantly. "You did nothing to earn your place in God's family. He loves you because he loves you. He loves you so much that he sent Jesus to pay the price for your sins. Loves you so much that he promises, 'Never will I leave you, never will I forsake you.' Loves you so much that he is with you wherever you go."

Wherever you go . . .

Lydia sniffled. It was getting ridiculous how many times she'd found herself in tears in church over the past two months. Somehow, God had used this time she'd spent in River Falls to crack the hard shell she'd built around her heart and call her back to him. But did that mean it was time for her to move on? Or that this was where she should stay? If she took Bryce Parker's offer, God would be with her. And if she stayed here in River Falls, he would be too.

Which didn't make it any easier to decide.

Chapter 40

"Why aren't you with Lydia?" Mama pushed her walker onto the porch.

Liam didn't look up from the landscape lighting he was installing in the flower bed. "She's over at Abe's." She'd gone right after church and been over there all day. "How's your headache?"

"I'm fine. Don't you usually go with her?" The rocker creaked as Mama lowered herself into it.

Liam glanced up to make sure she got settled okay. "I had things to do today." He'd put this project off much too long already.

"So you think avoiding her is the way to show her you love her?"

"Mama!" Liam dropped the spotlight he'd been holding, cringing as it hit the ground with a loud crack. "I don't love her. I—" But he choked on the denial. If he didn't love her, he sure didn't know what else to call it. "I don't want to influence her decision." He bent and picked up the light, examining it. He tried not to consider the possibility that she may have already decided.

"And influencing her would be a bad thing?" The persistent roll of the rocker against the wooden porch said Mama wasn't going to give up.

"It was for Molly," Liam said quietly. "I'm not going to ask Lydia to give up her big break." It was bad enough that he'd put his arm around her in church—but he'd only done that because she'd seemed to need the comfort.

"Some things are more important than a big break," Mama said. "If Molly were here, she'd tell you that."

Liam shook his head. Some things, yes. But what right did he have to convince Lydia he was one of them?

He ran a finger over the crack on the light. "I have to go buy a new one of these." He jogged up the steps, unwilling to look at Mama as he passed her rocker. But she touched his arm. "If things were the other way around, wouldn't you want to know how she felt before you made a decision like that?"

"I'll be back later, Mama." He dashed into the house, grabbed his keys, and escaped to his van. He started it up but just sat there. Memories of their first kiss in this van swirled with Mama's question. She wasn't wrong that he would want to know how Lydia felt if the situation were reversed.

His hand went to the keys.

But what if she said no? Or, maybe worse, what if she said yes—and then regretted it for the rest of their lives?

He let go of the keys and shifted into gear.

Although River Falls had a small hardware store, he'd gotten the light fixture from the larger store in Brampton. He used the hour-long drive there, the twenty minutes at the store, and the hour-long drive home to attempt to clear his head.

But by the time he returned to River Falls, his thoughts were cloudier than even the sky, which threatened to break open at any moment. His eyes caught on the steeple of Beautiful Savior, and he pulled abruptly into the parking lot. He still couldn't believe what Simeon had told him this morning, but when he'd tried to talk to his friend after the service, Simeon had waved him off with a reassurance that he was just tired and everything would be fine.

Liam parked the van, offering a silent prayer for Simeon and Abigail, then opened his door. The air was thick with the pending rain, but he made his way around the church, to the green space where the picnic had been held a few weeks ago. A stone bench sat among the flower beds back here, and Liam sat, running his hand over the rough but warm surface.

He pulled in a deep breath, somehow smelling Lydia's pomegranate scent instead of the flowers that surrounded him. He tipped his head toward the sky, watching the clouds pull and stretch and reshape themselves.

What do I do here, Lord? It felt like he'd been saying that prayer a lot lately.

Birds twittered, leaves rustled, but there was no answer.

He lowered his head, remembering the day Lydia had dunked him at the picnic, the night they'd gone bowling, their trip to Chattanooga. Lunches with her family, dinners with his, walking Buck. Every single moment bringing another spark of life to the heart she'd reawakened the very first night he'd met her.

Suddenly, everything was clear.

So what was he doing, sitting here?

Chapter 41

Lydia lifted her head from her notebook, staring down the driveway.

Still no Liam.

She'd taken up her post on the carriage house balcony the moment she'd gotten home from Abe's and found Liam's van missing. He had to come home at some point, didn't he?

She sent an apprehensive glance skyward. Hopefully it would be before the clouds let loose. She supposed she could retreat inside, but she didn't want to risk missing him.

She needed to tell him that she'd made her decision about Bryce Parker's offer—and the longer she waited, the more nerves multiplied in her belly.

She pressed a hand to it and directed her attention to the song she'd been working on to distract herself. It'd been inspired by Pastor Cooper's sermon this morning and had come to her so quickly it'd left her giddy.

She sang it quietly to herself, experimenting with a few melodies and settling on a folksy one.

Stumbling through the dark, I thought I was alone
Couldn't see you there, didn't know where you had gone
And then you whispered to me: "You don't need to see.
Only believe."
Because faith means walking with my eyes closed,
Faith means stepping into your heart,
Faith means knowing you will never leave, never forsake me,

Faith means I don't have to see
To believe.

She frowned as the last note trailed off. She wasn't quite satisfied with the chorus. Maybe if she—

The crunch of tires on the gravel pulled her attention off the paper. Her heart sprang up even faster than she did. It was beating at triple tempo by the time she reached the bottom of the carriage house steps.

Liam must have parked and gotten out of the van at record speed because he was right there waiting for her.

"Hi." His greeting was abrupt, his gaze intense and unsmiling, and her resolve wavered. Maybe she was making the wrong decision.

But she swallowed against the nerves blocking her vocal cords. "Liam, I have to—" She gasped as his lips met hers and his arms wrapped all the way around her.

Oh, she needed this. She slid her arms around his shoulders and let herself get lost in the kiss.

When they finally pulled apart, Liam's gaze was still intense, but it was softened by a smile. "Sorry I interrupted you. But there's something I have to tell you before you make a decision about Bryce Parker's offer." He slid a hand over her cheek and into her hair.

Lydia shook her head. She didn't need to hear what he was going to say. Because whatever it was, it wasn't going to change her mind. "I already—"

A loud blast of music made her jump. It took a second to figure out it was coming from her pocket. She pulled her phone out in exasperation. "Sorry. Benjamin was playing with my phone this afternoon. He said I—" Her eyes fell on the screen. "It's Mia."

Liam lifted his eyebrows. "I didn't realize you two talked on the phone."

"We don't." The only time Mia had ever called had been when she'd gotten that flat tire. What if she needed something again? "I'd better answer."

Liam nodded.

Lydia lifted the phone to her ear, letting her eyes go back to Liam, who stood close enough that she could have kissed him again.

Instead, she spoke into the phone. "Mia?"

"Lydia." It was more of a sob than a word and was followed by something indistinguishable.

Lydia grabbed Liam's arm. "Mia, what's wrong?"

Panic shot across Liam's face, and he reached for the phone, but Lydia shook her head. Mia was talking again, and it took every ounce of concentration to make out the words through her sobs.

"Mia, shh. It's okay. Did you say an accident?"

Liam tore the phone out of her hand. "Mia? It's Dad. Where are you? Are you all right?"

Lydia strained to hear, but the sounds coming from the other end of the phone were too garbled. She dug her fingers into Liam's arm. Her heart thudded painfully.

"She's okay," Liam murmured after a moment, the phone still pressed to his ear. "She rear-ended someone, but no one is hurt."

Lydia let out a hard breath. As long as Mia was all right, everything would be fine. Cars could be replaced.

"I'll be there in a minute," Liam said into the phone. "Where are you?"

At first there was no answer from the other end of the phone, and Lydia thought maybe the call had dropped.

"Mia?" Liam asked.

A muffled sound came through—and whatever Mia said caused Liam's face to grow darker than the storm clouds above them.

A raindrop splatted on Lydia's head.

"What do you mean, Nashville?" Liam growled into the phone.

Lydia inhaled so sharply the air burned her throat. Mia had *promised* she wouldn't go again.

"We'll talk about it when I get there," Liam barked. "Let me talk to the police officer."

Liam wandered away as he continued the conversation, apparently talking to the officer on the scene.

Although the rain had picked up to a hard sprinkle, Lydia lowered herself onto the steps, her legs wobbly.

A minute later, Liam hung up and jogged toward her, holding out her phone. "I have to go pick her up. She's in Nashville." Water drops scattered around him as he shook his head.

"I know. I'm so sorry, Liam." She blinked back her tears. She never should have presumed to know what was best for the girl. She should have let Liam decide that—because she was clearly not cut out to be any kind of parental figure.

"Hey." Liam caressed her cheek. "She's okay. There's nothing for you to be sorry about."

But Lydia shook her head. "I should have told you. But she promised me she wouldn't go again."

Liam froze, his face hardening. "What do you mean again? She's gone before? When?"

Lydia bit her lip, trying to remember. "The Fourth of July. And when she had that flat tire. I don't think there were any other times, but . . ." Who knew how many times the girl had lied to her?

"And you knew?" He looked like someone had just punched him in the gut. "You didn't tell me?"

Lydia took a step forward, reaching for his arm, but he dodged away.

"I didn't know until she got home," she tried to explain. "She begged me not to tell you. And she promised she wouldn't do it again."

Liam snorted.

"I know. It was stupid of me to believe her. I thought that maybe if I could earn her trust, get her to like me, maybe I could help her. I promise, Liam, I thought—"

"Maybe in your world everything is about getting likes and being popular." Liam's voice was icier than the rain that pounded them. "But this is real life, and parenting isn't a popularity contest."

"I—" She couldn't blink the tears away any longer, and they fell faster than the rain. Was that really what he thought of her?

Liam strode toward the van.

"Wait." She scrambled down the steps, wincing as the sharp gravel stabbed into her bare feet. "Let me come with you. It's a long drive, and—"

"I think you've done enough." Liam jumped into the vehicle and slammed his door.

Lydia watched as the van disappeared into the rain, its wheels kicking her heart out from underneath them.

It turned out she'd been right to think Liam could break her heart even worse than Dallas had.

At least this time she had one thing going for her—it hadn't happened in front of the whole world.

That, and she hadn't given Bryce Parker her decision yet. She'd wanted Liam to be the first to know.

Thankfully, it wasn't too late to change her mind.

Chapter 42

Liam clutched the steering wheel in a death grip, but his hands wouldn't stop shaking. Sniffles came from the passenger seat, where Mia had folded herself into a little ball in the dark.

He couldn't decide if he was more relieved that she was okay, angry that she'd gone to Nashville without permission, or disgusted with himself for the way he'd treated Lydia.

It wasn't her job to know where his daughter was—it was his. And that was the part that killed him. He hadn't had a clue—he'd taken Mia's word for it that she was working. If something had happened to her . . .

He scrubbed a hand over his rough face, then checked the time. Midnight. He did a mental calculation. They were about an hour from River Falls. Maybe Lydia would still be awake when they got home.

And if she wasn't, maybe he'd wake her up and apologize and tell her what he'd been planning to say before the call from Mia had interrupted.

He glanced at his daughter again, though it was too dark to make out more than her profile. When he'd first gotten to the precinct, where the officer had agreed to let her wait for him, Liam hadn't been able to put two words together as she'd fallen into his arms. All he could do was hold her and thank God she was okay.

But he couldn't pretend it hadn't happened. He had to talk to her—discipline her—even if it was unpleasant for both of them. Being a parent wasn't an optional battle.

Give me wisdom, Lord, he prayed silently, then said out loud, "We have to talk about this."

Mia didn't say anything, but she sniffled again.

"I don't understand what you were thinking. You could have been hurt or—" He couldn't give voice to his worst nightmare. "And I wouldn't have known where you were."

"I know." Mia's voice was subdued, her usual fiery defensiveness gone. "I promise I'll never do it again."

"That's what you told Lydia." He still couldn't believe Lydia had kept Mia's behavior a secret, but he'd had a long enough drive to think about why she'd done it, and he thought he understood, even if he didn't necessarily agree with it.

"She told you." Mia didn't sound surprised.

"I can't believe you put her in that position, Mia. She just wanted to be there for you."

"I know." Mia's head was turned away from him, but the full weight of her sigh reached him. "I'm sorry. For all of it."

"I—" Liam was at a loss. Was this a ploy to get out of punishment? "I'm glad you're sorry. But there will be no driving until further notice. Your paychecks will be going toward replacing the car. You'll go to work and school and nowhere else. It's going to take a long time to earn back my trust."

"Okay." Mia didn't put up a fight. "Anything else?"

Liam considered his options. "Yeah. I forgive you."

"Really?" Mia turned to him. "Shouldn't you yell at me some more first?"

Liam chuckled. "Your mother always used to say that grace went a lot farther than a lecture."

"I miss her," Mia whispered, and Liam's heart broke for her all over again. Though he'd tried to be everything to her over the years, he knew he had fallen far short of what Molly could have given her. He had to admit that lately he'd been hoping maybe Mia and Lydia could have that kind of relationship someday.

"Hey, Dad?" Mia cut into his thoughts.

"Yeah, kiddo?"

"I'm sorry I said I wished you had died instead of Mom." She sniffed. "I don't wish that. I wish neither of you had died."

Liam let out a long breath. "I know, kiddo. Me too." He squeezed her arm, and she leaned over and rested her head on his shoulder.

His heart lifted as she drifted off to sleep. He had no delusions that things between them would suddenly be perfect. But at least they'd made a start.

Now he could only hope that things would go as well with Lydia.

Chapter 43

Lydia eyed her suitcase, already heaped full. Her eyes went to the mess of clothes still scattered on the bed. She'd acquired several new out-fits—mostly t-shirts and shorts—on shopping trips with Ava and Ireland since she'd arrived in River Falls. And then there were all the birthday presents from her family. There was no way it was all going to fit.

She was pretty sure she had a grocery bag or two in the kitchen she could use. As she walked, she pulled her phone out of her pocket. She'd been texting back and forth all night with Benjamin about her decision to accept Bryce Parker's offer. Her brother seemed excited for her—and he'd made her promise to get him tickets—but he'd spent the past hour trying to convince her to stay long enough for them to throw a goodbye party for her.

What if I promise to make you the world's biggest cake? his latest text read. *Then will you stay for a party?*

Lydia laughed. *Tempting. But I can't.*

Technically, she could. Bryce wouldn't be in Nashville for another two weeks, so she had some time before she had to go. But she couldn't stay here any longer. Not after tonight.

You can make me a cake when you come to visit me in Nashville, she added.

Like you'll have time for me, with Liam coming to visit you every weekend. Benjamin's reply sank to the bottom of Lydia's stomach. She clicked her screen off and shoved her phone back in her pocket.

Benjamin wouldn't have to worry about competing with Liam for her time. Liam had made it perfectly clear earlier that he was done with her.

She scrubbed her palms over her cheeks to wipe away a fresh batch of tears and went to grab the bags.

She was supposed to be happy. This was the biggest opportunity of her life. Everything she'd been working for. It was better not to have Liam around to complicate things. Now she could give her all to her music. Make Mama and Daddy proud. Live up to their legacy.

She returned to the bedroom and stuffed things willy-nilly into the bags. She needed to get this done and get some sleep so she could get an early start on the road—maybe even before Liam woke in the morning.

She had one bag filled and the other half-full when a loud knock made her jump. She dropped the bag on the bed and crept to peek around the curtain. Her heart leapt straight to her throat as she spotted Liam's van. She hadn't heard him drive up.

She rushed for the door. As much as she dreaded seeing Liam, she needed to know that Mia was okay. She'd ask about the girl, tell Liam her decision, and say goodbye.

That word nearly kept her from opening the door, but she made herself turn the knob. Mia stood in front of Liam, looking disheveled and small—but in one piece. Lydia dove forward and pulled her into a fierce hug. "You're okay."

Mia's thin frame stiffened, but then she nodded against Lydia's shoulder and reached around her to return the hug.

After a moment, Liam cleared his throat.

Right. He probably didn't want her anywhere near his daughter right now. Or ever. If anything had happened to Mia, it would have been all Lydia's fault.

But Liam's eyes were on Mia, who toed the worn wood of the carriage house balcony.

"I'm sorry." Mia met her eyes, and Lydia could read the sincerity there. "I shouldn't have asked you to lie for me."

"Oh." Lydia looked from Mia to Liam. He stood stiff, with his arms crossed, his expression impossible to read in the dark. Had he told Mia to make the apology, or had that been her own choice?

"All right," Liam said to his daughter. "Go home and go to bed."

Mia didn't turn away. "I should have listened to you." Then she trod down the steps, Lydia and Liam both watching until she reached the bottom.

"Can we talk?" Liam asked.

Lydia nodded without looking at him. She stepped out onto the balcony, pulling the carriage house door closed behind her. The night was sticky but cool, and she shivered.

"Are you cold? I think I still have my shirt in my van."

Lydia closed her eyes, remembering the warmth of that shirt against her skin. "I'm fine."

Liam stepped closer, but she couldn't handle his nearness. Not if she was going to keep her resolve.

She led him to the rattan chairs on the other end of the balcony. But instead of sitting when she did, Liam squatted in front of her chair.

"Lydia, I'm sorry."

She shook her head. "There's nothing for you to be sorry about. You were right. I should have told you."

"I understand why you didn't. I know you care about Mia. It's one of the things—" He touched her arm, and she could feel the electricity traveling nerve by nerve to her heart.

It jolted her into action. She sprang from the seat, nearly knocking him over. "Apology accepted."

She took off across the balcony toward the carriage house door. *You have to tell him.*

But she couldn't. Not right now. Not with the way he had just looked at her.

Maybe she could leave him a note.

"Wait, Lydia." He must have recovered his balance quickly because his footsteps were right behind her. "There's something I need to tell you. Before you decide about Bryce Parker's offer."

Lydia stopped. She couldn't avoid it now.

She turned, not meeting his eyes. "That's what I was going to tell you earlier." She felt numb, disembodied, like she was walking in the dark all over again. But she made herself continue. "I already made my decision. I accepted the offer."

Please stay, Lydia. What would she do if he said that?

But he didn't say anything, though the sharp in and out of his breath punctured the night air.

She gestured toward the carriage house. "I'd better finish packing. I'm leaving in the morning."

"Already?" His voice had gone flat, lifeless, and for half a second, Lydia considered saying no, of course she wasn't leaving tomorrow. She wasn't leaving ever.

But clearly Liam didn't have a problem with her going. Otherwise, he'd try to stop her.

She pressed her hands to her sides, feeling abandoned all over again, even though she was the one doing the leaving.

"Yeah." She swallowed the storm cloud of tears growing in her throat. "Goodbye, Liam." She opened the carriage house door and dove inside before the cloud could break.

Chapter 44

Liam stared at the carriage house door Lydia had just closed. It needed a new coat of paint. He'd thought maybe it was a project he and Lydia could work on together, but . . .

Don't be an idiot. Open that door back up and tell her you love her.

But he couldn't. He'd already kept one woman from living her dreams. He couldn't do that to another.

He felt about a hundred years older as he dragged himself down the steps and across the yard. Inside, a light glowed from the kitchen, and he moved to turn it off. But Mia was at the table, playing absently with a water bottle.

"Hey. I thought you went to bed," he said. She had to be as exhausted as he was.

She shrugged. "I wanted to find out how it went with Lydia."

Liam sighed and sat down heavily, dropping his face into his hands. "She's taking Bryce Parker's offer. She leaves tomorrow."

"How do you feel about that?"

Liam snorted. "You've been spending too much time with Uncle Simeon." It was the name Mia had always called his best friend. Liam tried not to think about the fact that Simeon could have been Mia's uncle for real if Liam had married Lydia someday.

"Enough time to know you're avoiding the question." Mia smirked at him.

"I'm happy for her," Liam said finally. "This is her dream. I'm not going to get in the way of that like I did to—" He caught himself just in time. He'd always been careful not to talk about Molly's dream of playing for the Boston Symphony Orchestra. He didn't want Mia to feel the same guilt he did.

But Mia raised an eyebrow. "To Mom?"

Reluctantly, Liam nodded. Maybe Mia was old enough to know.

"That's really what you think?" Mia pushed her chair back. "Wait here. There's something you need to see."

She disappeared from the room, and Liam bowed his head. He couldn't possibly have screwed this day up more if he'd tried.

Mia returned a few minutes later, carrying a tattered shoebox. She set it on the table and opened it with care, as if it held precious jewels. After a few seconds of rummaging, she passed him a well-worn piece of paper.

"What's this?" But as his eyes fell on the handwriting, he knew.

He drew in a sharp breath. Molly had given him a letter like this too—one he could rarely bring himself to pull out and reread.

"Mia, I—"

"Just read it." Mia gathered up her box. "Goodnight, Dad." She disappeared from the room, leaving him staring at Molly's sloping handwriting.

He let out a shaky breath as he carefully unfolded the paper, running a finger over the words. It had been seven years since he'd seen his wife, and yet, right now, he could almost imagine her standing in front of him.

My dearest Mia,

I know you're young and this is a lot to understand, but I also know that you'll grow into a lovely young lady. As you reread this letter over the years, there are three things I want you to always remember:

1) Jesus loves you. More even than your daddy and I do, which feels impossible because we love you so much, but it's true.

2) Listen to your daddy. There may be times when you don't see eye-to-eye. Times you don't understand him or he doesn't understand you. But in the end, there is no one in this world who will love and care for you more.

Liam looked up with a laugh, even as his vision blurred. Somehow Molly had known what the future held better than he had. He let his eyes drop back to the paper, wondering what else Molly had known that he hadn't yet figured out.

3) Always reach for your dreams, whatever they are. My prayer for you is that your dreams make you as happy as mine made me. You and your daddy, Mia—you are my dreams come true.

With all my love and kisses,

Mama

With a shaky hand, Liam wiped his eyes and refolded the letter. If he and Mia had been Molly's dream, maybe they could be Lydia's too.

Chapter 45

Lydia had never had such a terrible headache in her life.

She couldn't have slept more than five minutes last night, and her swollen eyes, red nose, and raw cheeks served as evidence enough of what she'd done instead.

She considered climbing back into bed and giving sleep one more chance before her three-hour drive. But she knew it would be useless.

Besides, she could sleep when she got to Nashville.

When she got home.

But the word no longer felt like it applied to that city. River Falls had become home.

She moved to the door. It might take time to stop thinking of River Falls as home, but eventually she would. A sick feeling gathered in her stomach, but she ignored it.

She'd already loaded her bags in the car and placed the carriage house keys on the kitchen table, along with a copy of the song Liam had been waiting for the second verse of. Maybe it was silly, leaving it, but for some reason, she felt better knowing he'd have it. Sort of like an apology and a wish for what could have been.

All that was left to do was leave.

The hardest part.

She let her eyes roam the cozy space she'd come to love one more time, then pushed the door open. She stepped through and pulled it closed quickly, before she could change her mind.

She was doing the right thing.

Better a little regret now than a lifetime of pain later when things with Liam inevitably ended.

Tears pooled again, but she sniffed them back and pushed her feet to the stairs.

She was halfway down them before she noticed the shadow. Her head jerked up at the same time her heart stopped.

"Liam, what—" But he took the steps two at a time, until he was standing right in front of her. And then his arms were around her and his lips were pressed to hers.

She should pull away, should tell him he was only making things more difficult—but she couldn't. Her arms went to his shoulders, around his neck, pulling him closer, a sharp slice of hope cutting through her.

When he finally let go, looking at her but not saying anything, the hope that had been building in her gave way to doubt. "What are you doing? I have to go."

"I know," he murmured. "But there's something I've been trying to tell you. And I couldn't let you go without saying it." He took both of her hands in his.

Joy and terror and longing clanged against her chest, and Liam's smile unraveled her. But she couldn't let him say it. It would make this impossible. "Liam, don't—"

But his finger came to her lips. "I love you."

She gulped and tried to take a step backward, but the stairs got in the way. "Liam, you can't—"

But instead of letting her go, he pulled her closer. "I have to. I love you. After Molly, my heart felt dead. . . . But you—" His smile strengthened. "You brought it back to life. And it's one hundred percent yours. I love you like . . . like electricity loves metal."

A soft laugh chased her tears away.

Liam wiped her cheek. "Sorry. I know it's not a good comparison, but—"

She shook her head. "It's actually really poetic."

"Good." Liam's Adam's apple bobbed. "Because I think you feel the same."

She tried to shake her head, tried to swallow, tried to move. But she was paralyzed.

She couldn't let herself think about loving him. Because if she loved him . . .

"Don't be afraid," Liam whispered.

But how could she not be afraid? When everyone she'd ever loved had left her in one way or another?

"I'm not asking you to give up your dreams." Liam tugged her the rest of the way to him and wrapped her in his arms, kissing the top of her head. "I'm asking you to make us part of them. Whether you go on this tour or don't go on this tour, it doesn't change anything. I'll be here waiting for you. I'll fly around the world to visit you. Whatever you want. I'm not going anywhere."

His fingers went to her chin, lifting her head so that she could see every ounce of truth in his eyes. "I love you," he repeated.

And suddenly she wasn't afraid anymore.

"I love you too." The words burst from her like a song. She barely had time to register his gigantic smile before his lips came to hers. She didn't know how she hadn't realized it sooner.

It didn't matter what she did next, where she went. Because when she was with Liam, she was home.

Epilogue

"I missed you." Liam wrapped his arm around Lydia's shoulder, pulling her closer to him as they sat on the carriage house stairs. The warmth of the early spring evening surrounded them, and he inhaled a deep breath of her pomegranate shampoo, its scent sending waves of contentment over him. The same contentment he'd felt every day of the past eight months with her.

"I was only gone for two days." Lydia rested her hand on his knee, her head warm on his shoulder.

"It was two days too long." He pressed his lips to her forehead.

"Mmm. I'm glad to be back." Lydia slipped her fingers between his.

"Why's that?" he teased.

"Mia and I have a date to go prom dress shopping tomorrow, remember?" she teased back, smiling up at him.

"I don't know why you're encouraging her to go to that dance," he grumbled, though he couldn't hold his grumpy expression for long. In reality, nothing made his heart happier than the way Lydia and Mia had bonded.

Lydia elbowed his side. "You're not fooling me. You know you like Cole."

Liam grunted. He didn't love the idea that his little girl was dating anyone, though he supposed if she had to, he was happy it was Cole. The two had even started attending Pastor Cooper's teen Bible study together,

248

and Liam was finally certain that bringing Mia to River Falls had been the right move.

He hoped he wasn't the only one who thought River Falls was the perfect place.

Lydia leaned into him. "How's Simeon?"

Liam sighed. He and Simeon had gone golfing yesterday, and he'd hoped to finally get something real out of his friend. "For a counselor, that guy sure doesn't like to talk about his feelings. According to him, everything is fine."

"That's what Abigail said last time I talked to her too."

"I guess we'll have to take them at their word." Liam nuzzled his face into her hair again. "So you're happy with how things went in Nashville?"

She nodded against him. "Really happy. I think it's going to be a decent album."

Liam snorted. "Decent? It's going to be fabulous."

After declining the tour with Bryce Parker, Lydia had signed with a small record label that gave her the level of creative control she'd been looking for. Her first album had dropped a month ago, and already her song "Love A Mess Like Me" was all over the radio. Her open and real posts on social media about discovering that God loved her even through the mess she was had gone viral as well, and Liam was so proud of the way she was using her new platform to reach others with God's love.

"While I was there, I met with a real estate agent." She slid her finger under her bracelet, playing with the charm he'd given her for her birthday. "I think it might be time to sell Mama and Daddy's house—if you don't mind if I crash in your carriage house indefinitely."

"I don't know about indefinitely," Liam teased. "I sort of had other plans."

"Oh yeah?" Lydia tilted her face up, offering her lips to him with a smile. "And what are those?"

Liam let his lips linger on hers, then shifted to unwrap his arm from around her. "Let me show you."

He stood, digging for the box he'd tucked into his pocket, then eyed the steps. He hadn't thought this through.

It took a moment to balance himself on one knee on the staircase, and when he'd finally managed to get into position, he looked up to find Lydia already in tears.

"I didn't say anything yet," he joked, running a hand over her wet cheek. Moisture sprang to his own eyes.

"Lydia—" He wrapped his hand around hers. "When you came running into my life that night in Nashville, I thought you were amazing and beautiful and—"

"Crazy," Lydia filled in with a laugh as she sniffled.

"Maybe a little crazy," he conceded. "But I had no idea how you would change my life. Restart my heart. I love you, Lydia. And I don't want you to stay in the carriage house indefinitely. I want you to be my wife and live with me and make a home with me. Lydia St. Peter, will—"

"Yes."

"Yes?" Liam's heart jumped straight to the stratosphere.

"Sorry." Lydia clapped a hand over her mouth. "I didn't mean to interrupt you. I just couldn't wait to give you my answer. Which is yes. Assuming you were going to ask what I think you were going to ask."

Liam chuckled. "Would your answer still be yes if I said I was going to ask you to marry me?"

"The most definite yes I've ever said in my life."

"In that case—" Liam opened the ring box clutched in his hand. "You'd better put this on." He slipped the ring onto her finger, then gathered her into his arms.

He brought his lips to hers, murmuring, "Welcome home."

Thanks for reading SONGS OF HOME! I hope you loved Lydia and Liam's story! Catch up with them and the whole Calvano family in the next River Falls book, MEMORIES OF THE HEART, where Simeon will fight to keep his marriage with Abigail alive. You'll also get to attend Lydia and Liam's wedding!

Also, be sure to sign up for my newsletter to get Asher and Ireland's story, REFLECTIONS OF LOVE, as a free gift.

Visit https://www.valeriembodden.com/freebook or use the QR code below to sign up.

A preview of *Memories of the Heart* (River Falls book 3)

Chapter 1

Abigail made sure to keep her eyes closed lightly—not scrunched—and her breathing deep and even as she heard Simeon drop his toothbrush back into the holder. She knew his routine well. Next he'd spritz on a dash of the light, earthy wild sage cologne she loved so much, pat the spot where his hair stuck up in a perpetual cowlick on the right side of his head, then reappear in the bedroom to say goodbye to her before heading off to work.

Only she wouldn't say it back.

Because she was still sleeping.

The soft swish of the cologne spray was followed two beats later by the bathroom door creaking open. Then a sigh, deep and long, that tore at Abigail's insides. It was her fault, that sigh.

All of it was her fault.

Simeon's footsteps shuffled across the hardwood floor to her side of the bed.

Abigail let out a slow, even breath, careful not to let her eyelids flutter as Simeon brushed a lock of hair off her forehead. His scent drifted over her as his lips pressed to her skin, his breath breezing across her cheek with a whispered, "I love you."

She forced herself to inhale, slow and even, eyes still closed, as he pulled away. It was a moment before she heard his footsteps retreat and the bedroom door click softly closed.

A tear trickled slowly from the corner of her eye, following the line of her nose until it reached her lips. Still she didn't open her eyes. Getting out of bed would be too much work.

She crunched the pillow under her head, scooting toward Simeon's side of the bed to soak up any warmth he may have left behind. But it had grown cold.

The sound of Simeon moving around the kitchen drifted up the stairs, and Abigail let herself remember the days when she used to get up with him, when they'd laugh as they got in each other's way in the small bathroom, when they'd linger over a kiss or two in the kitchen, even if it made them late for work.

It hadn't been that long ago. They hadn't even been married for five years yet.

So why did it feel like a lifetime stood between them?

You know why.

Abigail punched at the pillow as the front door opened and closed, its sound echoing up the stairs even though Simeon hadn't slammed it—he would never slam it. His dress shoes clicked across the driveway, followed by the rumble of his SUV's engine. She pictured him buckling his seatbelt, adjusting the mirror—he did it every time even though no one else drove the vehicle—and turning down the volume of the radio so he could use his short morning drive time for prayer. She wondered briefly if those prayers included her.

She had tried to work up the energy for her own prayers, but her mind was one big blank when she tried to think about God these days. Well, not so much a blank as cluttered with all the lies and accusations and blame. With all the things she'd done wrong. All the lies she'd told. All the reasons she deserved this punishment he was putting her through.

With a groan, she pressed her fists to her eyes, then opened them. The only thing harder than getting up was lying here and letting her thoughts continue down this path. She peeled herself off her pillow and ran a hand through her tangled hair. Though it was May, the chill of the hardwood bit at her feet as she dragged herself to the bathroom.

The scent of Simeon's cologne still lingered in the air, and she sucked in a big breath of it. If she closed her eyes, she could probably imagine his arms around her, imagine burying her nose in his shirt and drowning in the comfort of his embrace.

She shook her head and turned on the shower, cranking the temperature to maximum. Steam quickly filled the room, blocking her view of the mirror. Good. She peeled off the sweats she'd slept in, trying hard to avoid looking at the body that had let her down so many times. It didn't even seem to belong to her anymore, soft and spongy in places that used to be firm and toned. A mom body. Only she wasn't a mom.

With a sigh, she stepped into the shower, wincing as the scalding water stabbed her shoulders. But even the heat couldn't drive the thoughts away.

She flipped the water to cold, showered quickly, pulled on a new pair of sweatpants and a t-shirt, and brushed her teeth, then headed for the kitchen. Simeon had left her favorite mug next to the full coffee carafe. A bright yellow sticky note clung to the front of the mug, and curiosity pulled Abigail forward to read it.

I'll be home early for our doctor appointment. I love you.

She ran her fingers over the letters. *I love you.* She'd always teased Simeon that his handwriting was way too neat to be a doctor. To which he'd always reminded her that he wasn't a *doctor*, he was a counselor.

It was one of the things that had drawn her to him. He'd been so easy to talk to.

And all you told him was lies.

Abigail set the note down, the *I love you* still seared against her fingertips, joined by the prickle of guilt. She loved him too. But she was starting to wonder if that was enough. He was such a good man. And she was . . . not who he thought she was. She'd thought she could leave that behind. That she could be someone new. But instead she'd only dragged him into her mess.

She poured herself a cup of coffee and moved to the kitchen table, which overlooked the spacious backyard. The outdoor space was the whole reason they'd bought this house. There was supposed to be a tire swing back there by now. And a sand box. And maybe even a tree house. Instead, it was immaculate. And empty. There was no reason to have all those things when there were no children to use them.

Chapter 2

Simeon tipped his coffee cup back, grimacing as the lukewarm liquid coated his tongue. With a sigh, he plunked the mug on the corner of his desk, resisting the urge to venture into the small reception area to refill it. He'd already had three cups, and he needed to save some for his clients. He glanced at the time on his computer screen. Eleven o'clock. Three more hours until Abigail's doctor appointment. He scrubbed a hand down his freshly shaved cheek, wondering if he should call to make sure she'd gotten out of bed.

Not that she'd been sleeping when he'd left. They'd been married long enough that he could tell the difference between her fake sleep, with its deep, even breaths, and her real sleep, with its uneven, soft half-snores. But he hadn't had the energy to call her out. And even if he had, it wouldn't have changed anything. She would have said everything was fine, just as she always did, then rolled over and gone back to sleep for real.

He tried not to take it personally. It was the depression. Diagnosing it wasn't the problem. Neither was discerning the cause. The losses they'd experienced over the last two years would leave anyone reeling.

No, the problem was that she wouldn't let him—or anyone else—help her.

So he went on, day after day, acting like he knew exactly how to help other people sort out their lives, how to help couples renew their marriages, when his own was unraveling. It felt like there were only a few stitches left. And once those let go, he wasn't sure there'd be any way to mend their relationship.

He picked up the framed photo of the two of them in Ecuador that adorned his desk, rubbing at a smudge that marred the glass over Abigail's smile. Maybe they'd rushed into things too quickly. He certainly hadn't planned to meet anyone on that mission trip—let alone propose marriage to her. But she'd upturned all his carefully laid plans with that smile. And he'd known almost immediately that it was a smile he wanted to wake up to every day for the rest of his life.

He tried to remember the last time he'd seen it—a real, genuine smile—rather than the strained "everything's fine" smile she'd put on for months now. Maybe his own certainty that they were right for each other hadn't been enough. Maybe he should have given her more time

. . .

A bell jingled as the exterior door out in the waiting area opened, and Simeon set the picture down, giving a quick glance at his schedule. Wendy Storm. Good. He needed a relatively "easy" client right now, and Wendy was always more than willing to talk—and eager to hear his suggestions and report on her progress. He only wished he could have helped her and her husband Jeff more—but Simeon had only met with them a few times before Jeff had decided he'd had enough and left her. The day she'd walked into his office alone, crying, Simeon had been devastated. It wasn't his first failure as a counselor, but he'd really thought they'd been making progress.

Wendy's depression after the divorce had been hard, but she'd been willing to seek help. Willing to talk. Willing to do all the things Abigail refused to do.

Simeon shook his head and closed the file of notes he'd been making. That wasn't fair. It wasn't that Abigail refused. It was that she was so far down, she couldn't see the way out. That was what he needed to help her with—no matter how long it took. He wouldn't give up on her.

Simeon blew out a breath and tried to refocus his attention on the client he was about to counsel. He closed his eyes and bowed his head to pray as he did before every session. *Dear Lord, Give me wisdom and guidance as I counsel Wendy. Help her to see that even when the love of people fails, your love never will. Help my love for my wife never to fail. Help me figure out how to reach her, Lord.* He cut himself off. This prayer was supposed to be for Wendy. *Help Wendy continue to heal, Lord. Amen.*

Simeon opened his eyes and got up slowly, still working to let go of thoughts of Abigail. Being a counselor meant he had to put his personal life aside, even when it was hard.

He opened the door that led from his office to the small waiting area.

"Good morning." Wendy jumped up from one of the cozy armchairs Abigail had helped him pick out a few years ago to replace the stiff chairs he'd had before.

"It's a beautiful day, isn't it?" Wendy smiled broadly.

"I— Uh." Simeon glanced toward the large windows that looked over the small parking lot and the Serenity River beyond it. He hadn't even noticed the weather when he left home this morning, but the sky was a bright, cloudless blue, the mountains that skirted the town carpeted in the green of late spring. "Yes, it is. Come on in."

He stood aside to let her pass through the doorway into his office, then followed her to the leather chairs arranged around a small coffee table. The furniture made the space feel more like a living room than an office. That was Abigail's doing too.

Wendy dropped into what had become "her" chair, and Simeon sat across from her.

"So, how are you today?" Wendy slid off her shoes and folded her feet under her.

Simeon laughed. "I think that's supposed to be my question to you."

"Who asks you then?" Wendy peered shrewdly at him.

Simeon swallowed. It used to be Abigail. But it had been a long time since she had asked anything about him—how was work, how was he. None of that seemed to matter to her anymore.

"I'm fine, thanks," he answered Wendy's first question, skipping the second.

He was always fine. That was his job. To be fine so he could help others who weren't fine. "And how are you doing?"

"Really great." Wendy leaned forward, as if the momentum of her happiness might pull her out of her chair. "You know that job I applied for? At Zelensky and Baker? I got it!"

"That's great." Simeon felt his own lips lift into a smile. He spent so much time listening to clients' troubles that it made him extra joyful when he had cause to celebrate good news with them. "Congratulations."

"Thanks." Wendy's cheeks flushed. "And that's not my only good news."

"No? What else?"

"I'm in love." Wendy pressed her palms together in front of her heart.

Simeon had years of practice in not registering surprise or skepticism at clients' revelations. And this certainly wasn't the wildest he'd ever heard.

But it still tested his ability to retain a neutral expression. "That's rather sudden, don't you think?" he asked.

Wendy shook her head. "Actually, I think it's been coming on for a long time now. I was just too caught up in everything with Jeff to recognize it at first. But he was there for me through all of that, and now—" She pressed a hand to her heart. "I think I'm finally ready."

Simeon considered his next words. He didn't want to put a damper on her enthusiasm, and yet he had a responsibility to make sure she wasn't being taken advantage of. "You said he was there for you through the divorce. You were very vulnerable during that time. Is there a chance he took advantage of that fact?"

Wendy shook her head emphatically. "It's not like that. He has no idea I feel this way. I didn't even realize it myself until I was journaling like you told me to. I was kind of daydreaming, I guess, about the ideal man, and it hit me—" She slapped herself on the forehead. "I already know him."

"Okay. I feel like there are a few things to unpack there." Simeon made a quick list in his head.

"I knew you would." Wendy's smile lit up her whole face. Maybe she really was in love.

Simeon thought wistfully of Abigail's smile but pushed the image out. This wasn't about him and his wife.

"Let's start with this." He directed his attention back to Wendy. "What were some of the things you wrote about this ideal man you're looking for?" Simeon could only hope her answer wouldn't be too wildly unrealistic.

"Well, a good listener. Someone who really hears me, you know? Who doesn't just nod and smile when I talk."

Simeon found himself nodding with relief. Those were realistic expectations. "And you feel like this guy is a good listener?"

"Oh yes," Wendy gushed. "We've talked for *hours*, and he never tires of listening to me. And I can tell he really cares what I think."

You're a really good listener, do you know that? Abigail had said that to Simeon moments before their first kiss.

He forced his thoughts back to the present. "How can you tell that?" he asked Wendy.

She tapped her lip, then leaned forward. "He asks questions, like he wants to understand me better. And he remembers what I say, even weeks later."

"That's good. But you said he doesn't know how you feel?" Simeon asked carefully. The last thing Wendy needed was to have her heart broken by some guy who didn't reciprocate her feelings.

"No." Wendy bit her lip. "Not yet."

"So you're thinking about telling him?"

Wendy shrugged, looking uncertain. "Do you think I should?"

Simeon hesitated. This wasn't a matter of right or wrong, so he couldn't really give her a yes or no answer. What he could do, though, was give her some things to consider.

"Do you think he reciprocates your feelings?"

Wendy nodded slowly. "I think he might."

"And if he doesn't?" Simeon asked gently. "Are you ready to deal with that?"

Wendy's head stopped bobbing. "I'm not sure," she said quietly. "I don't want him to hate me."

"I'm sure he wouldn't hate you," Simeon reassured her. "But it might change your relationship. You need to be prepared for that."

"So you don't think I should tell him?" Wendy's face fell.

"I'm not saying that." Simeon considered how to phrase it. "I'm saying there's a risk. But some things are worth the risk." He happened to believe love was one of them. After all, that was how he'd ended up proposing to Abigail after only three months.

But then, given the current state of their relationship, maybe that wasn't the best example. "It's just something to think about," he told Wendy. "Before you move forward."

Wendy chewed her lip. "Okay, I'll think about it."

"Good." Their talk turned to other topics Wendy had journaled about, including her childhood trauma in the foster care system. Every time she talked about it, Simeon wondered if this was what Abigail's experience in the system had been like too. But unlike Wendy, who talked about it openly, Abigail had said she'd rather forget the past. But maybe, if he—

"So anyway—"

Simeon startled as he realized he had no idea what Wendy had just said. How long had he tuned her out?

"I think maybe that's why I was drawn to Jeff, don't you?" Wendy continued.

"It could be," Simeon answered hesitantly.

"You don't think so?" Wendy leaned forward.

Simeon kicked himself. He couldn't agree or disagree with something he hadn't heard—but he couldn't really explain to Wendy that he hadn't been listening to her.

"There are probably a lot of reasons." Simeon tried to cover his lapse. "It's rarely one simple answer." He glanced at the clock on the wall behind her. "Oops. It looks like we went over our time."

Wendy giggled. "That's nothing new."

"True." Simeon stood and waited for her to do the same.

He escorted her toward the door, but halfway there, she stopped and turned toward him so abruptly that he nearly plowed her over. She grabbed his arm to steady herself.

"Sorry." Though she was wearing heels, she came up only to his chin, and she tipped her head back to meet his eyes. "Thank you."

"You're welcome."

"No, I mean, for everything. For listening. For not laughing me out of here when I said I was in love. I know it sounds crazy, but . . ."

"It's not crazy." Simeon subtly maneuvered his arm out from under her hand and started toward the door again. "I just want you to be careful, that's all. So you don't end up getting hurt."

"That's sweet of you."

Simeon shrugged uncomfortably. He hadn't said it to be sweet; this was his *job*.

"Can I ask you one more favor?" Wendy paused in the doorway to the waiting area. "Would you pray for me?"

"I always do." Simeon opened the office door and ushered her out.

"Thank you," she said with another wide smile. "I always feel so much better after talking to you."

Simeon waited until she was outside to close his office door. He let out a breath and rubbed at his temples. He was fortunate Wendy hadn't noticed how much his mind had wandered during their session. He had better get it together before his next client showed up. It was his job to help them with their problems. Regardless of his own.

KEEP READING MEMORIES OF THE HEART

Also By Valerie M. Bodden

More River Falls Books

While the books in the River Falls series are linked, each is a complete romance featuring a different couple.
Pieces of Forever (Joseph & Ava)
Songs of Home (Lydia & Liam)
Memories of the Heart (Simeon & Abigail)
Whispers of Truth (Benjamin & Summer)
Promises of Mercy (Judah & Faith)

River Falls Christmas Romances

Wondering about some of the side characters in River Falls who aren't members of the Calvano family? Join them as they get their own happily-ever-afters in the River Falls Christmas Romances.
Christmas of Joy (Madison & Luke)

VALERIE M. BODDEN

The Hope Springs Series

While the books in the Hope Springs series are linked, each is a complete romance featuring a different couple.

Not Until Forever (Sophie & Spencer)
Not Until This Moment (Jared & Peyton)
Not Until You (Nate & Violet)
Not Until Us (Dan & Jade)
Not Until Christmas Morning (Leah & Austin)
Not Until This Day (Tyler & Isabel)
Not Until Someday (Grace & Levi)
Not Until Now (Cam & Kayla)
Not Until Then (Bethany & James)
Not Until The End (Emma & Owen)

Want to know when my next book releases?

You can follow me on Amazon to be the first to know when my next book releases! Just visit amazon.com/author/valeriembodden and click the follow button.

Acknowledgements

As this book hits shelves (and Kindles), our family has been in our new home in Texas for nine months, more than a thousand miles from our family and everything we've ever known. But the funny thing is, I first started writing this book before the thought of Texas was even a glimmer in our eyes. But God already knew then that I was going to need that reminder that belonging isn't a matter of *where* we are, it's a matter of *who* we belong to—the One who calls us his own. I am so grateful to him, first of all, for that incredible gift and the promise it carries that he will bring us to be with him one day. But also for promising to be with us on the journey through this world, wherever we go. To him be all glory and praise!

I am also so very thankful for the partners he's given me on this journey, my incredible husband and our four children. What an adventure we've been on together, and I wouldn't choose to go on it with anyone else. Wherever y'all are (I told you we moved to Texas!), that's where home is for me. And though the miles separate us now, I am also grateful for my parents, sister, in-laws, and extended family and friends who continue to show their love and support as if we were right there next to them.

And speaking of support, I couldn't do this without the support of my incredible advance reader team. Special thanks to: Vickie, Debra Payne, Sharon, Paula Hurdle, Kathy Winchell, Michelle M., Rhondia Cannon, Trista Heuer, Judy L., Margaret N., Patty Bohuslav, Chris Green, Ilona, Mary S., Jeanne Olynick, Karen Jernigan, Joy Lacey, Jean S., Sandy

Golinger, Mary T., Connie, Judith, Vickie Escalante, Terri Camp, Seyi A., B.J. Frey, Lynn Sell, Jenny M., Tonya C., Becky C., Becky, Ann Diener, Jenny Kilgallen, Chinye Ukwu, C. Beck, Diana A., Diana Austin, Barbara M., Haley Powell, Melanie A. Tate, Jan Truhler, Korkoi Boret, Deb Galloway, Kathryn Rebernick, Gary L. Richards, Lincoln Clark, Judith Barillas, Teresa Martin, Pam Williams, Lisa Gallup, Nancy Fudge, Mary, Vikki W., Jerilyn, Sherene, Tonya C., Jan Gilmour, Korin Thomas, Jaime Fipp, Bonny Rambarran, Kellie P., and Carol Witzenburger.

And of course, thank you for reading! I hope you've enjoyed your visit to River Falls—and most of all, that you've been reminded once again of God's great love for you. A love so great that he calls you his own! I'm so grateful for your support and encouragement of my books. God's blessings to you!

About the Author

Valerie M. Bodden has three great loves: Jesus, her family, and books. And chocolate (okay, four great loves). She is living out her happily ever after with her high-school-sweetheart-turned-husband and their four children. Her life wouldn't make a terribly exciting book, as it has a happy beginning and middle, and someday when she goes to her heavenly home, it will have a happy end.

She was born and raised in Wisconsin but recently moved with her family to Texas, where they're all getting used to the warm weather (she doesn't miss the snow even a little bit, though the rest of the family does) and saying y'all instead of you guys.

Valerie writes emotion-filled Christian fiction that weaves real-life problems, real-life people, and real-life faith. Her characters may (okay, will) experience some heartache along the way, but she will always give them a happy ending.

Feel free to stop by www.valeriembodden.com to say hi. She loves visitors! And while you're there, you can sign up for your free story.

Made in the USA
Columbia, SC
22 December 2024

50449340R00164